THE
EVERLASTING

ELAINE MILTON

To Sara

I hope you enjoy the book!

Elaine

ONE

The first time Tallin had the dream was the night of her twenty-fifth name day.

She awoke feeling unsettled, a lingering picture in her mind of a crystalline orb full of colours which swirled in wisps of magenta, green and gold. A shrouded figure had been hunched over it, drawing the colours to the surface with a fingertip.

Afterwards, every time she closed her eyes at night, the figure was waiting for her.

Each time, she remembered more detail. She dreamed of an ancient fortress, winds whipping around the crenellations so sharply that she sometimes woke shivering. In her sleep, she wandered through barren halls, feet catching on broken flagstones, the smell of damp and decay making her nostrils twitch. Always, there was the orb, tendrils of colour churning inside the crystal as if they were alive and trapped in a nightmare just as she was. The night she dreamed of the dungeons for the first time, she awoke screaming.

Ithal was knocking on her door within minutes, as she would have expected. He fussed over her as if he were her surrogate father, no matter that she was no longer a child.

"Tallin, let me in," he called, breathless with panic.

She swung her legs off the mattress and padded over to the door.

"I'm fine, just a bad dream," she said, forcing a smile on to her face. "Nothing to worry about. Honestly."

Ithal's face outside the door was pale and drawn.

"You have to get dressed and come to the main hall. Hurry."

The High Cleric sat on the polished mahogany throne usually reserved for meeting nobles and powerful politicians. His face was expressionless beneath his neatly trimmed beard, but the way his hands twisted in his robes belied his true feelings.

"Tallin. I'm glad you are here," he said without preamble. "We have a problem on the Iveson Farmstead four miles to the east."

"What sort of problem?" Tallin looked around the almost empty room, her eyes widening at the sight of a stranger kneeling between two guards – an older man, perhaps sixty, dressed in the rough linens of a farmhand. There were dirty streaks on the man's leathery cheeks where he had swiped at tears, and his eyes were red-rimmed and sore.

"This is Loran Iveson," the cleric said, "whose wife, Sophia, passed away yesterday evening. This morning, she tried to kill him."

"She was confused, Your Worship," Loran said. "She didn't know what she was doing."

Tallin shook her head and frowned.

"If she died last night, how could she try to kill him this morning?"

"That is a question we are all asking ourselves," the cleric said. "We fear there has been a disturbance in the shroud and some poor souls are not passing on to Everlasting, or are being pulled back through."

"That's impossible," Tallin said.

The High Cleric got to his feet, his lilac robes dragging across the dusty flagstone floor. He took Tallin's hands in his own, his skin wrinkled and warm.

"There is a man in the library asking to speak with you. He has been knocking on our door for the last three weeks telling our gatekeepers wild stories about souls coming through the shroud and saying that your magic is needed to put things right. Naturally, we threw him out every time – the ravings of a madman, you understand. Yet now..."

"You think he's right," Tallin said.

"Yes."

She let out a heavy sigh. "Then I should see what he has to say."

"The gods go with you, child. Do what you must to lay these souls at rest." The old man lifted her hands and pressed his dry lips to her knuckles.

Tallin bowed to him, a quick bob of her shoulders, and headed to the library, the low murmurs of the monks and Loren Iveson's gentle sobs fading away behind her. She took several deep breaths, trying to settle the fluttering in her stomach as she thought about what might lie ahead.

It was not unusual for people to come to the abbey seeking her help. She was a sibylant, a rarity in these times. It meant that she was born with magic, powers few understood and even fewer wielded. She was the first born in Glendoran for seven generations and, before her, most thought that magic had disappeared from the land.

Many people felt she was an aberration, one that fascinated and disgusted them in equal measure. It did not stop them from asking for help, and she had always tried to do her best. And here was someone else, she thought disconsolately as she pushed the carved oak door of the library open. Someone who wanted assistance with far more than the wheat harvest or a rat infestation.

The man perched on one of the dark green velveteen window seats, looking out across the grounds of the abbey. His back was ramrod-straight, his face obscured by a pale, hooded travelling cape.

Tallin hesitated, the skin on the back of her neck prickling.

"You came to see me?"

"Yes," the man said, not moving from his position.

Tallin swallowed. She had no idea what she was supposed to say to him.

"Why?"

The man slid back his cloak and turned his gaze on her. She took an involuntary step back at the intensity in his expression and the shock of his appearance.

She had never seen anyone like him before, despite being brought up surrounded by boys and men. He was fair-skinned to the point of translucently pale, his cheekbones high and defined, raven-black hair falling in scruffy waves to his shoulders. His eyes were what made her catch her breath. They were strange and unnerving, yet as beautiful as a clear lake on a sunny day. She supposed they would be called blue, but they were the blue of the sky trapped beneath glass, streaks of silver highlighting them so they shone.

And they were trained directly on her.

"You are not what I expected," he said.

"What?"

Tallin wondered if she would be able to say anything more than a single word.

"You. I thought you would be older, more experienced. This is no task for a youngling."

His words hit Tallin like blades, and fury bubbled up inside her and spilled out before she could stop it.

"I am no child. I have studied my magic for sixteen years, and many of the priests have praised my control and mastery. Who are you to come here asking for my help and be so rude?"

The man's eyebrows knitted, his stern face softening into an expression of confusion.

"I am sorry. I did not mean to offend you," he said. "My name is Kirian, and I bring news of a terrible event."

"Yes, the High Cleric mentioned something about souls not going through the shroud," Tallin said. "It's difficult to believe, to be honest."

"It is the truth," Kirian said. "For some weeks now, souls of those who have passed over to Everlasting have been drawn back into the world of the living. It means that nobody can truly lie at rest until whoever controls them is stopped."

"How do you know all this?" Tallin asked.

"I am what you might call a sensitive," Kirian said, "which means that I can tune into the world beyond ours. I can feel the presence of magic, which is why I was drawn here, to you. It is also how I can sense the other, the one holding the souls."

"And what are you asking of me?"

For all her bluster and anger at being questioned, Tallin knew that she was little more than an apprentice. She had no idea how to begin to deal with a situation like this.

"The person I seek is a powerful necromancer," Kirian said, "and I fear it will be nothing short of impossible to return balance to the world. Yet we need to try, and you are the only other person with magic I have found. I need your talents."

"I thought I was the only one in Glendoran." Tallin frowned. "How can someone so strong in magic have been able to go undetected until now?"

"That I cannot answer." Kirian sighed. He turned and gazed back out of the window. "We need to move soon. The other dwells far north, and it will be a long journey."

"I'm sorry, but I still don't know how we're supposed to put this right. I'm just one person, and I have no idea where to start. The most I've ever done with my magic before is help the crops to grow. This is, well, it's totally beyond me." Tallin shook her head. "I can't do this. It's like you said - I'm not who you think I am."

"You are all we have," Kirian said, his face cracking into an unexpected smile. He looked different, younger somehow. "Besides, you might surprise me."

"You'd better hope so," she said. "So. What do I need to do?"

Tallin sat on the edge of her bed, her head in her hands, thinking about everything she had heard. Her skin pebbled with gooseflesh, and she couldn't seem to get warmer. She was terrified of what lay ahead, yet at the same time there was a small part of her which felt almost excited. She had rarely left the grounds of the monastery, and when she had she had never travelled farther than the two or three small villages within a day's ride. She hadn't pictured seeing the world in quite this way, but she had to admit she would not miss the confined space of her little room or the many hours spent in study with Brother Yip and Brother Juris.

Three days to prepare, three days to be fitted for travelling clothes and armour and to get the horses ready, and then she would be leaving these walls behind her. She had no idea when, if ever, she would return.

Tallin opened the little dresser beside the bed and began to carefully sort through her meagre possessions. A small locket with a few strands of her mother's hair inside – black like her own. A bottle of perfume, the scent of which transported her back to her childhood in the days before her magic manifested. A little notebook and pen, a mirror, flint and tinder, a sewing kit, a slice of heavy fruit cake she had been saving, wrapped in a napkin. They all went into her pack.

She wondered if Ithal had told the High Cleric yet, wondered what his reaction would have been. She couldn't imagine that he would be happy to let her go, but he had seen for himself what was happening in the world when he set light to Sophia Iveson's still-twitching corpse. Such things were an affront to all they knew and believed about the peace found in death, and in the absence of an army, Tallin would have to do.

She wouldn't be entirely on her own. Ithal had told her that Cearul and Fianna would travel with her. They'd volunteered as soon as the word went round about her unusual mission. Probably keen to get some time away from the monastery themselves, she thought. She knew the pair of them were lovers, and it was frowned upon for sworn-in guards to fraternise inside monastery grounds. She was fond of them both, though, particularly Fianna, who was one of the few women living there. It would be no hardship to spend more time with them.

And, of course, there would be Kirian. She still didn't know who he was and where he had come from. He was certainly strange, with a way of talking which seemed overly correct, as if he was measuring every word before he spoke it. She had never met anyone like him before, and yet she was entrusting him with her safety on a journey through the wildest parts of Glendoran. She snorted and rubbed her temples. This whole situation was ridiculous.

"Are you there?"

Ithal's voice carried through the door, and she called for him to enter.

"I've informed the High Cleric that we will be departing in three days, and I asked Heini to select eight of his sturdiest horses to accompany us," Ithal said, sinking down on to the tatty bench which ran along one wall of the little room.

"We?" Tallin said, raising an eyebrow. "You speak as if you're coming with us."

"That's because I am," Ithal said. "You don't think I'd let you go by yourself, do you?"

Tallin sighed. She was fond of the old man, but he would not see his half century again, and his waistline showed his love for his sedentary lifestyle. He was clearly in no shape for an arduous journey into the north.

"You can't, Ithal, it'll kill you," Tallin said. "I'd rather not have your death on my conscience."

Ithal laughed, a familiar rumbling baritone. "Nobody seems to be passing over properly at the moment anyway, isn't that the problem? Look, if I send you off to your own death with a stranger, I couldn't live with myself anyway. I'm coming with you, and I won't hear any more argument about it."

"You'll hold us back, old man." Tallin grinned despite herself.

"Ouch," Ithal said, gripping his chest. "Though I hear your point. I promise, if I become a liability I'll let you go on without me. Until that happens, I will be by your side as I should be."

Tallin shook her head, still smiling. "If I can't dissuade you, I suppose you have three days to butter up the kitchen staff for the best supplies to take with us."

Ithal patted his stomach. "You certainly know my strengths, my dear."

The dreams were worse that night, as if the necromancer knew they were coming. Before, it had felt like watching a scene unfold in front of her, but this was different. She could feel the emotions in the old castle where the necromancer was keeping the souls. The crystal orb pulsed with the energy of the souls trapped within it, panic and fear evident in the disturbed thrashing of the bright coloured wisps. It felt as if she truly stood in the broken-down great hall, and she felt disoriented when she woke tangled in her blankets in the warmth of her bedroom.

It was well before dawn, but she knew she would not sleep again that night. She made her way to the library, her favourite room in the house, where she knew she could always find a peaceful spot to gather her thoughts.

She pulled an old history book from one of the tall, overcrowded shelves and settled down in an ancient, upholstered leather chair in front of the cast iron fireplace, toasting her toes on the low flames which burned slowly to embers.

Kirian found her there about an hour later.

"I did not expect to see you awake," he said, hovering beside her. Tallin thought he seemed nervous in her presence, and she could not think why. She was hardly intimidating.

"Please, sit down," she said, indicating the chair opposite hers. "I was just reading through some old maps and books about Glendoran. I don't know much about the places outside South Inwold, so I thought I'd try to find out what I'm letting myself in for."

"Have you never travelled?" Kirian perched awkwardly on the edge of the chair.

Tallin shrugged her shoulders, focusing on the book in front of her.

"I came here when I was nine after my mother caught me making bubbles out of the sunlight in the garden. I've lived within the walls of the monastery ever since. I've been to a couple of the nearby villages to help people when they needed my magic to grow crops or repair their houses, but mostly I don't even go outside."

"You are a prisoner?"

Tallin gave a bitter laugh. "No, I'm just far too important to risk. At least until the dead start walking our streets, it seems."

"Yes, that tends to make people reassess matters."

Tallin looked at the man curiously. "What about you? Have you seen much of the world?"

"Ah... I suppose you could say I have," Kirian said, glancing away. "I am quite familiar with most parts of the land."

"Where are you from, originally?"

Kirian chuckled, a rich, low sound. "Here and there. It was so long ago that I have almost forgotten."

"It's not like you're as ancient as Ithal," Tallin said. "But I get the message. I'll stop being so nosy."

"I am not offended," Kirian said, "but I never stay in the same place for long, and it seems like an eternity since I have been anywhere that felt like home."

Tallin nodded. "I may not have travelled like you have, but that's a feeling I can relate to."

"Are you not happy here? The people seem kind."

"They are," she said, "but I don't know, it seems like

home should be about more than kindness and a roof over your head."

"There are those in the world who do not have these things."

"I know that," she said. "That doesn't mean that I feel any less lonely."

"I apologise. I did not intend to make you seem ungrateful," Kirian said.

"That's fine, but I'm not ungrateful at all. Everyone here has always looked after me. If anything, it's been a bit weird the way they celebrate my magic. I suppose I remember the look on my mother's face when she used to talk about my Da, and..." she trailed off, "I must be boring you. I'm sorry."

"It is so long since I have talked to another person that I am far from bored," Kirian said.

"I suppose anyone would be interesting in that case, even me." Tallin shut the book with a thud and put it down on the little side table beside her chair. "Well then. I should get ready for breakfast. It must be nearly daybreak."

"Forty minutes, perhaps. I will see you later?"

"I've no doubt you will."

It was a difficult day. The news had spread through the monastery that there was a disturbance in the shroud between the living and the dead and that Tallin would soon be leaving to find the source. Tallin spent the whole day fielding anxious questions and feeling as if her shoulders would be worn away with all the awkward patting.

The sun was well past middle-light before she managed to escape to the little stone tower overlooking the gardens where she would often spend time alone with her thoughts. She was leaning over the chipped stone balcony watching the birds digging for worms in the soil below when Ithal joined her.

"Sorry to disturb your peace," he said.

Tallin wrinkled her nose. "I don't think I'll be getting much of that any time soon."

"That's the truth."

Tallin let out a long sigh. "Am I needed?"

"Later will be fine. The armourer has brought some leatherwork for you to try. Isbel has taken it to your room."

"Thank you."

"They don't want you to go, you know."

"I'm not exactly looking forward to it myself, Ithal," Tallin said. "It's not going to be a relaxing walking holiday, is it?"

"Hardly," Ithal said, mopping sweat from his brow with his sleeve. "To make matters worse, the High Cleric says he can't spare any more guards to travel with us."

Tallin frowned. "That's not many people to overthrow a necromancer."

"Kirian seems to think he only needs you," Ithal said, "but even if you are strong enough to seal the shroud, we still have to get there. It's apparently a long way north, so we're going to need all the help we can get."

"If the High Cleric says no, I don't see what else we can do."

Ithal exhaled loudly. "We could try petitioning the emperor. Explain the situation and ask him to spare some of his soldiers to travel with us."

"You think he'll listen?" Tallin didn't feel enamoured with the plan. Emperor Joacci was considered to be a good and fair ruler, but he was known to be a logical and stubborn man who had a particular dislike for the spiritual. She couldn't imagine telling him about their mission and expecting him to take it seriously.

"Unless you feel confident taking on an unknown evil with five people, one of whom is twenty fisks overweight, I don't see that we have a choice. We have to go to Harrintown."

"You're right," Tallin sighed. "Ithal, this is ridiculous. I don't know what I'm doing."

The older man put his arm around her shoulders and squeezed her arm gently. "Does anyone ever really know? If anyone can sort this mess out, Tal, it's you. We all have faith in you."

Tallin scraped her boots against the rough wall of the balcony, pieces of dark moss catching on her toes and crumbling to the floor. "Glad someone does."

"Every one of us," Ithal said. "Now, we'll be packing up tomorrow so I suggest you start saying your goodbyes. Lot of people here going to miss you, you know."

"I don't think that's true, Ithal," she said, "but thank you for trying to make me feel better."

Tallin turned away to walk back to her room, listing in her head all the important people she might not ever see again once she departed. There were not too many. There was her favourite person, Cook, a rail-thin, mousy woman who, Tallin remembered, had been the first person to show her kindness when she first came to live at the monastery. There were always extra treats squirrelled away for her in the kitchen, including Tallin's favourite sticky orange buns. There was the High Cleric himself, a kindly old man despite his revered position. Heini, the stable master, who had taught her to ride. Yip and Juris, her tutors. And, of course, Isbel, her maidservant and friend, the one person she saw every day.

The clothing fit. She looked at herself in the mirror atop her small dresser and wondered who she was turning into, wondered where the simple country girl with the big feet and crooked nose had gone. The plain cotton shift she wore most days lay on the floor at her feet as she twisted her hips to look at the straps which held the long, silken tunic against her body and marvelled at the shape of her thighs in the tight breeches designed for riding. The gold of the tunic shimmered against her dark skin, and she thought that perhaps, for once, she looked striking. There was a thick scabbard on her hip to hold the dagger she had been given in case her magic wasn't enough to deter attackers, though she had no idea how to use a blade, and a solid-feeling leather vest which she could buckle over the tunic when she needed extra protection.

She struck a pose, waving her dagger inexpertly in an attempt to look threatening. She just looked silly.

"Tell me honestly, Isbel, if you were a tough, road-hardened bandit, would you look at me and run away screaming?"

Her maid gave her The Look. The one that usually meant she was asking a stupid question. Which, Tallin supposed, she was.

"I'd shit meself, Ma'am," the young woman said.

"With laughter, I suppose."

"Din't say that, did I?"

"You didn't need to."

Tallin sighed and slid the dagger back into its scabbard. She hoped the emperor could be persuaded to send some assistance, if they even made it that far. Harrintown was a distance away, and it would be many days of travel just to reach the palace. Aside from Kirian, none of them had ever travelled that far. Her mouth watered with a sudden rush of nausea from the pit of her stomach.

"You all right, Ma'am? You're looking awful pale."

"I'll be okay, Isbel. I'll be getting to see the world, what more could I ask for?"

"Comfy blanket and a warm man?"

Tallin forced a smile. "I don't think either of those things are part of the plan, sadly."

"Ah well, you never know, right?" Isbel poked her in the side and giggled. "That weird guy's a bit alright if you ask me."

"Weird guy, just what every woman looks for." Tallin couldn't help but chuckle. The young woman made most of the monks' hair curl with her inappropriate familiarity, but she could always cheer Tallin up. She wondered what the maid would do after she had gone.

"I'll be back before you know it, Isbel," Tallin said, her smile disappearing as she took the maid's hand between hers. "You take care of everyone here, won't you?"

Isbel snorted. "Course. Except that arse Rinam. You sure you don't want to take him with you? Feed him to the dragon or whatever it is you lot are looking for."

Tallin shook her head. "One weird guy's enough for me to deal with. You're stuck with him, I'm afraid."

"Thought you'd say that. Bugger."

"I'm going to miss you, you know."

"Ah, don't be so soft, yeah? Like you said, you'll be back soon. Won't even know you're gone."

Tallin pulled the girl into a brief hug, making her squawk in indignation, before making her way down to the kitchens to speak to her old friends.

It had been harder than she expected it would be. Tallin was pensive as she trudged back to her room, chewing on a sticky roll. Cook had smiled and wished her luck and health, but Tallin could tell from the shake in her voice that she was terrified.

She climbed into bed, exhausted from the sadness and fear which had swept over her all day like waves. Her eyes were hot and gritty as if they had been rubbed in sand, and she hoped it meant she would fall so deep that she would not be disturbed in sleep.

Yet the dream was even stronger that night.

The colours in the crystal were brighter and busier, and although they were silent behind the glass Tallin could somehow still sense the screams of despair they emitted. They swirled and twisted in a desperate dance, flailing against the orb as if trying to escape. Their panic was set to a terrible soundtrack: groans of metal dragging against stone and hammering sounds, which Tallin knew came from the enormous dungeons beneath the castle hall. When she awoke, sweating and gasping, she found that her magic had triggered in her sleep and small balls of light were spinning around her bed.

That had never happened before.

Briefly, she wondered if she could pull the blankets over her head and wish this whole mess away. Another knock at the door quickly put paid to that particular fantasy.

"Who is it?"

"It's just me, Ma'am. You were screaming."

Isbel hovered outside her door, her thick brows drawn together in a frown. "You look like death. You having bad dreams?"

"Every night," Tallin said wearily.

"Yeah, well. I'm here now, and I ain't going nowhere 'til morning. Like it or not, you're stuck with me."

Isbel crawled into the bed beside her and wrapped her scrawny arms around her waist. "You can sleep now, Ma'am. You're safe, yeah?"

Tears prickled in Tallin's eyes as she curled into the warmth of her friend. "Thank you."

"'Ere, watch out, I don't wanna get snot in my hair," Isbel said.

Tallin laughed and closed her eyes. For the first time in weeks, she slept without dreaming.

TWO

It was time to leave. The sky was unusually grey and overcast, sharp talons of rain biting into the exposed skin of their faces. Tallin rode Bridget, her chestnut mare, at a slow walk from the stables, through the cobbled courtyard, and under the wide granite arch which funnelled them out on to the smooth, grey stone bridge leading to the main abbey gates. The horse was restless, snorting softly, as if she could sense Tallin's anxiety.

The crowds of people come to see them off stood five deep all through the courtyard and along the bridge, so that the horses could barely pass between them. Tallin gazed down at the sea of faces, stunned into silence as every single person raised their hand to their hearts as she passed, a gesture of love and good fortune.

Isbel stood at the end of the line, a smile on her face and her eyes pink from crying. "Kick their arses, Ma'am!" she yelled, and Tallin grinned at the chorus of gasps she drew from the people standing near her.

"I'll kick 'em from here until Moonday," she shouted back with a wink as the horses trotted through the large, iron gates.

It was odd to see the monastery becoming smaller in

the distance, the noise of the crowd receding into the wind that bore them away. She was soaked through to the skin already, shivering so that her teeth clattered together like drumbeats. She hoped the canvas tents strapped to the saddles of the pack-bearing horses would still be dry enough when they stopped for the night.

They had planned to reach the outskirts of the Plains of Corah by dusk, hoping to find a small field to camp in before tackling the miles of wilderness. Tallin prayed the rains would stop and they would be able to light a fire, as the chill was beginning to set into her joints.

Despite the weather, they made good time. The sun was only just skirting the horizon when Fianna pulled her horse over, indicating a small, bare patch of land behind a row of trees, far enough away from the track that they could shelter comfortably and not be seen from the road once it was full dark.

The two guards were off their horses and the tents half way up before Tallin had even had a chance to properly stretch away the aches in her muscles. She watched them work, marvelling at their focused efficiency and the way they worked together in harmony, each of them knowing exactly where the other was and what they needed to do. She was not blind to the small touches that passed between them, the glitter in their eyes.

She noticed Kirian watching them too, his expression unreadable as he followed their every move from where he sat on the ground, undoing the pack that held their provisions.

"Do you think it helps, having someone to fight for?" Tallin asked, dropping to her knees beside him.

Kirian startled and whipped his head round to stare at her.

"I have no idea," he said eventually.

"Oh."

They lapsed into awkward silence, Tallin wondering if it would be rude to get up and walk away. Before she could, Kirian spoke again.

"What is it like, to love someone?"

Tallin blinked. "You've never..."

"If I had, would I be asking?"

She looked down at her hands, unable to hold his intense gaze.

"Um, well, it's hard to say. Hard to describe. Perhaps it depends upon the situation. My own experience," she inclined her head towards the guards, "was nothing like theirs."

"What do you mean?"

Tallin huffed a breath through her nose. "It might have been frowned on, for them to carry on together as they are, but that would be nothing compared to being in love with an apprenticed monk. We were only seventeen, and when he took his formal vows, it was all over. I couldn't hope to compete with the gods."

"Monks are not allowed to love?"

"You can't really stop someone from feeling love, but no, they aren't allowed to act on it."

She glanced up. The man was still staring at her, his head tilted to one side.

"I do not understand," he said, "how you can feel something yet not be acting upon it. Is loving not an action?"

"It feels like it," she said, "but it's the physical expression of that love which would be impossible."

"Why?"

Tallin's eyes were sad as they met his. "I could try to answer that, but my honest answer is, I don't know."

"So you have nobody to fight for?"

Tallin raised her eyebrows. She was unused to people being so direct with her. Most of the monks favoured strange roundabout ways of talking, using silly little metaphors for anything that might be considered uncomfortable.

"I fight for myself," she said, her voice so low that Kirian could barely hear her.

It was still too wet to light a fire, the branches of the trees soft and heavy with rain-soaked moss. Tallin lay in her bedroll, hungry, damp and cold, and wondered if she had ever felt this miserable in her life. It was so dark inside her tent that she couldn't see the clouds of her breath in the dank air, and the blackness was a perfect canvas for the pictures in her mind to come alive and taunt her.

Tonight, it wasn't just the necromancer who materialised in her imagination. Tallin couldn't stop thinking about what lay ahead of them tomorrow. She had never seen the great plains before, but imagined them as a wide mouth full of fangs, waiting to swallow them up. She knew the journey could end for them almost as soon as it had begun.

With a frustrated sigh, she got to her feet and wandered out to where Cearul was keeping watch.

The young elven man looked almost spectral in the darkness, she thought, the moonlight shimmering off long, silver hair which he had loosened around his shoulders. His skin was dark and peppered with pale freckles across his forehead which glittered like a galaxy of stars above his eyes.

"I may as well take over," she said, sinking to her knees beside him, the damp earth clinging and shaping around her skin.

"Can't sleep?"

"Not a chance. Too much on my mind."

"I can imagine," he said, "though you're going to need your strength for the plains crossing. We will be getting low on supplies by the end, and we can't have you fading."

"I know that," she said, a note of petulance creeping in to her tone. "I'm hardly keeping myself awake on purpose."

"I didn't say you were," Cearul said mildly.

Tallin sighed. "I'm not cut out for this. Perhaps if I'd stayed with my ma in our little hut, I'd be more prepared. I've barely even been outside the monastery, Cearul. I've been shut away and coddled, and everything I know about the world comes out of a book. Everyone's expecting too much. I can't do it."

Cearul levelled his gaze at her. "If not you, then who?"

She put her head in her hands and rubbed at her eyes. "I don't know. How do we even know that this isn't all an elaborate lie? Other than poor Missus Iveson, we have no proof that souls aren't moving through."

"Do you really think it is?"

"No. I've sensed it too, I've dreamed it. It's real. I just wish it wasn't."

"I think that's something we can all agree on."

"What do you make of Kirian?" Tallin asked, keeping her voice low.

"Can't really say," Cearul said. "He's been quiet so far, kept himself to himself. He's watching everyone carefully, though. Perhaps just to see where he fits in, but I'm not sure."

"You think we can trust him?"

"I don't know. Fi doesn't, but you know her. She doesn't trust anybody."

"True." Tallin rubbed her hands together and blew on them. It was cold without a fire, and she was beginning to regret volunteering to sit out on watch. Still, the elf had probably been out here since sundown, knowing him, and he needed his rest as much as she did. "You can go now, Cearul. Fianna's been keeping the bed warm for you, I expect."

"Are you sure?"

"I'll wake you if I need you."

Cearul smiled and disappeared into his tent without a backward look. Keen to get to his lover, no doubt. Tallin envied them their easy company and the close bond they had forged over the five years they had lived and worked together.

She sat quietly for several hours, deep in thought, her skin numb in the frosty night air. Time passed slowly, the only sign of the advancing night being the quietening of the chibchibs, which had finished their middle-dark song and flown to roost.

Ithal relieved her in the early hours, but she had not slept until the sky started to lighten through the gaps in her tent. She was exhausted, and she knew she had a long day ahead.

The watery sun was well past its central point when the grass and soil underfoot began to give way to a rough, stony sand. They hadn't seen any people or animals for miles, and the trees around the track were thinning away.

Tallin's head swam at the sight of the silvery plains stretching before them. She had never seen so much emptiness. The only movement was the gritty sand caught in the sharp winds which dusted across the land, whirling in prickly eddies which beat against their faces and caught in their hair. It was nothing like the salty sand of Cappa Bay where Tallin used to go swimming when she was a child. It was hot and earthy, the peaty smell lingering in her nostrils until they itched.

"How many miles?" she asked, turning to Kirian who sat motionless beside her on his pale grey gelding.

"It would take us two days to cross, if we do not stop," he said. "But the winds become cold at night, so we cannot ride after sundown. It will be more like four days."

"The horses cannot carry us for that length of time without a rest anyway," Ithal said. "We can't rush. We will just have to be very careful."

"What are we looking out for?" Fianna gazed at the horizon, her eyes wide and alert.

"There are dangers in the open," Kirian said. "Most of the smaller life forms are harmless, but we would not wish to meet culai or the varinyx."

Tallin frowned at the mention of the great sand-serpent. "I thought the varinyx was a myth."

"Far from it," Kirian said. "It takes several travelling merchants every year, and their horses."

"That'd be why the prices are so steep, then," Ithal

muttered.

"So long as we are alert for his presence, the beast will not harm us. His travels under the sand are indiscriminate, and he will not seek us out. The culai are another matter," Kirian said.

Cearul glanced over. "Do you need me to scout at all? You know my kind are immune to the culai glands."

"No," Kirian said. "You are better staying with us. Should we get bitten, you may be needed to help. I have some herbs in my pack – look, these purple ones with the veins. They are an antidote to the poison, if you boil them up."

Cearul nodded, and they kicked their horses into a slow trot.

Hours passed, and the terrain did not alter. Tallin's eyes ached from staring at the bright expanse of sand. She rode behind Kirian, whose sharp eyes were trained on the ground for any sign of vibration or movement beneath the surface, an indication that the varinyx was nearby.

Tallin was unused to riding for this length of time, and her thighs felt swollen against the saddle.

"When do we stop?" she called out to Kirian, who reined his horse back and turned to face her.

"Soon," he said, "since we will only have the sun for perhaps eighty more minutes. We should hobble the horses and pitch the tents before we lose the light."

"We may as well stop here," Ithal said, "since it all

looks the bloody same."

Nobody argued. It seemed to Tallin that she was not the only one fed up with sand getting everywhere.

The day had been dry, so the small fire they were able to cobble together from brown grasses and twigs lit easily. At least they would have hot food in their bellies, Tallin thought as she began to unpack the tents from their bags.

As the sky grew dark and the fire guttered, Tallin bid the group goodnight and retreated to her tent, reminding Cearul to wake her for last watch. She was exhausted; every time she blinked she felt her vision spin. She sank gratefully into her bedroll and closed her eyes.

It felt as if barely any time had passed when she was woken by a scream.

THREE

Tallin leapt to her feet, tripping over her pack in her haste to respond to the noise.

The sky outside her tent was grey with the first weak fingers of dawn, and Tallin blinked several times before her eyes adjusted to the gloom. A large, dark hump lay on the dull sand about twenty feet away from the tent. Nearer to her, Cearul stood wrestling with something she could not see, and Fianna was racing over to join the fray, her sword raised high and her face set firm for battle.

Tallin narrowed her eyes and called light from her hands, a large, glittering orb of pale yellow which threw out rays like a miniature sun. It reflected in the golden eyes of a pack of culai loping towards the camp. The hump she had seen was one of the horses who had been bitten on the stomach. It lay frozen on the sand, mouth open and eye rolling wildly. One of the beasts was on Cearul's chest, long, narrow snout pushing towards his neck, its jaws drooling and snapping. There were perhaps twenty of them in total – a small group, but still capable of real harm.

Tallin focused on the small, grey-furred animals, glanced again at the sweating horse, and drew on her fear. The light surrounding them intensified, and she clapped her hands together, pulling a column of magic from the sand which rose in a shimmering sheet to protect them from the culai on the other side.

The creatures threw themselves against the barrier, biting and clawing as the emerald glow of the magic slowly dimmed.

"Everyone ready?" she called, pulling more energy into her palms.

Cearul wiped his hands as he dropped the broken body of the culai that had attacked him to the ground, its neck snapped.

"Ready," he said, breathing heavily.

Tallin glanced around. Fianna was in position, her sword and shield raised. Cearul stood beside her, raising his bow. The other two were not fighters, she knew. Ithal had his club, and he could swing it with some force, but Kirian appeared to have no weapon to hand.

"Kirian?" she asked.

"Ready," he said, his voice clear and unwavering.

"Right," Tallin said. "Don't look directly at me if you value your sight."

Culai were nocturnal creatures with sensitive eyes. As soon as the first animal broke through, she threw her spell directly into its face. The light burst on its nose and rolled in a wave over its shivering body. It howled piteously and began to roll on the floor, blinded and writhing in pain.

Those behind it paused only momentarily before swarming towards the camp in a frenzied bundle.

Fianna was a whirlwind of slashing blade and solid shield, light on her feet despite her thick leather-and-iron armour. If Tallin had the time to watch her, she would have been impressed – the woman was muscular yet graceful, her long, red, braided hair swinging as she spun and stabbed at the small, snarling culai.

Tallin sent magic soaring towards the warrior, pale green light bathing her and adding a layer of protection to her skin. It would make it harder for the beasts to get their teeth into her flesh.

Tallin looked from side to side, trying to keep track of where the creatures were. She saw Ithal swing his club and crush the skull of a leaping culai and Kirian wrestling one with his bare hands. She breathed in and felt her panic, using it to form another bright spell which she threw towards the struggling man. The animal in his hands shuddered and died as the light passed through its skin and liquefied its innards.

Arrows flew as Cearul let them loose, one after another. They whipped through the air as if they were coming from different directions, and it was only after the thought cemented itself in her brain that Tallin realised that they were. A strange dark plains elf stood on a rock beside their tents, her large, carved bow raised as she joined their battle.

Ithal's shout rose above the growling of the culai, his voice breaking. Tallin watched in horror as he sank to the ground, his legs collapsing beneath him. He twitched and jerked for a short time before falling still.

Tallin heard herself scream, rage and pain swelling up inside her, making her magic bubble and boil in her veins. Sparks fizzed along her hair, and glittery flecks of light pulsed beneath her skin. She turned her mind inwards, tuning in to the burning sensation of her powers, before flicking her eyes open and focusing.

She was bathed in light, glowing beneath her skin and inside her eyes. Magic surrounded her like a corona, white hot and sizzling, and as she threw out her arms, it rose from her like a wind.

The culai wailed as they were caught in the silver beams of magic. It seeped outwards in shimmering rays, beautiful and deadly. The smell of burning fur filled the air, the high shrieking sounds of animals in pain. She watched Cearul drop to the ground and roll away from the streaking light, his eyes screwed shut.

Her magic had never been this strong, never so controlled, and she struggled to breathe with the shock of it. As the light died away, small grey bodies scattered around her, she fell to her knees, her vision swimming. Her legs were leaden with exhaustion and she could feel her veins fizzing and burning with the effort of her spells. She needed to sleep, but there was no time for that.

Fianna was quickly at her side, helping her to stand on shaky legs. As her vision cleared, she saw Kirian kneeling beside Ithal, peeling his tunic back from his shoulder.

"Is he hurt?"

Her voice was small and reedy, almost unrecognisable.

Kirian glanced up, his expression heavy with concern. "Yes. He has taken a nasty bite, and the poison is in his blood. We have little time."

"Can you help him?"

"I will try."

She looked down at Ithal, his body stiff as a statue on the ground. She knew that in less than a hundred minutes, the poison would stop his heart.

"I need a fire," Kirian said, rummaging in his pack for the herbs which would treat the wound and counter the poison. "The cure is effective but the herbs need to be steeped in boiling water."

Fianna frowned. "Our fire is long cold. We do not have enough kindling to start another."

"We have fire."

Tallin had forgotten about the elven woman. She stood on the edge of their camp, almost as still as if she had been bitten herself, her bow lowered to her side. As usual for elves, she was tall and imposing, dressed in a loose, flowing white robe which matched her hair and contrasted with her dark skin.

"Who are you?" Tallin asked.

"My name is Chraisa. We do not have time for question. This man needs help. Come."

The woman turned and began to walk away, her waist-length hair floating behind her like a silken curtain.

Cearul called out to Fianna to help him move Ithal. They lifted him on to his horse, lying him face down across the saddle. If he lived, he would have some bruises, but Tallin supposed they would be the least of his problems.

"Get the other horses," Cearul said to Tallin. "We will walk with him."

Ithal's gelding began to plod after Chraisa with its cumbersome burden, flanked by the two warriors. Tallin stumbled over to where Kirian sat on the sand beside the horse who had been bitten, stroking his hand along the animal's neck. It was the large bay gelding who had carried their tents.

"We may yet save Ithal, but there is little we can do for this fellow," Kirian said. His voice was quiet, and Tallin saw tears glisten in his eyes.

The horse was sweating but unmoving, the whites of his eyes stark against the warm mahogany skin.

Tallin knelt beside the distressed animal, crooning soft words of comfort into his furry ear as she placed her dagger against the soft, damp skin of his neck. She took a deep breath and pushed, the sharp steel severing the arteries and jugular vein.

There was a lot of blood. She stood back, watching it soak into the slate grey sand, blinking away tears. The horse had been a gentle and faithful servant to the monks for years, and had good-naturedly carried their packs for many miles without complaint or hesitation.

"Sorry," she whispered into the wind.

Kirian held the reins of the remaining horses, who were shuffling their feet and whinnying nervously.

"You did the right thing," he said.

"I know," she said. "The right thing, but not the easy thing."

"Yet you did it," he said. "Perhaps I underestimated you."

She shook her head and walked slowly over to mount her mare, taking the reins of a horse either side to lead.

"We'll see," she said.

Tallin hadn't known what to expect from the plains elf, but the camp was beyond anything she could have imagined. Set around a deep, circular watering hole dug into the sand and fortified with rocks, it was large and bustling, and *colourful*. Bushes heavy with red, purple and green berries surrounded the central pool, and there were even small trees bearing what appeared to be apples.

Her eyes widened as she took in the sight of the tents where the elves lived. They were large, domed and circular, made from a thick, dark green fabric that she had never seen before. Each of them had been intricately embroidered with a pattern in gold thread, and the tents were clustered together in groups of four or five, each bearing identical stitching.

The camp was surrounded by pillars of rock sunk deep into the sand. Each pillar bore detailed carvings of the varinyx, the serpent's fangs sharp and shining. Tallin gazed at them in wonder. It must have taken a long time to bring this amount of rock to the middle of the plain, and even longer to shape them so creatively.

Kirian dismounted and ran over to Ithal, who lay prone on the ground next to a small fire that Chraisa was kindling. He rummaged in his pack and came out with a handful of purple and amber herbs which he crushed in his fingers and dropped into a small tin of water ready to heat on the fire.

A spicy scent filled the air as the herbs began to bubble. Tallin crouched beside Kirian, watching him work. The man was intently focused on his task, frowning as he stirred the pot and tested the consistency of the poultice forming inside.

It was then Tallin noticed the puncture wounds on the back of Kirian's hand. They had bled and clotted, and looked swollen and painful.

"You were bitten?"

Kirian glanced up at her, a scowl on his fine features. "I am busy. You must not disturb me. This is important."

Tallin lapsed into silence, stung by the man's sharp tone. He continued to mix the herbs, leaning over to breathe in the fumes, adding some more of the purple leaf. Eventually, he nodded and separated the saturated herbs from the water, pressing them – still hot and steaming – against Ithal's wound.

"Help me lift his head," Kirian said to Chraisa, who

had been looking on silently. Between them, they raised Ithal up and Kirian lifted the tin to his lips, forcing the fragrant water into his mouth.

Much of the water dribbled back out, running down the old man's chin and neck and staining his beard, but enough must have made it into his throat as within a few minutes he coughed and gasped.

Tallin felt as if a bubble was expanding in her chest as she watched the colour returning to Ithal's face.

Kirian exhaled a shaky breath. "He will live."

"I don't know how to thank you," Tallin said. "I had no idea you were a herbalist."

Kirian smiled, and again she was disconcerted by how much it changed his face. "Plants are fascinating things. They can save life and sustain it, and they can take it away."

"Fortunately it was the saving part, this time," she said, holding his gaze with a smile of her own.

Chraisa interrupted the silence that fell as they stared at each other. "That is no dabble. You know plants. You take my Ruari with you so he learns?"

Kirian turned to the elf. "I beg your pardon?"

She tilted her head back imperiously, regal as an Empress. "I help you today, you pay back. You take my son as apprentice. Teach him healing herbs."

"We're on a very dangerous mission," Tallin said. "We are risking our lives; we can't be responsible for anyone else."

"He is strong. You take him." The woman was firm.

Tallin and Kirian looked at each other in stunned silence.

"He might die," Kirian said eventually. "You would risk your son for the sake of a little knowledge about herbs?"

"Knowing is everything," Chraisa said. "It is the only value."

"If you're sure," Tallin said, "I suppose he can come with us. So long as he can look after himself."

"We are elven," Chraisa replied with a dismissive wave of her hand. "We all look after ourselves."

"Then it is settled," Kirian said, crouching to check Ithal's poultice. "It will be some time before this heals enough for us to move on. We need to retrieve our belongings."

In their haste to follow Chraisa and heal Ithal, they had left everything behind except the horses. Tallin paled, her stomach churning at the thought of returning to the scene of the skirmish, not wanting to look again at the dead animals. She still could not get the smell of blood out of her nostrils.

"We will go," Cearul said, "if Chraisa does not mind providing us with a guide?"

"My son will help," the elven woman said, and whistled long and loud. "Ruari!"

A small, red-headed boy, perhaps ten years of age, appeared from one of the nearby tents, his face breaking into a gap-toothed smile.

"Mama?"

Tallin huffed a loud breath. "Wait – this is your son?"

Chraisa nodded. "My son."

"He is not elven," Kirian said with a frown.

"Never mind that," Tallin said. "You said he could look after himself, but he's just a child. We can't possibly take him with us." ·

"Ruari knows the plain. More than you," Chraisa said.

"I don't doubt that," Tallin said, "but we are going to a place far beyond here. It's no place for a child."

Chraisa made a noise which reminded Tallin of Brother Yip when he had eaten too much rich food.

"Ruari lives here, on plain. You think he does not know risk?"

"But -"

"He goes with you. Or you leave now."

The woman seemed to grow taller, her hand stretching out to touch the bow across her back.

Tallin swallowed hard. "We had an agreement. We will honour it."

Kirian shook his head. "But this boy, who is he?"

"He is my son."

"How can that be?" Cearul asked, looking from the woman's dark and delicate elven features to those of the boy, pale and freckled and distinctly round-eared.

"A man came, brought woman and babe to plain, left them there to die. She was wounded, had been beaten, did not live. Many broken bones. Babe in arms, we saved. Became my son."

"I see," Cearul said. "Well, Ruari, are you going to help us fetch our tents and packs?"

"Yes." The boy half-bowed, half-curtseyed, almost tripping over himself in his excitement to meet the strangers in camp.

Tallin watched them leave, the elven and human warriors and one small boy riding beside them. Almost like a family, she thought. It felt as if, for a moment, she had taken a glimpse into a different lifetime.

She returned to Ithal, checking his temperature as Kirian began to make a fresh herbal draught. The man looked much better – his limbs were no longer cold, and he was beginning to lift his head and move his lips.

"What are we to do with the boy?" Kirian asked her, his voice low.

"I believe I heard her say he was your apprentice,"

Tallin said, "so I think by that token he's your responsibility."

She tried not to laugh at the shock on Kirian's face, a twitch of panic giving away his feelings about the situation.

"I take it you haven't got much experience with children," she said.

"No," Kirian said. "Those I have met, I have not spent a long time with, and they have for the most part not been in happy moods."

"They can be rather grumpy. At least, I was, when I was a girl."

"Was?"

Tallin looked up in surprise at the unexpected humour, the grin playing over Kirian's lips.

"I thank you not to be so rude, sir, or I shall bring down the full force of my magic upon you," she said, her tone light.

"And as I saw earlier, that is quite some force," he said. "I was impressed."

"Yes, well. I'm not sure where that came from. I've never been able to call that much power at once before. Look at the state of me, though, I've never felt so drained. I hope I won't need to do that again any time soon."

Kirian chuckled. "Nothing a bit of sleep will not cure. Your magic is connected to emotions, I believe?"

"Yes," she said. "I've never been able to do much unless I am feeling something. Anger, fear, pain, joy… as long as it is in my heart, I can call on my magic."

Kirian smiled. "Then it is understandable that you had more strength today. You have lived your life in the monastery, safe and secure."

"Some would say boring," she said drily.

He chuckled. "Boring. So it is. Then today, on the road, tired and aching, ambushed by deadly animals and seeing your friend wounded… it is only natural that your emotions would be running high."

"That's a good thing, then," she said. "Given that I'm feeling scared out of my wits half the time, this necromancer had better watch out."

"You are dreaming about him."

Tallin took a sharp breath. "Yes. How did you know?"

"Like I said, I am a sensitive. I understand things about people, but do not ask me how. I could not give an answer."

"Could not, or would not?"

Kirian shook his head. "If I knew, I would tell you."

"Like you told me about that bite?"

Tallin reached out to take his hand, but he pulled sharply away from her.

"How come you weren't paralysed?" she asked.

Kirian shrugged. "It seems I have immunity somehow. Perhaps something to do with my blood."

"That's fortunate," Tallin said.

"Yes."

"I thought only the elven were immune."

"They are the only race who are entirely immune. That does not mean others cannot be."

"I suppose so," Tallin said, regarding Kirian through narrowed eyes. It wasn't unheard of, she knew, for people who appeared human to have elven blood from generations back, but it seemed unlikely that Kirian, with his pale skin and round ears, would have a single drop.

FOUR

The sun was well past middle-light when the others returned to camp, heads low and disconsolate.

"We have only one tent, two bedrolls and a few pots and pans," Fianna explained. "By the time we got there, the sand was all churned up and everything else was gone. It must have been the varinyx."

The famed and feared serpent was blind and lived beneath the surface of the plains. It would drag sand through its body as it moved, filtering out anything edible and discarding the rest, and it was capable of swallowing creatures the size of a horse. Tallin thought it must have enjoyed quite a meal on the remains of the animals left behind at the camp.

The tents and belongings would have been less edible, but nonetheless, they had been processed and lost to them.

"This is why we have stone serpents," Chraisa said. "They sink into ground, varinyx senses them and moves around. Keeps camp safe."

"We can't exactly carry huge stone pillars around with us," Tallin said.

Chraisa made a dismissive noise.

"When we move on, we will have nowhere for your boy to stay," Cearul said, fixing his gaze on Chraisa.

"We can provide," Chraisa said. "Small garn. Have spare."

"Garn?" Tallin looked confused.

"Our tents," Ruari said. "We call them garn."

"You will stay tonight," Chraisa said, "while man recovers."

"Thank you," Tallin said. She was grateful for the help, especially as the plains elves were renowned for keeping their distance from people. Even elves such as Cearul, from the same lineage but brought up to live among humans, would often be disdained by those who still lived in the traditional way.

Later, as they all sat around a cooking pot, Tallin couldn't help but dwell upon what would have happened if Chraisa had not been hunting in the area, or had chosen not to intervene. Ithal would be dead, almost certainly, and perhaps they would all have gone into the belly of the serpent. She had much to be grateful to the woman for, and she resolved to help take care of Ruari and not to complain again.

Dinner was a curious affair. The elves produced a strange, sweet stew of unidentifiable meat, berries and leaves which tasted like nothing Tallin had ever eaten before. They all sat together in a circle to eat, watching the slowly dying cooking fire in virtual silence. Occasionally, one of the elves would smile at Tallin and

47

raise their bowl in acknowledgement, but no words were exchanged.

Afterwards, she watched the elves work – rubbing down the horses, cleaning the pots and stripping leaves from plants for the next day's meal. It was as if they were all parts of an efficient machine – everyone knew their task and went about it quietly and with purpose.

She felt a tugging on the hem of her tunic and turned to find young Ruari hopping on the spot, a wide smile on his face.

"Garn is up. Come see," he said, pulling at her wrist so that she had no option but to follow.

It was larger than their own tents, which was just as well as they had lost two of those. Less embroidered than the other garn in the camp, it nevertheless stood tall and impressive, the strange, thick green fabric draping heavily to the sand.

Tallin untied the door panel and pushed inside, stopping in her tracks so that Ruari walked into her back.

"How have you managed this?" she asked him.

Their own tents had been functional affairs, plain canvas hung over a folding softwood frame which tended to get damp and smelly in the rain. There was space for their belongings and a small, flat bedroll each, which were uncomfortable and scratchy and designed only to keep them off the muddy ground. The garn was very different.

The beds were simple, upholstered wooden boxes covered with the same green fabric of the garn. They were draped in thick bedspreads made of a rich-looking velvet the colour of rubies and embroidered in a fine gold thread which ran in a zigzag pattern around the edges. Large, soft cushions of all colours were strewn liberally around the floor, some big enough to comfortably sit upon. The garn was lit by tiny silver lanterns which hung from its frame, sparkling in different colours like blazing jewels.

Tallin picked up a lantern and examined it closely. The light it gave out appeared to come from a small, round stone set inside the metal.

"How does this work?"

"Stone is called chrysellium. Takes in light during day if put in sun, then when sun goes, light comes out of stone."

"Impressive."

Tallin turned the lantern in her hands, admiring the craft of the intricately worked metal. She knew many people felt the elves were barbarians, but it was clear to her that they had knowledge and skills beyond that which was understood.

She was glad that, at least for a night or two, they would be able to sleep more comfortably.

By nightfall, Ithal was beginning to talk. His eyes were more focused, and he smiled when he saw Tallin sitting beside him, her hands wrapped around one of his. He was still weak and his limbs would not support him, but Kirian thought the poison would be out of his system by the following day.

"You gave us all a scare," she said, rubbing his fingers to warm them.

Ithal chuckled, rough and harsh in his dry throat.

"You won't get rid of me that easily," he whispered. "Where are we?"

Tallin smiled. "You won't believe me if I tell you."

"When I first woke, I wondered if I'd gone to Everlasting until I realised that sand in my trousers was not the sort of thing you expect in the afterlife."

"The elves helped us," Tallin said. "This is one of their camps."

Ithal raised an eyebrow.

"I haven't questioned it," Tallin said. "Though, really, you owe your life to Kirian. He had the herbs that saved you and knew how to do it."

"I remember," Ithal said. "He was leaning over me like a ghost carved from marble when I opened my eyes. That was another reason I thought I was dead and gone over."

"Not yet you're not," she said. "Now, you need to sleep. We plan to spend another day here, then move on. We should get off the plains as soon as we can. I'm beginning to hate them."

"You and me both."

Ithal was soon settled in the garn, cocooned among cushions and blankets like a king. Tallin smoothed his matted grey hair back from his damp brow. "Rest now," she said, kissing his forehead as his eyes grew heavy with sleep.

The elves guarded the camp that night so they could sleep for all the hours of dark. Tallin shared the small tent with Fianna while the men took the garn.

The dreams she had were strange and disturbing. She saw the golden eyes of the culai in the dawn light, the blood streaming from the horse's neck, scarlet and steaming. Ithal's scream echoed in her ears as she spun and spun, the laughing faces of plains elves swimming in and out of focus around her. Through it all, in the background, she could sense the power of the necromancer and see him as a cloaked shadow on the horizon of her nightmare. Always there, always just in the corner of her eye.

Tallin heard him laugh, a mocking sound which scraped along the dream like shards of glass on soft skin. She felt the darkness in his voice as if it was within her bones, in her lungs, choking her slowly.

She was gasping for breath when she awoke, too panicked to scream. Fianna lay snoring opposite her, and she covered her mouth to stop herself from waking the other woman. Tallin lay awake for the rest of the night, wondering how she was going to be able to confront a man of such power that he could find her in her dreams when she was already almost too exhausted to sit on a horse.

Ithal was much better in the morning. He was up on his feet, a little shaky but strong enough to bear weight. The wound on his shoulder had crusted over and was beginning to look pink around the edges rather than the angry violet it had been the previous day.

He was also well enough to argue.

"A child! What were you all thinking?"

"He's not a spoiled bratling attached to his mother's knee, you know," Cearul said. The archer had become rather fond of the boy since he had guided them back from the old camp the previous day.

"But where we are going is not suitable for him," Ithal persevered.

Tallin shrugged. "It's not for anyone. Least of all you, as I remember telling you quite clearly before we left Clestead."

"That's different. I'm a grown man, I can make my own decisions."

"Ruari has also made his decision, have you not?" Tallin looked over at the child, who nodded energetically. "Being young doesn't mean he doesn't know his own mind."

"Well I suppose you'd know," Ithal said with a scowl. Tallin had been quite a handful when she was a child, furious at having been taken away from her mother and rebelling against her unwanted magic. She had driven many of the monks to distraction with her tantrums and argumentative shouting. Disrespectful, some had said.

Still, Tallin thought, she hadn't turned out too badly considering she had been raised through her teenage years in the confines of the monastery, away from all she had known and loved as a small child. She was, at least, good enough to rely on to save the world. A thought which would probably give at least five of the Brothers heart palpitations. Tallin grinned to herself.

"I don't know why you're smiling," Ithal said. "You're the one who will have to look after the boy."

"Already delegated to Kirian," she said.

Ithal swivelled his head to look at the dark-haired man, who, as usual, was sitting apart from everyone else and watching in concentrated silence, his face impassive and still.

"Now that's something I would like to see. Fine. You win," he said.

"As if there was ever any doubt," she said, squeezing his uninjured shoulder. "Will you be ready to travel later?"

"Perhaps."

In the end, they decided to stay a further night in the encampment and leave at sunup. Ithal's eyes were still sunken with exhaustion, and they all needed rest. By Kirian's calculations, it would take them another three days to reach the other side of the plain, and they would need to be awake and alert to the dangers. Tallin knew she wouldn't feel safe again until she could feel solid earth beneath their feet instead of the soft, grey sand.

The elves were more generous than any of them had

any right to expect. Tallin felt that things would be different had they not agreed to take Ruari with them, but none of them were about to pass up the offer of food and water that Chraisa made on the morning they departed. Most of their own provisions were gone with the tents, deep beneath the shifting sands. It would have been a hungry journey to Harrintown on the little they had left.

Ruari wrapped the dried plants and berries in a wide napkin and tied it tightly before stowing it in one of the remaining backpacks. It was plain fare, but it would sustain them for a few more days. There were handfuls of grain for the horses in another napkin. Tallin hoped it would be enough to keep them going. She felt sorry for the poor beasts, caught up in a journey not of their making. Scratching Bridget's ears, she silently promised her a warm stable and sweet hay when they reached the next town.

Chraisa stood, stern and severe, watching them leave. Ruari hugged her and she said some words in a language Tallin did not know as the boy clambered up behind Kirian on his tall, grey gelding, clutching the man tightly around his waist. When Tallin turned to look again at the elven woman, she had disappeared back into the camp.

The weather had changed, as it often did in the south, and the sun was shining brightly well before the middle of the morning. Tallin could feel the heat on her hair as they rode in a line across the shimmering plain, the sand almost glowing silver in the brilliance of the day. She kicked her mare up to ride beside Kirian and Ruari at the front of the procession.

"You know the way?" she asked.

Kirian turned his head slightly, regarding her from the corner of his eye.

"Yes. I have a good memory for locations."

"I need to thank you for what you did for Ithal. I know he won't say anything to you, he's stubborn like that, but you should know how grateful we are," she said.

The man's eyes softened. "I am glad I could help."

They rode on in silence for some time before he turned to her again.

"Forgive me if this is rude, but I am trying to become familiar with everyone. You and Ithal, are you... are you like Fianna and Cearul?"

Tallin choked on her breath in shock, before filling her lungs and roaring with laughter so that Bridget jinked beneath her.

"Gods, no! What in the name of Ceremor gave you that idea?"

Kirian blushed faintly, which Tallin thought looked surprisingly appealing. "I am not sure. You seem close. I wondered..." his voice trailed off, and he coughed in embarrassment. "That was a stupid thing to say."

"No, not really," Tallin was feeling generous. "We are close. Just not in the same way as the others. I suppose I can see how you might think otherwise."

"Thank you for explaining," Kirian said. "I have trouble understanding people sometimes."

"I've noticed," Tallin said. "Is that why you watch us all so closely?"

"Something like that," Kirian looked away, his face becoming pinker.

"We're all quite boring really."

"You are hardly boring." Kirian half-smiled.

"Well, thank you," she said, then grinned as she had a sudden thought. "Anyway, was there a reason you wanted to know? About me and Ithal?"

It was Kirian's turn to choke on his own tongue, the scarlet blush spreading down his throat into his tunic.

"What? No, I was simply curious," he stuttered, as Ruari giggled behind him.

"You two need garn," the boy shouted, his eyes twinkling with laughter. There was no doubt what he meant by his comment, and Tallin flushed at the thought.

"Ruari," Kirian began, his voice stern.

"Varinyx!"

The shout came from Cearul at the end of the line. Tallin whipped her mare around and saw the unmistakeable movement beneath the sand, heading towards them at a fast pace.

"Run," she yelled, tugging at Bridget's mouth and kicking her into a gallop. Harsh air blew from the horses' nostrils as they reached speed, surrounded by whimpers and high, rattling shouts of encouragement from Cearul and Fianna which nearly drowned out the muffled thud of hooves as they raced through the soft surface.

She heard the hush-shush of the grains of sand moving as the varinyx drew closer, the startled whinny of a horse cut short, the rough gasps of the riders and animals around her as they pushed through their exhaustion, racing towards safety.

Tallin's mind was blank, her muscles aching and her throat tight as she clung on to Bridget's neck, urging her forward. She couldn't breathe and could barely see through the dust that was being flung into her face by the hooves of the horse in front of her.

"Stop," Cearul called, and it took the others mere seconds to comply. Tallin and Bridget were both drenched in sweat, the mare's eyes rolling in distress. Tallin glanced around, the ground under their feet smooth and unmoving, the varinyx gone. She let out the breath that she felt she had been holding for hours, her hand shaking on Bridget's reins.

"Is everyone here?" Fianna shouted as they all glanced around. All that could be seen of the varinyx was a whirlpool of sand which was now moving rapidly off into the distance.

"We lost another horse," Ithal said. "And that means we've lost the garn too."

Tallin swore softly under her breath.

"At least it was enough," Kirian said. "The serpent has fed, and it was not one of us."

"I'm sure that poor old horse doesn't care about that," Ithal said.

Fianna nodded. "I agree. It's a blow to lose our belongings, but it could have been worse."

FIVE

After that, they barely stopped riding until they had reached the other side of the plain. They rode through the night, the chill biting through their clothes and freezing Tallin's fingers into claws around her horse's reins. By the time the sand began to turn to grit and clods of earth beneath their horses' hooves, it was well past middle-light of the following day and the sun was beating down hard on their skin. The horses had slowed to a grudging walk, exhausted and thirsty, and Tallin's head was beginning to pound.

"We should stop," she said, and her voice cracked in her throat. "The horses will need water as much as we do."

"They can't have a lot," Fianna said. "We only have ten waterskins left now, and they need to last until Harrintown."

"How far are we from the city?" Tallin asked.

Kirian sighed. "At least three nights, if we ride straight there."

Ten waterskins, six horses and six people. It didn't take a clever person to know that they would struggle.

"And if we don't?" Fianna asked.

"There is a waterfall in the forest to the southwest of the city, less than two days ride away. We could divert, and that should give us enough water to make it to the palace," Kirian said.

"What about our food?" Tallin asked.

"Ah, yes," Kirian said. "We may need to hunt for some more of that."

"Let's stop now for a short while. We all need to eat and drink, and we can decide what to do after that." Ithal was the voice of reason, Tallin thought, as she reined her mare in and dismounted. Bridget was all too willing to stop, her head drooping and her eyes glazed.

"We have to go to the waterfall," she said. "Look at her – she's drained. We can't lose any more horses, or we'll be lost ourselves."

"I agree," Cearul said. "It's no use rushing. We need to be sensible. It's easier to hunt game and collect berries than to deal with collapsing horses."

"Do you know how to get there?" Tallin asked Kirian.

"I do," he said. "I have been there before, and I have a good memory for places."

"You're certainly well-travelled."

"I have visited most areas," Kirian said.

"How come?" Tallin asked. "What takes you to these

places?"

Kirian took a deep breath. "I am just a traveller," he said, "moving from one place to another looking for work or for people I can help. It is surprising where such a life takes you."

"What sort of work do you do?"

"You saw me earlier," he said, his eyes shifting away from hers. "I am a herbalist, and I collect plants from all over Glendoran for potions and poultices which can help in many ways. They can reduce fever, they can counter poison, they can even imbue strength. People want potions for all number of reasons."

"So that's why you've been to this waterfall, then?"

"Yes. A rare plant grows there, umber leaf. It is used to reduce swelling in the skin."

"I see."

Tallin poured some water from one of the skins into one of the few remaining pans and held it out for her mare. The animal buried her nose in the pan gratefully. Tallin waited until the horse had finished drinking before taking a draught for herself, the liquid soothing her dry throat like an ointment.

Cearul was kneeling on the long, pale grass which grew beside the stony track they were following, sorting through what remained of their belongings.

"One tent, big enough for two, or three at a push. Three pans. Two bedrolls, two blankets. A few chrysellium lamps. Ten waterskins, as we already know.

61

Two pouches of herbs. A bag of dried plants. And we all still have our backpacks, except Ithal."

"Wait, didn't Ithal have the coin in his?" Tallin frowned, wondering how they would be able to bargain for fresh supplies in Harrintown without it.

Fianna chuckled. "He did, but it became too heavy for him to carry so he passed it on to me."

"Now you're grateful I'm old and weak, eh?" Ithal smiled ruefully.

Once the horses were watered and rested, they mounted and began to ride towards Bertalg Forest, where Kirian said the waterfall would be found. They would be travelling along the main merchant's trail at least until nightfall, the horses almost automatically following the path of stone and compacted earth flattened out by many hooves and wheels over the years. Tallin was able to relax slightly and began to relax as her body swayed to the rhythm of her big mare's loping gait.

Lapsing into reverie, she found herself thinking about what the waterfall would be like. She had never seen such a thing, and she wondered if it would be as majestic and glorious as she pictured. In her mind, it was a tower of silver water, sparkling in the sun as it cascaded into a deep blue pool, crashing with a roar around the smooth, dark rocks at its base. She imagined it beautiful, imagined herself stepping into the water and feeling the spray on her face and her body.

She imagined the others there with her. Ruari would be playful, she thought. She was almost certain he would never have seen a waterfall either and would share in her childlike joy. Ithal would watch from dry ground, of course. He wasn't one for play.

Fianna and Cearul might be able to have some time alone in a beautiful place. It would be nice for them, she thought, to be able to be together without care, even if it was just for one stolen moment.

As for Kirian, well, he would have seen it all before. She pictured him standing beside her and smiling indulgently at her enthusiasm, the water droplets catching in his hair and the sun's sparkle reflecting in his eyes. She would be looking up at him and laughing, and perhaps. Perhaps...

Tallin shook her head fiercely and blinked her eyes. Was she daydreaming about "the weird man," as Isbel had called him? The sun had clearly got to her far worse than she had realised.

Sleep that night was difficult, although at least the ground was dry and the air was not too chill. They found a spot off the main track, hidden behind some thick, scrubby bushes full of fat, round berries which Kirian announced were edible, and Tallin picked and ate them until her fingers and lips were bright purple.

Ithal, still weak after his injury, slept in the tent. Everyone else managed as best they could outside, huddled around a fire built using wood from the trees that were once again growing beside the roadside. It was nearing middle-dark and Ruari was the only one who had managed to doze off, curled into a little ball in a patch of granny-tongue ferns beneath a tree.

"Is it possible to die from lack of sleep?" Tallin

grumbled.

"Eventually," Kirian said. "Likely your body would shut down, or you could make a fatal mistake through exhaustion."

"Cheerful," Fianna said. "I don't think she wanted an actual answer."

"Oh."

"It's fine," Tallin said. "I just want you to promise that if I do die of exhaustion, you'll burn my cold, dead corpse before I reanimate and try to murder you all."

"I suppose," Kirian said doubtfully.

Tallin shook her head. She should know better than to confuse the poor man, but it was just too easy to do.

"I wouldn't actually try to murder you," she said, patting his shoulder.

"You cannot know what you would do," Kirian said. "If you were under the control of the necromancer, you might be forced to kill people."

"Again, cheerful," Fianna said. "Can we change the subject?"

"Gladly," Tallin said. "So, has anyone got any good campfire stories?"

"Ithal's the storyteller," Cearul said, "and he's asleep."

Kirian coughed pointedly, and everyone looked at

him.

"Would you tell me about how the two of you met?"

Fianna and Cearul looked at each other and smiled.

"I'll let you tell that one," Fianna said.

Cearul nodded. "All right. It must have been five or six years ago when I was twenty. Until then, I lived in Clestead village, just outside the abbey, with my mother and father who had worked in service to the monks since before I was born. When I reached my majority, I was apprenticed as a guard."

"He was sent to me for training," Fianna said.

"Am I telling this story or are you?" Cearul raised an eyebrow.

"Sorry. Carry on."

"My first day, I was given a greatsword and a set of clothes made of leather. Then I was sent to the guardroom and told to look for a tall, red-haired warrior who would show me where I was to stay and who would guide me through what I needed to learn," Cearul said. "I didn't expect it to be a woman."

"Do elven women not fight, then? Chraisa had a bow," Kirian asked.

"Oh, elven women fight. I wasn't brought up among elves. In my home, my father was always in charge, always the one who would do the heavy work. He would be the one to hunt and skin animals; my mother was, I suppose the word would be soft. It was a shock to me to meet a woman who was so fierce and tough."

"Admit it, you were scared of me." Fianna grinned.

"Terrified," Cearul said. "You shouted at me four times that first afternoon. I thought I'd be going home in shame within days."

Fianna snorted. "So did I."

"I was pretty hopeless with the greatsword. It was Fianna who suggested I change to the bow. I think if it weren't for that, I wouldn't have made it as a guard at all."

"You're a little clumsy on your feet, my love," Fianna said. "You've got as good an eye as anyone I've met, but you're stronger when you can take someone by surprise. You're clever and tactical, whereas I'm a bit more about the brute force."

"I wouldn't even try to compete in that respect," Cearul said with a smile.

"So when did you fall in love?" Kirian asked.

Cearul spat out a laugh. "For me, about three days after we met. For her, it took a lot longer."

"You were so young," Fianna said. "I thought you were strangely appealing from the first moment, but love? No, that was some months away."

"Strangely appealing," Cearul mused. "Thank you. Such high praise."

"How did you know?" Kirian asked.

"What, that I loved her? I don't know. It's hard to describe. I suppose I was drawn to her as I watched her spar with her sword. She was so strong, and she was so graceful, and the look on her face – all concentration and focus. And then she'd stop, and she'd be shining with sweat and her wonderful red hair would be plastered to her face, and she'd look at me with those eyes as green as the forest, and all I could think was how much I wanted to touch her."

Fianna made an amused sound. "You know it's love when you still want to touch someone even when they're sweaty and they stink."

"So what did you do?" Kirian asked.

Tallin had never heard this story before. She leaned closer and smiled in encouragement for Cearul to go on.

"Well, I didn't touch her, if that's what you're wondering. I didn't have a death wish."

"No, it wasn't until around Juilin of that year, remember, when we went hunting and you were attacked by that bear?" Fianna said, turning to the others. "He was pinned by a black bear, and I honestly thought he was dead. Swung my sword so hard that it sliced clean into the bear's throat."

"Almost mine, too," Cearul laughed.

"Yes, well. I was upset. I think it was then that I realised how I felt about him. I had to check him over for any injuries" – and here, Fianna actually blushed – "and I suppose it just happened."

"You kissed me," Cearul said triumphantly. "You know it's love when you still want to kiss someone even when they're covered in bear blood and filth."

"It was memorable at least, if not for the taste," Fianna said.

"Well, I think it's a lovely story," Tallin said, "horrible, violent bear attack and all."

"You know what they say," Cearul said, "the truest love never walks the easiest path."

Kirian frowned. "What do you mean?"

"It's just a phrase," Fianna said. "It doesn't really mean anything, just one of those things people say when they're being all serious."

"And people are serious a lot when they talk about love," Tallin said, "which is ridiculous. Surely it's one of the best feelings you can have. I don't know why everyone gets all uptight about it."

"I think you'll find it's not love they have a problem with," Fianna said with a grin. "It's sex. Those monks think that the world will end if they stick it in someone."

Kirian looked shocked. Tallin laughed.

"Lucky we don't all feel that way, or it'd be pointless trying to save it," she said.

"Indeed," Fianna said. "Now, while we're on the subject, Cearul and I are going to go for a little walk. We won't wander far."

"Just keep the noise down," Tallin said with a smile.

"Naturally."

Tallin watched them walk away hand in hand. It was people like that, she thought, who made the world worth fighting for. Love like that. It warmed her heart more than any fire could, to see them together.

"Are they really going to...?"

She looked up at Kirian whose face was a picture in the firelight. His eyes were wide and so clear that she could see the flickering flames reflected in their depths.

"Of course," she said. "We don't have tents now, so it's the only privacy they'll get. And considering the danger we're going into, I don't blame them for taking every chance they can to be together."

"You are feeling mortal," Kirian said. This time, there was no question in his voice.

"We all are," she said.

"I try not to think about it."

"Good for you," she said. "Some of us find it a bit harder to distance ourselves from impending doom."

"You sound scared," Kirian said.

"It'd be strange if I wasn't."

"But what are you really scared of?" he said, focusing on her intently as if he could see right through her skin to the thoughts that lay behind her eyes.

Tallin sighed and lowered her head, staring at her hands. Gods, her fingernails were disgusting, she thought. Not that it mattered. Nobody cared.

"Nobody would miss me if I died out here," she said, raising her hand to stop Kirian from interrupting. "No, really, they wouldn't. Oh, they'd miss my magic, they'd miss what I stood for – they wouldn't be able to brag about the powerful sibylant living in Clestead Abbey any more – but me? No, most of them don't even know who I am, not really."

"What about Ithal?"

Tallin shrugged. "Perhaps. He'd be the only one, and given that he'd put himself in the way of any danger, the chances are he'd not be about to do any grieving."

"There must be someone else who would," Kirian said.

"Ha. My maid, I suppose, and Cook. But they'd get over it soon enough."

Kirian shook his head. "That all sounds a little self-pitying to me."

Tallin stared at him for several silent beats, then laughed aloud. "I thought you said you couldn't understand people."

He shrugged. "Good guess."

"Tell me then," she said, feeling daring. "Would you mourn me if I died?"

Their eyes met and, for a transient moment, she saw something strange and dark in his expression. He opened his mouth but didn't answer, his jaw working over silent words.

"Fine, I get it," she said quickly. "Forget I asked. Not important."

"It is complicated," he said finally, his voice low.

"I don't understand. How can it be complicated? You'd either miss me or you wouldn't."

"I enjoy your company," he said, "and I would miss that. I am not used to being around people for so long, and when this is all over I think I will miss that. Is that an answer?"

"It's an answer," she said, "just not a very good one."

"I am not sure what else I can say. It is strange for me, to spend time getting to know someone else. But I am glad it is you."

Tallin gave him a wry smile as she threw more sticks on to the fire. "For what it's worth, I'm glad too. Even if it does mean sleeping in the wet grass and worrying about the end of the world."

"There is little I can do about that," Kirian said.

"I know. At least we can worry together, though, right?"

"We can."

Kirian smiled at her, that face-changing expression

she wished she would see more often. As she held his gaze, the air in her chest grew thin and she had to look away.

Tallin lay down on a patch of soft moss between the protruding roots of one of the larger oak trees and pulled a threadbare blanket over herself. She closed her eyes and feigned the steady breathing of sleep, listening to Kirian methodically cracking twigs between his fingers close by.

After a time, she did not have to pretend any longer.

Her back ached when she awoke, chilled and stiff in the early morning dewfall. Strangely, she could not remember dreaming. Perhaps, she thought, her body was too busy conserving its energy in the cold night air.

After the drama of the past days, the journey to the falls was uneventful. Cearul's black gelding got a stone in its shoe, but Kirian plucked it out with a thin-bladed knife which he pulled from his own small pack, and the horse walked on happily, to everyone's relief.

They made good time, and an hour after middle-light they were riding through the depths of Bertalg Forest. The forest was very different to the sparse woodland which grew in South Inwold, the other side of the plains. Tallin had never seen so many trees, their trunks thick and gnarled so she could almost see the shapes of faces in the wood. The leaves were abundant, shiny and a rich, dark green, and they formed a canopy over their heads as they rode between the trunks. Sunlight pushed through small gaps in the foliage, lighting up their path in stripes, dust motes dancing in the rays like glitter.

"I hope you know where you're leading us," Fianna said to Kirian.

"I know," Kirian said simply.

Tallin gazed with wide eyes at the strange surroundings. She hoped that Kirian was right. She had no idea where she was, and the thought was unsettling.

SIX

The sun was nearly all the way across the sky by the time they rode into a wide clearing of pale grass dotted with the deep orange of the umber leaf.

"It's smaller than I thought it would be," Tallin said, gazing at the falls.

The water trailed in thin, grey ropes from a sharply-jutting rock face into a small, rocky pool below, about the width of Tallin's bedroom at the monastery. A narrow river – more like a puddle, she thought ungraciously - wound its way from the pool into the trees, becoming more shallow and sluggish as it went. Even the low rays of sunlight sparkling across the surface didn't do anything to make it look any more attractive.

Cearul and Ruari went to hunt before the light was lost, the boy taking with him a small catapult as a weapon. According to Kirian, wild boar and wood raftan lived in the forest in large numbers, and there would be enough meat on a boar to feed them for several days.

It was while they were gone that the underbrush rustled and a small, grey culai came leaping out into the clearing, lowering its head between its front paws as if it were bowing to them.

Fianna immediately drew her sword, and Tallin felt her fingertips itch with magic.

"Wait," Kirian called, just as she was about to unleash a spell.

"What do you mean, wait?" Ithal said. "One of those things nearly killed me. Why are you stopping? Get rid of it."

"Culai never come inland from the plains, and they are pack animals. There is something strange about this one," Kirian said, frowning as he slowly began to approach the animal. He knelt down, feet from its face.

"What are you doing here?" he said, his voice hushed and soft. "Why would you come to us alone when it is clear we have weapons?"

The culai whined and blinked.

"I cannot understand you," Kirian continued. "Do you want something from us?"

It began to turn in circles, nose to tail, still whining.

"Show me, then," Kirian said.

The culai turned tail and trotted off into the trees. Kirian made to follow.

"What are you doing?" Fianna called, concern in her voice.

"It wants me to see," Kirian said, not looking back.

"Well, if he's going, then so am I," Tallin said.

"Oh, in the name of the gods," Ithal swore. "It's probably just trying to draw us away so it can pick us off one by one."

"Then perhaps we should all go together," Fianna said, following with her sword still in her hand.

"What about the horses?" Ithal said plaintively.

"They're hobbled. They won't go far," Fianna said. "Come on."

Tallin pressed forward through the trees until she almost stumbled over Kirian on his knees behind an overgrown bush.

"What's happening?" she asked, touching his shoulder lightly.

He jumped, and as he moved back she could see, over his shoulder, a tiny human-shaped creature, caught in a rusty wire trap, unconscious and wounded. Kirian was working at the trap with deft fingers, trying to free it.

"An aulin," she breathed, eyes going wide. She had heard tales of these little creatures but had never dreamed she would see one. This one was female, the mossy daubings of her tribe still visible beneath the crusted blood staining her body. The skin underneath was a rich conker-brown, dotted with large dark blotches and freckles. If not for her grass-green hair, which was corded and thicker than a human's, she would look almost like a yearling human child. She looked as vulnerable as a babe, lying on the ground.

"She has lain here for days," Kirian said. "This trap

is old, set many years ago to catch boar. Nobody would have checked it. If not for the culai, she would have died. She may still."

"Do you know how to help her?" Tallin asked.

"I will try."

Kirian gathered the aulin into his arms, gently and carefully, and began a slow, steady walk back to the clearing.

"Well, isn't that a thing," Ithal muttered. "Ain't never seen one of them in my life."

"They're secretive creatures," Fianna said. "Cearul told me stories about one he met, once, but mostly they live where people do not."

"Can't say I blame them," Ithal said.

They lay the aulin down on one of the remaining bedrolls, and Kirian tore a strip from the hem of his tunic, moistening it in the waterfall to clean her skin. .

"The injury is deep, and she has lost a lot of blood," he said, shaking his head. "I can heal the flesh, but she may be too weak to recover."

A twig snapped, and Tallin twisted towards the sound. The culai had returned and was lingering at the edge of the clearing, hesitant and trembling.

"That thing's back," Ithal muttered.

"Thank you, Ithal, we all have eyes," Fianna said.

Kirian glanced over at the animal. "It means no harm. It is bonded somehow with this aulin. It wanted our help."

"Leave it alone," Tallin said. "Kirian is right. It wanted to save her."

"And once we do, it'll feast on our bones," Ithal said bitterly.

Fianna chuckled. "You think a single culai would be a match for us?"

"As I know," Ithal said, "it only takes one bite. I don't trust it."

"Well, I trust Kirian," Tallin said. "And he says it won't hurt us, so let's not worry."

"You can sit nearest it then," Ithal said, "if you're so confident."

"Fine."

Tallin pointedly sat on the grass, closer to the animal than anyone else in the group, turning her back to it. She pulled a face at Ithal.

"Childish," he said.

She stuck out her tongue.

A large stone flew past her ear and crashed into the undergrowth behind her, sending the culai skittering frantically into the forest. Ruari popped his head up from behind a large trunk, waving his catapult triumphantly.

"Culai gone. I save you."

"It was not hurting us," Kirian said with a sigh.

"Thank you, Ruari," Tallin said. "How did you get on with the hunting?"

"Three raftan," the boy said. "I killed two."

"He is a fine hunter indeed," Cearul said, emerging from the trees with the kills. The small, brown animals dangled from their bushy tails, tied to a stick in the elf's hand. "These will feed us well tonight."

Cearul's eyes went wide as he noticed the aulin, Kirian continuing to dab at her injuries. "An aulin? What's going on?"

"We found her caught in a trap," Tallin said. "Kirian's trying to heal her."

"I never thought I'd see another one of those," Cearul said. "Years ago when I was a teenager, I saved a fox cub from drowning in a bog. Turned out it was the totem animal for a young aulin, who gave me a gemstone."

Fianna pulled out a thin necklace set with a bright, polished emerald. "This one."

"Perhaps you will bring luck," Kirian said. "She will need it."

"Totem animal?" Tallin asked.

"Aulin are born into tribes, and each tribe is linked to an animal as a symbol of their god. The markings on their skin represent that animal," Cearul said. Tallin looked at the unconscious aulin. She supposed she could see, from the remaining clots of green dye daubed across her skin, that they were in the shape of an animal with four legs and a long snout.

"I guess that explains why the culai was hanging around," Fianna said.

"Kirian said they were bonded," Tallin said.

"And the child scared the animal away," Kirian said sternly. Ruari's lower lip trembled.

"Don't worry, kid, he's like that to everybody," Ithal said.

Kirian frowned at him before returning to his task. Tallin watched him crush herbs between his fingers, making them into a paste which he sniffed and tasted before working it into the open wounds on the aulin's legs.

Eventually, he stood up. "That is all I can do. We will need to keep her as warm as we can and get some fluids into her somehow. Only time will tell if she wakes up."

"Thank you for trying," Tallin said.

They ate well that evening, the raftan meat rich and tender. They decided that the watch would be taken in pairs, and Tallin was teamed with Kirian for their shift. They stoked the fire and watched night fall while the others huddled in the tent and under blankets, trying to keep warm.

"May I ask you something?" Kirian said, almost in a whisper.

Tallin wondered what he wanted to say that he didn't want to be overheard. "Of course."

"I was thinking about what Ithal said earlier," Kirian said, "about being 'like that' to everybody. What does he mean?"

Tallin felt pinned by the man's earnest gaze. She wasn't sure how to answer the question without offending him.

"Sometimes you can be a little short with people," she said eventually.

"There is little I can do about my height."

Tallin shook her head. "I meant that you can be a bit abrupt at times."

"I do not mean to be," Kirian said. "I do not want anyone to think me rude, especially you."

"I don't think you're rude," she said. "I think you're quite charming, in your own way."

Kirian looked away into the fire, a smile playing over his lips. "Thank you."

Over the next hours, she found herself telling Kirian about her childhood growing up in Skiffield with her mother. She told him all about how her father had died when she was four, bitten by a snake while tilling the fields behind their cottage. About how her mother had worked hard to put food on the table, sewing wonderful gowns for the nobility from the finest silks and beads. About how she had always wanted to be able to wear the gowns instead of watching her mother's creations be shipped off to yet another spoiled duchess.

About the day she was taken away to spend her days sitting in a small room at the monastery, the scent of the lavender in their cottage garden a distant memory. How she missed her mother's hugs, the warmth of her arms and her heart.

She couldn't remember ever telling anyone these stories, yet sitting beside the fire looking into Kirian's eyes, she felt the words spill out as if they were an uncontrollable wave. When she finally stopped talking, her eyes were red and itchy with barely-held tears.

"Would you like me to hug you?" Kirian asked, his voice hesitant.

"I'd like that very much," she said.

Tallin stood and walked into his embrace, her cheek resting against his shoulder as he wrapped his arms around her tightly and held her. His breath played lightly over her hair, and she closed her eyes and cried silently into the rough cloth of his tunic.

After a few minutes, she stepped back and rubbed her eyes. "I'm sorry. I feel a very long way from home here."

"I understand," he said. "I hope I helped."

"You did. And I am grateful."

The tent rustled behind her, and Ithal clambered out, Ruari just behind him.

"Time for me and the boy to take over, I think. You may as well use the tent. Fianna and Cearul are fast asleep over by the waterfall, and the aulin doesn't take up much space."

Tallin nodded and pulled open the tent flap. "Luck for the watch. Hope nothing comes out of the night for you."

"You sleep well," Ithal said.

Kirian hesitated.

"There's room for you as well," Tallin said. "Better than being cold."

He smiled and followed her into the tent. The aulin was wrapped up in blankets on the far side of the tent, her breathing shallow but steady. Tallin sat down on a thin bedroll next to the aulin, leaving Kirian with the spot nearest the entrance.

"You get the draughty bed," she said with a grin.

"That is fine," he said. "I can sleep anywhere."

Tallin lay on her back staring into the darkness. It had been a strange evening. She was embarrassed that she had cried all over Kirian's shoulder, but he hadn't seemed to mind. Instead, he had held her so tightly that she had felt the tremble in his arms, the beating of his heart against hers. He had felt so real beside her, soft and warm and vibrantly alive. His touch had brought her comfort when she had needed it most.

"Are you awake?" she murmured.

"I am," Kirian replied.

"Thank you for tonight," she said. "You made me feel less alone."

"I am glad," he said. "You should never feel alone."

His gentle words sent silent tears coursing down her cheeks, and she fell asleep with a smile on her face and with no nightmares waiting to pounce as soon as she closed her eyes.

SEVEN

When she cracked her eyes open again, she found that Kirian had curled his body around hers during the night. His arm was thrown across her waist, and she could feel the heat of his breath on the back of her neck. She lay very still, not daring to move in case she woke him.

Time passed slowly and the morning outside became lighter. Perhaps forty minutes after she had woken, Kirian stirred, inhaling with a startled gasp as he realised his position. He rolled away from her as if he was on fire.

"I apologise. I did not mean to."

"It's fine, Kirian," she said, turning to face him. "I don't mind. You kept me warm, at least."

He stared at her like a scared mouse.

"We should get up," he said, his voice shaky. "And I need to check on the aulin."

As he moved past her on his knees to look at the still-unconscious creature, Tallin grabbed his arm.

"Wait."

Kirian froze, and she could feel the tension thrumming through his body.

"What are you frightened of?" she asked.

"I am not sure what you mean," he said, his eyes sliding away from hers.

"Do you know," she said conversationally, "last night I didn't have any nightmares. That was the best sleep I've had for months."

Kirian nodded, still refusing to look at her.

Tallin took a deep breath, trying to settle the quivering in her stomach.

"I'd like to sleep like that again," she said, "if you want to."

He finally turned his head to meet her gaze. That lost look was in his eyes again, sorrowful and intense.

"Perhaps we should not," he said, his voice cracking over the words.

"Why not?" She was aware she sounded like a petulant child and closed her eyes, wincing inwardly.

"You are right," he said. "I am afraid. Afraid of how I feel."

Her eyes flicked open, and a lump formed in her throat. "And how do you feel?" she asked, her voice barely a whisper.

"You would not understand."

She reached up and ran her fingers through his hair, the palm of her hand coming to rest against his jaw.

"Would this," she said, leaning forward and pressing her lips against his lightly, once, twice before pulling away. "Would it be so terrible?"

He stared at her, wide eyed, a look of almost comical surprise on his face. She moved in to kiss him again, and he turned his face to the side, his throat working furiously.

"I am sorry," he said, his voice soft and wavering, sounding as if it came from a distant place.

"Tell me you don't want to," Tallin said.

"I cannot," he said after a long pause, "but this would not be right. It would not be fair on you, in the end."

Tallin frowned, her cheeks beginning to flush with heat.

"How do you know?" she asked. "We could win. We could do this, and then everything would be back to normal. All of us could get our lives back."

"Even if we do," Kirian said, "I would have to leave. We would have no future."

"Why not?"

He shook his head. "I wish I could tell you. I am sorry."

"And I wish you'd stop saying sorry," Tallin said.

He moved away from her, kneeling over the aulin and bending his head so she could not see his face. She felt like screaming, but instead turned away and pushed out of the tent, the bright, sunny morning outside doing nothing to improve her mood.

Ithal was frying the remaining raftan meat in a pan over the campfire. He looked up at her with a smile. "Sleep well?"

She grunted and sat down beside him, reaching out to poke the meat with a stick.

"Well, you're cheerful this morning," Ithal said.

"Shut up, Ithal."

"Ah, I see."

She turned on him, irritated. "What do you mean, you see?"

He was saved from answering by the arrival of Cearul, Fianna and Ruari.

"We need to think about packing up and setting off," Cearul said, "if we want to make good progress before nightfall."

"What about aulin?" Ruari said.

"Good point," Ithal said. "Is she still unconscious?"

"Yes," Tallin said "as far as I know. Kirian is checking on her now."

"So what are we going to do? We can't leave her here," Fianna said.

"Either we stay here another day to see if she recovers, or we take her with us," Ithal said.

Tallin shrugged. "Don't look at me."

"We'll decide once we've spoken to Kirian," Ithal said.

The aulin had shown no signs of waking, but some colour had returned to her face, which according to Kirian was a good sign.

"She may wake soon, but we should not tarry," Kirian said. "She is small enough and slight enough to travel with one of us, if we are careful."

And so they had packed their gear, filled their waterskins and wrapped up the last of the cooked meat. The horses were wide awake and content, their bellies full of lush grass, and they were soon back on the trail, the aulin strapped to Fianna's waist with the rope from the tent. Tallin was reminded of a mother carrying a yearling child in a sling, though she wouldn't dare tell Fianna that.

Kirian glanced over his shoulder. "We are just under two days' travel from Harrintown by my estimation. We will have one more night to set camp, but we should reach the city tomorrow just before dusk."

"And what then?" Fianna asked.

"We'll need to persuade the emperor to allow us an audience," Ithal said. "Just like that. Easy."

Tallin huffed loudly. "This is ridiculous. We all know he's going to send us away."

"What harm is there in asking?" Ithal said. "We can't do this by ourselves. We need to get whatever help we can."

"Well, I hope he's in a better mood than Tallin," Fianna said, grinning as Tallin shot her a wicked glance. "Someone had ants in the bed last night, by the look of her."

"Shut up."

Ithal chuckled. "That's pretty much what I've had all morning so far, too."

"Shut up."

They rode until the trees began to thin and they were once again travelling on a clearly marked track.

"The culai is following us," Cearul remarked, glancing back over his shoulder. Tallin followed his gaze. The small animal was some distance back but was loping along the side of the road from tree to tree, trailing them.

"It will do," Kirian said. "It is bound to the aulin and cannot leave her."

"What if she dies?" Fianna asked.

"Then it will pine away," Kirian said.

It kept tabs on them for hours, hovering in the distance when they stopped to feed and water the horses, and it was still there when the sun began to lower on the horizon. Just as Tallin felt herself start to sag in the saddle, they came across the ruins of an old cathedral on a hillside overlooking a smattering of farmhouses.

"We could knock at a door and see if we could get beds for the night?" Fianna said hopefully.

Ithal shook his head. "Look at us. We are too many, and we have an elf and an aulin. No stranger in the middle of nowhere would share their home with us tonight."

"He is right," Kirian said. "There is shelter aplenty here. Half the roof is still intact on the cathedral, and we will be out of the worst of the cold."

Tallin gazed around the ruins. The cathedral must have been regal once, she thought, the grey stone walls tall and imposing. The large, arched windows were damaged but still held some of their original coloured glass, cracked and grubby but clear enough to catch the last rays of the evening light which rippled and flickered across the remains of the old marble floor.

The tombs around the building were mostly overgrown, stones rising from the grassy earth like golem's fingers. Several mausoleums still stood on the grounds, each one carved with a family insignia. One or two of them were cracked open, as if grave robbers had paid a visit. Tallin shivered. For all its beauty, the place was creepy, and she wasn't at all sure about sleeping there.

"Let's get the tent up and a fire started," Cearul said. "It's as good a place as any to stop."

Tallin let out a heavy sigh.

"What's the matter with you?" Fianna asked. "Face like a smacked arse all day."

"Nothing," Tallin said. "This place is just giving me the shivers."

"Better than being out in the open," Fianna said. "Come on, give us a hand with the tent."

The watch rota was set the same as the previous night. Tallin wanted to object but she knew that would only draw attention to her awkwardness around Kirian, and she decided it would be better to grit her teeth and try her best to ignore him. A plan which worked well until a man loomed out of the darkness.

"Who's there?" Kirian called, his eyes trained on the shadows of the night. Tallin stared but could not see anything. She closed her eyes and thought about the anger she had felt that morning, bringing shards of magic fizzing to her fingertips.

In the light of her spell, she could see a figure shambling towards them, slightly lopsided and limping.

"Who are you?" she asked. "What are you doing out here?"

There was no answer. The person kept moving.

Tallin clenched her fists, and the light strengthened. She could see now that it was an old man, perhaps seventy. He was pale and thin, and there were clods of damp earth in his hair and clinging to his rough clothing.

Next to her, Kirian let out a harsh breath. "He has come back through."

"Gods," Tallin said, her voice catching in her throat. "What are we going to do?"

"Give me your dagger," Kirian said.

She handed the blade over silently, her fingers trembling around the hilt. "What do you need it for?"

"What do you think? He should not be here."

Tallin felt her magic bubble in her veins, fear and horror sparking the fiery rush of it. This had been someone's loved one, someone they had carefully buried and grieved over. Someone's husband, perhaps, father, grandfather. She wondered briefly what sort of life he had led, what kind of man he had been.

This man should be lying at rest, she thought, the downy hairs on her skin standing up with the prickle of her fury. This man should be in the arms of Afallach, deep in his eternal slumber. Not here, shuffling through the mud in a used-up body.

Kirian had gone over to the man and was ducking the weak swings of his fists. The man was making incoherent growling noises, his mouth open and yellowed eyes filmy and wet.

"Shhh," Kirian said softly, reaching out to hold the

man's flailing arms. "Quiet. I will help you."

With a gentle push, Kirian had the man down on his knees. He crouched alongside him, wrapping his arms around the man's thin, filthy body. Tallin drew closer, watching with wide eyes. Kirian was speaking in a low, melodic voice.

"I will walk with you into the silver clouds, into the twilight where the shadows grow long and silent. I will walk alongside you and guide you into the Everlasting. For it is I who will make the path sweet, who will make it soft and easy. May your footsteps be light and your heart be quiet. May your sleep be dreamless and may you forever be at peace."

Kirian kissed the man's forehead and slid the dagger deep into his eye. The corpse fell backwards with a thump as Tallin winced and stifled a scream.

Kirian stood up, wiping the dagger on his tunic. "We will need to burn the body."

"What?"

"If we do not, there is a chance he will not pass over. He has been dragged back to his earthly body and will remain tied unless it is destroyed. He will suffer."

"Right. I'll wake the others. We'll need to collect fuel."

It was Fianna who found the recently-dug grave in the hillside below the cathedral. Now empty, the walls had caved in and there was a trail of dirt to mark the dead man's path. Wild flowers still lay scattered in the earth, their petals only just beginning to brown.

"They've only just buried him," she said, as they all piled wood into a mound.

"Only the newly dead can retake their bodies," Kirian said. "The older souls will be drawn to the necromancer. He is collecting them."

"I think I've seen them in my dreams," Tallin said. "He has them caught in a glass orb."

"Why?" Fianna asked.

"I cannot answer," Kirian said. "I only know it is happening, not for what reason."

Tallin shuddered. She recalled the anguish of the trapped spirits, the way their colours merged and swirled frantically, beating against the crystal as if desperate to escape.

"It needs to stop," she murmured, as Cearul and Fianna lifted the dead man on to the pyre they had built for him. Fianna leaned over and reverently placed the flowers from the grave on the man's chest before she struck her tinder and lit the fire.

"Afallach take you and keep you safe," Fianna said as the flames began to lick at his clothes.

The pyre would take hours to burn. The smell was sweet, earthy, clinging. Tallin wondered if she would ever get it out of her nostrils. Resuming her watch as the others went back to sleep, she sank down in the soft grass next to Kirian, upwind of the smoke and flames.

"You spoke to him, before he died," Tallin said. "Was

that a prayer?"

"He was already dead," Kirian said.

"You know what I mean."

Kirian blinked at her and inclined his head. "Indeed it was a prayer. One I have repeated countless times. I cannot remember where I learned it."

"The words were beautiful," Tallin said.

"I can but hope they bring some comfort at a difficult time."

"You have seen people die, then, before?"

Kirian looked down at his hands. "I have."

"Is it always peaceful?"

"I would be lying if I said so. Many times it is far from it."

"Will you tell me about it?" Tallin asked.

"About dying?"

"Yes."

It was morbid, she knew, but they faced it every day. None of them knew whether they would make it back home alive or if they would end up the same way as the poor man they had sent back to Everlasting that evening.

"I was in Tramante when they had the plague," Kirian said.

Tallin nodded. She knew about that. Many people still referred to the island as the Plaguelands.

"Hundreds of people died over the months it took to spread across the isle," Kirian said. "I sat beside many unfortunate souls in their last moments. It was not a good death."

"You were lucky not to catch it yourself," Tallin said.

"I was."

"Were you frightened?"

"I watched people's lungs foam through their lips. I watched their bodies stiffen and rack with pain. I looked into their eyes as they died and saw the agony that they could no longer express with sound. Yet, no. I was not afraid."

Tallin sighed. "I'm not afraid, either. Of dying, that is."

"What are you afraid of?"

She waved a hand towards the guttering pyre. "Not dying. I'm terrified of failing and ending up like him."

Kirian looked her in the eye. "I would not let that happen."

"You might not be able to stop it."

He gave her a tight smile. "I would tell Afallach himself to take you home."

"Right, so you're on first name terms with the Soulkeeper, are you?" Tallin rolled her eyes. "You know, while you're at it, why don't you have a word with Ysgwyn and ask him to come help us out here. We could do with a battlemaster, and he's been distinctly absent for all the prayers he gets."

"You mock your gods so casually?" Kirian asked.

"Comes from being brought up in a monastery," Tallin said. "There's only so much of all that stuff you can listen to before you start wondering where these so-called gods actually are."

"So you do not believe?"

Tallin shrugged. "Don't know. All I do know is, if these gods do exist, then surely they'd rather I did something productive with my life instead of spending it on my knees praying and wailing."

"That sounds sensible."

"The monks would not agree," Tallin said.

"Well then. It is lucky for you that you are not a monk," Kirian said with a smile.

Tallin snickered, then forced her face into a serious expression. "I'm still angry with you, you know."

"I know. And I am still sorry."

Tallin opened her mouth to shoot out an irritated response when she saw his lips twitch.

"Are you teasing me?" she asked.

"Perhaps. I could not resist."

Tallin exhaled heavily through her nose and shook her head. Kirian's humour had been unexpected and had taken the sting out of an awkward situation. Perhaps they could at least manage to be civil, if not friendly. They were, after all, going to have to spend a lot more time together.

"You are impossible," she said.

"I do not know how a person can be possible," Kirian replied.

Tallin squealed and threw a large handful of grass at him, which hit him directly in the face and made him splutter. He sighed and began to pick loose blades out of the strands of his hair.

"I am beginning to think Ithal was right about you," he said.

"What? What did he say?" she demanded, her eyes flashing.

"I am trying to think. Something about being as sweet as sugar and as much trouble as a rampant bear in mating season."

"A rampant bear?"

"In mating season. I am just repeating his words. Do not blame me."

Tallin felt her mouth hanging open and closed her jaw with a snap. She would have something to say to

Ithal in the morning, that was for sure.

In the morning, the pyre had burned down to ash
and scorched bone. Kirian used a large, flat stone from
the cathedral floor to sweep the remains into a swiftly-
dug hole while Fianna tidied up the open grave. They had
been fortunate to avoid the attentions of the farm
dwellers beneath the hill, and it would be much better if
nobody was ever aware that the dead man had left his
burial place.

They headed northeast towards the city. The aulin
remained unconscious, and the culai still followed
diligently at a distance. Tallin wondered what would
happen if she had not woken by the time they arrived at
Harrintown. Carrying her into the palace would not be
an option.

North Inwold was more heavily populated than its
southern cousin. They passed through small villages and
townships, occasionally stopping to purchase supplies
from the market stalls which tended to spring up beside
the roads in such places. Their rough southern accents
drew curious stares, and Tallin wondered how they
would fare in the capital. Maybe it would be easier there
to disappear among the crowds.

Half a day outside the city, they set up camp. Only a
few would go on from there into the city. Kirian, Cearul
and Ruari would stay to guard the camp and watch over
the aulin.

Evening was falling as Tallin, Fianna and Ithal
reached Harrintown. The sky was clear and speckled
with stars, and the sharp wind chilled their bones. The

walls of the city loomed like flat mountains as they rode up to the large steel gates, the guards at their posts outside fixing them with cold stares.

"What is your business?" the tallest of the guards asked, a burly man with a long, curly moustache.

"We wish to speak with the emperor," Tallin said. "We have important news and a favour to ask of him."

"I doubt he will be interested in your stories," a second guard said, a woman by the sound of her voice, although her face was hidden beneath a heavy iron helm. "He has enough trouble at the moment without outsiders bothering him."

"What sort of trouble?" Tallin asked.

"The sort which is none of your business," the woman snapped. "Now, be on your way. The emperor has no time for commoners like you."

Tallin raised an eyebrow. "If it has to do with the dead rising, it's our business."

The woman pulled herself to attention, her body going stiff. She would probably be glaring at them if they could see her face. "What do you know of this?"

"We have important information," Tallin said. "We need to speak to Emperor Joacci immediately."

The older guard narrowed his eyes and stroked his moustache with a forefinger. "We should take them to the palace."

The woman grunted. "We don't even know who they

are."

"The emperor will find out soon enough."

"You take them then."

The man shrugged. "Fine. Follow me," he said, beckoning them through the gates.

EIGHT

Tallin was a country girl at heart, used to the small villages and rolling fields of the south. She gazed in naked awe at the sights which surrounded her as they trekked through the city streets towards the palace grounds. Even at dusk the city was busy, people sitting in groups within large, canopied areas lit by torches, eating fragrant curries with shovel-shaped bread. Around them, travelling musicians played cheerful tunes on lute and pipes. A woman was singing, her voice high and clear, although Tallin did not know the language of the song. Small children wandered between tables, selling many different home-made goods from small, brown sweets to candles. The air was heavy with smoke and smelled of burnt oil and spices, with a distinctive undertone of sewage.

She felt a tug at her tunic and turned to find a small, grubby-looking girl holding a tray of fruit.

"Oranges for the lady?" the girl said with a slight lisp. "Only twenny pessles."

"No, thank you," Tallin said, turning away. The girl spat on the ground and began to tug at Ithal's cloak.

"Oranges for the gennelman?"

"For the sake of Ceremor, girl, will you stop pestering everyone?" the guard said, his voice loud and strident. The girl quailed and curtseyed an apology before hurrying away into the crowds.

"Sorry about these people," the guard said. "Terrible hawkers, not much better than beggars really. Wish they'd get 'em off the streets but our emperor has these fancy ideas about human rights or whatever rubbish it is they're talking about now. Bloody nuisance, the lot of 'em, you ask me."

"I don't think we did," Fianna said dryly. The guard harrumphed and lapsed into silence.

The streets became smoother and cleaner underfoot, and the houses larger, as they moved through the city. The people who lived here did not eat in public with their fingers. Tallin could see clearly through the plate glass windows, peering at the families who reclined on soft velvet sofas, candlelight shimmering over richly painted rooms.

"It's rude to stare," the guard said sharply as Tallin craned her neck to look into one particularly interesting home, the furnishings of a style she had never seen before. She blushed and quickly looked away.

Rounding a corner, they came upon another set of iron gates topped with elaborately worked silver stags. Four guards stood alert outside, spears and swords raised and ready. They were dressed in similar armour to the guards from the city gate except they had large, red feathers atop their helms, and each wore an armband with the royal coat of arms stitched into it.

"Halt," one shouted as they approached. "Taliesin.

What brings you here?"

The guard who had accompanied them saluted. "Hail, sister. These people arrived at the gate this evening. Reckon they know why the dead are rising. Asking to see the emperor, of all things. I've brought them so you can decide what to do with them."

"Go on then," the woman said.

"What d'you mean?"

"They can tell me why we have undead walking around our city. We'd all like to know more about that."

Tallin swallowed at the combative tone of the woman's voice. "The shroud between the worlds is damaged. Souls are not staying in Everlasting. Those who are newly-dead are being dragged back through."

"How did this happen?"

"We don't know," Tallin said, "only that souls are being kept by a necromancer somewhere in the northern reaches. We are trying to find him, but we will need help."

The guard narrowed her eyes. "Just how do you know all this?"

"I am a sibylant, Ma'am, and I have dreamed about the necromancer. One of my companions is a sensitive, also, which means they can connect to the souls. We will head north when we leave here, but we were hoping that the emperor might provide us with a small army to protect us on our journey."

"The sibylant from the south, eh? I've heard the stories. Never thought to see you round these parts."

"I had no choice, I was needed," Tallin said.

The guard shook her head. "How do I know you're not causing all this trouble?"

Tallin blinked. "What?"

"You heard me. Why should I trust you? Three days ago, we have reports of the dead climbing out of their graves, and now we have the Southern witch here. What am I supposed to think?"

"We have nothing to do with the break in the shroud," Tallin said.

"Then how come you know so much about it?"

"I explained to you about my dreams," Tallin said, "and my friend who is a sensitive."

"Which one of you is that?" the guard asked.

"He isn't with us," Tallin said.

"Well, that's fortunate for him," said the guard, "because it means he won't be thrown in jail like the rest of you. Cuff them!"

"Hey, wait a moment," Ithal said. "We're trying to help."

"You will have to prove that to the emperor," the woman said as several other guards surrounded them. Tallin hissed as the cold metal of the cuffs snapped tightly around her wrists. Fianna bit out a curse behind her and the sounds of a scuffle ended with the unmistakeable crack of a hand on bare skin.

"Leave her alone," Tallin said. "We'll come with you, I don't want to fight you. But I swear, we've done nothing wrong."

"Emperor Joacci will be the judge of that," an older guard said in her ear, his face so close that his beard tickled her cheek. Tallin shuddered.

The guards marched them into the lower reaches of the palace, the dungeon cold and damp and everything Tallin might have pictured a dungeon to be. She had never imagined herself inside one, however, and her skin prickled with the chill and the fear of being alone down here in the gloomy cells. Shards of magic glimmered beneath the skin of her hands, and she heard the guard draw in a sharp breath.

"She ain't lying, this one," he said to the first guard. "Look at 'er. Fingers all lit up like a Brumalia branch."

"Get her in the cells, quick," the woman said. "She's going to need sedating, too. Not taking no chances with that stuff."

Tallin fell to her knees as the man pushed her roughly through the iron-barred door of one of the cells, crying out as the coarse stone floor tore her leggings and grazed her knee.

"You even try using them spells, girl, and your friends will pay for it," the guard spat as he shut the door with a clang. "Now, get over here and give me your hands if you don't want us to hurt them."

Tallin pictured her friends being tortured, imagined how Fianna would fight and, probably, pay the ultimate price. She sighed and held her wrists up to a sliding panel on the door, trying not to look as the man slid a needle into the vein on the back of her hand and a chill began to creep along her arm. The guard reached through the gap, then, and took the cuffs from her aching arms. She rubbed fruitlessly at the raw skin beneath, tears springing to her eyes as her head began to swim.

Tallin sat in silence, fighting the heaviness of her eyelids, the only light coming from the occasional spark of magic from her fingertips. Her breath was thick in the darkness, the icy air knifing through her chest with every inhalation. The cell smelled of moss and damp, and she imagined insects skittering down her throat and into her lungs. She couldn't stop shivering.

She'd known that it would be no easy task to persuade Emperor Joacci to assist them, but she had expected the worst that would happen would be that they were thrown out of the city and told not to return. She hoped the emperor himself would be more sympathetic in the morning.

With a loud sigh, she lay on the hard floor and gave in to the swimming of her vision, eyes closed, gritting her teeth against the cold that seeped into her joints as the drug began to drag her down. Her mind wandered to Kirian, Ruari and Cearul, wondering how long it would be before they realised that something had gone wrong. They'd come after them, she knew, and she passed out with a prayer on her lips that they would be more careful and less trusting than she had been.

The dreams she had were vibrant and violent. The crystal orb was there, as ever; this time, it was almost full of roiling colours, the surface of the orb seeming to stretch and bubble as the souls tried to push their way free. She could feel the panic and hatred oozing from them, the confusion of people who were once alive reduced to tendrils of light cocooned within glass.

She dreamed of the necromancer, his face hidden beneath his cloak as he worked on the constructs in the castle basement. The metal giants were large, clumsy-looking beasts held together with screws and plates, mismatched and ugly. They stood in silent rows, a synthetic army awaiting the spark which would stir them into being.

In her nightmare, Tallin conjured up pictures of a future world, one in which there was no death, only enslavement. Each time one of the giant constructs would kill, the soul would be captured and used to animate another. Even within the dream, she understood that this was the future that lay in wait for them all, should they fail.

When her eyes finally cracked open to the sound of clattering iron doors, she had no idea how long she had lain in her drugged sleep, only that her mouth was dry and her stomach was twisting in pain. Despite the cold air, her skin was sheened in sweat.

"Breakfast," a guard said, sliding a bowl of cold oats through the opening in the door. "The emperor will see you in thirty minutes."

Tallin forced herself to eat the bland, sticky oats. They stuck to her teeth and made her gag, but she knew she needed the sustenance. Once the bowl was empty, the guard fastened the cuffs around her sore wrists once again, and sat watching over her until the Emperor's own guard called for her attendance.

She followed the guards back up the stone stairwells, several others walking behind her with sword drawn, presumably to prevent her escape. She didn't know how far she was meant to be able to get with her hands clasped together in irons, but she supposed they thought her magic dangerous enough not to take any risks. Little did they know, she thought bitterly. The drugs that they had pumped into her system had left her sluggish and drained, and she couldn't even begin to summon up the energy needed for her spells.

They went along several narrow corridors and through a small, wooden door. It was plain and innocuous looking, yet it led into a grand hall many steps removed from the dungeons where she had been kept. Tallin looked around incredulously. She had thought the main hall of the monastery extravagant, but it was nothing compared to this.

The room was so long that she could barely see the emperor, perched on an enormous, silver throne at the far end. The floor was polished marble, pale grey with glittering silver striations running through the stone. Around the walls hung elaborate, jewel-coloured tapestries depicting scenes of palace life, from balls to hunting. Each wall hanging must have taken months to create, Tallin thought. She had never seen such craft.

Despite the quality of the tapestries, Tallin's eyes were drawn upwards to the ceiling of the room, high above her head and curved in a pronounced arch. Edged in fine gilt, elaborate paintings covered the surface, knights and dragons depicted in scenes which looked almost as if they could be real. All the folk tales of Glendoran were rendered upon the stone, and Tallin found herself tripping over her own feet as she tried to take in the artwork. Here there was the story of Empress Jasca single-handedly defeating the Commander of the Jotunn with her famous silver sword Soraidh. Next to that battle scene was the story of Captain Kemmis destroying Rhosilian, the last dragon ever seen in Glendoran. Tallin had always felt sad when she had heard that tale for, despite their danger, dragons were majestic creatures. They had been extinct now for a very long time.

Eventually, she reached the dais holding the emperor's throne. She knelt before him, her forehead scraping against the cold floor.

"Your Majesty," she said, her voice trembling.

"Rise," he said, his voice deep and rich, carrying easily through the room. "So, I hear you are the false southern witch I have heard tale of. What is the meaning of your appearance here?"

"I travel with my companions on a mission to repair the broken Shroud," Tallin said. "Souls are no longer safe in Everlasting, and we have reason to believe an evil magic has drawn them back through, Your Majesty. We came here to seek an army to help us on our way."

The emperor frowned, deep wrinkles appearing in his olive skin. "I do not believe that magic truly exists. Perhaps once, in the time of legend, but no longer. You are but a charlatan, come here to seek riches for a virus you have no power over."

Tallin blinked up at the man, his expression still and

severe beneath his heavy brows. She took a deep breath and curled her hands into fists, drawing on the last of her strength to create a ball of weak silver light which shimmered over the iron of her cuffs. She heard the guards beside her hiss and move closer.

"Stop," the emperor commanded. "Enough! This is an evil which cannot be tolerated."

He rose from his throne and took two steps closer to Tallin, who shrank back instinctively. Emperor Joacci was not a tall man, but he felt like a giant to Tallin as he looked down on her from the dais.

"This is no coincidence. We have the dead crawling from their graves, and three days later the southern witch arrives and shows her power. You have something to do with this," he said, waving away her squawk of protest, "and you shall remain in jail until we can arrange a trial. Now, begone!"

The guards immediately grabbed Tallin by the arms and began to drag her away. She cried out in panic and pain, her eyes rolling as she implored the people around the room to do something, to intervene.

"Please," she pleaded, "you have to believe me. We can stop this. We need your help!"

"We cannot trust one who would use magic so lightly," the emperor said as she reached the door, her heels scraping a dark line on the polished floor. "You will stay where we know you are safe."

Back in the cell, Tallin sat with her head in her

hands, tears streaking the dirt on her face. She wondered how long it would take for Kirian, Cearul and Ruari to realise that something was wrong. Even then, she had no idea how the three of them could hope to mount any form of rescue mission. The dungeons were well guarded, and each door was triple-locked with big iron keys carried on the belts of the jailers.

She tested her magic, concentrating on the anger she felt at her ill-treatment, but even then she could still only summon a feeble light with no strength behind it. The drugs that still coursed through her bloodstream were dulling her powers. She cursed quietly, so wrapped up in her thoughts that she didn't notice that a guard stood pressed up against the bars of her cell.

"Hey," he said, his voice low. She whirled and stared at him. The man was *koroni*, a race of people rarely seen on the mainland. His skin was like oil in the rain, a kalcidoscope of glossy purple, green and gold stretched tight over sharp bones. The scales that dappled his cheeks were clear even in the low light. Lizard men, some people called them, and she could see why.

The koroni were known as much for their strength as for their unusual appearance, and this guard was no exception. He stood a full head taller than any human man Tallin had seen, and his shoulders were broad and muscular. There was no doubt why many nobles liked to employ koroni as soldiers and guardsmen, Tallin thought.

This one was clearly trying to get her attention. She wandered over to the door.

"What do you want?" she asked.

"I'm supposed to sedate you again," the man said, his eyes flicking from side to side.

"Supposed to?"

"I heard about what you said to the emperor. I wanted to know if it was true."

Tallin shook her head. "What's the point?"

The koroni stared at her through the bars of the door, his dark eyes faintly glowing in the gloom.

"They say that you know who is raising the dead. They say that you think a necromancer has power over the souls of those who have passed over, that he is drawing them back. Is it true?"

"It's true. You'll all find out, soon enough."

"I want to come with you," the man said, his voice urgent.

"I'm not going anywhere, it seems."

"I can free you."

Tallin stared up at him, narrowing her eyes. "How do you intend to do that?"

"I can slip your guards the sedative instead of giving it to you, and use their keys to get you out of here."

"And then what, just dance on out through the palace?"

"No. There's a supply chute in the basement behind

the kitchens, not far from here. We should be able to climb out that way."

Tallin felt a prickle of hope in her chest. "And what about my friends?"

"They are in other cells," the koroni said.

"I'm not leaving without them," Tallin said.

"I will free you all. Tonight."

"Why would you do that? You would be in serious trouble, if someone caught you."

"I believe what you say. I want to stop the necromancer, too. I want to help," the man said, his eyes sparkling as his voice became more fervent.

"And you trust me?"

"It is worth the risk. I need you to work with me, though, pretend to be drugged, until later tonight when the way will be safer."

Tallin snorted. "Don't see that I have much choice, really. Got to be worth a try."

"I will return later, then," the man said, and slunk silently away into the dungeons.

Tallin had no idea how long she had waited. She lay on her side, her back to the door, and stared at the plain grey walls, running dark with damp. She thought constantly about the man, wondering if he really would come back, whether they would be able to get to safety. It had been quiet for hours when she finally heard footsteps in the corridor outside her cell.

The guard's hand shook as he turned the keys in the locks.

"We have to hurry. The other guards are out cold, but I only had one dose for the three of them. I don't know how long it will hold for. Come on," he said, tugging at her arm.

Tallin didn't need telling twice. She followed the man down into the depths of the dungeons, trying not to catch the eye of the prisoners in the cells either side of her.

"Where are the others?"

"They're further along here. We won't leave them," the man said.

They came across Fianna first. She sat cross-legged on the grubby floor of a tiny cell, her hair matted with blood from a cut on her temple. Her eye was blackened, and her lip was swollen from a cut.

Tallin cursed. "What did they do to you?"

Fianna's head shot up at the sound of Tallin's voice. "Gods, Tallin, I thought we were all doomed. It's damn good to see you."

"Your face?" Tallin asked.

"Ah, just roughed me up a bit, is all. Some of these guys really don't like a woman with a smart mouth, I think that's what they said," Fianna smiled, her lips looking oddly crooked. "Who's this guy anyway?"

The koroni bowed. "My name is Ystril. I want to come with you, to help."

Fianna raised her eyebrows. "Wasn't expecting that. I guess right now we'll take all the help we can get."

Ithal was in the same block of cells. He came with them silently and unquestioning, his eyes tired and drained of emotion.

"The chute is in the store rooms behind the kitchens," Ystril said. "They should be cold at this time of night, but even so we will need to be quiet."

They crept through the narrow stone halls, Ystril leading the way. Tallin's head spun from holding her breath, and her stomach was in knots. Somehow, they managed to make it to the little store room without discovery, but Tallin's sigh of relief soon turned into concern about the chute Ystril had informed them would be their exit route. It wasn't an easy climb, and Ithal eyed the narrow opening with a look of doubt. "I'm not going to fit up there," he said, frowning.

"It's wider than it looks," Ystril said. "They get whole sacks of grain and potatoes down there with no trouble. You'll be fine."

Fianna went first, her knuckles gripping white around the thick steel rope of the pulley which hung down the length of the chute. She hauled herself up, using her knees to push against the stone as she began to shimmy slowly towards the trapdoor at the top. Agile as she was, it still took her about ten minutes.

117

"I'm never going to do it," Ithal moaned.

"We don't have any choice," Tallin said.

Tallin went next, the knotted metal of the pulley rough against the palms of her hands. She twisted her body, curling like a caterpillar in the confines of the chute, trying to get enough momentum to push her way to the top. It took her longer than it had for Fianna, and she could sense the waves of tension rising from Ithal and Ystril who waited below her until the way was clear enough for Ithal to proceed.

Finally, she reached the top, Fianna leaning down to offer her hand and tug her the rest of the way out of the shaft. The air was fresh, and Tallin took a deep draught, feeling it fill her lungs with sweetness. She crawled some way along the damp grass and collapsed in a heap, staring up at the clear night sky.

Behind her, she could hear the grunts and scrapes of Ithal making his slow, laborious way up to freedom. He took longer than either she or Fianna had, his body too burly to easily manoeuvre in such a tight space. Tallin leaned over beside Fianna, each of them taking one of Ithal's arms as they hauled him out on to the grass, gasping and shaking.

"We're to wait here, behind the barn," Ithal said, once he had caught his breath. "The guard will come through the palace and join us."

"Have we got time to wait?" Fianna asked.

"We wouldn't even be here if he hadn't helped us," Tallin said. "We can't go without him."

Fianna nodded once, and the three of them walked slowly over to the large, wooden barns in the palace grounds. They crouched in the long grass which grew behind the structures, the scent of damp hay in their nostrils, and waited.

It wasn't long before the shape of Ystril loomed out of the darkness. He was carrying their backpacks and Fianna's sword and shield, taken from her when they were first locked away. Fianna hugged him joyfully as she slid the sword back into its scabbard. Tallin knew that the weapon had been a gift from the woman's mother when she had first been sworn into service, and since that day she had used no other.

"Follow me," he said, "and be quiet. We won't be safe until we are clear of the city. If anyone stops us, I'll just say that I am removing you from the city on the emperor's orders, but it's likely that will be challenged."

"Let's go then," Tallin said.

They took a rather different path out of the city than the one they had followed on their way to the palace. Ystril led them down narrow alleyways that smelled of mould and human waste. Tallin's feet were wet, and she didn't want to think too hard about why.

This late at night, well past middle-dark, few people were on the streets of the city. They passed a handful of beggars dressed in thick rags, gazing up at them from doorways with pleading, rheumy eyes. Tallin felt guilty that she had no time to stop to help, but she knew that they needed to avoid any attention being drawn to them. She pulled her hood a little closer around her face and turned her eyes to the road. They skirted the main square, the last of the evening traders packing away their stalls, a few people who had stayed late in the tavern staggering around drunkenly and giggling.

"How are we going to get past the guards on the gate?" Tallin whispered.

"Wait here," Ystril said, as he headed off into the square. They watched in silence as he struck up a conversation with one of the merchants who was busy packing bags of nuts and dried fruit into boxes stacked on a large cart. Tallin couldn't tell from their body language what was going on, but it wasn't long before Ystril turned in their direction and raised his hand in a beckoning gesture.

They scurried over to him. "Quick, get up on to the cart," Ystril said, his voice husky and low. "Squeeze in between the crates, and we will cover you. This man has agreed to transport us all out of the city, if you can pay him."

Fianna rooted in her pack for the coin purse. Thank the Gods that Ystril had managed to salvage their belongings, Tallin thought, for they would be in a difficult situation without them.

The cart was cramped and dark beneath the canvas sheeting that had been pulled over them. Tallin's skin prickled with clammy moisture in the cold, confined space, a shiver running through her veins. The old, brown draught horse who pulled the cart was slow and deliberate, the wheels hitting every single bump and dip in the road, causing the wooden crates to judder and dig painfully into Tallin's back. It was not comfortable but, if it got them away from here, it would do.

She heard the clang of the gates and the muffled voices of the guards as they spoke to the merchant. She couldn't make out what was being said, and her breath stilled in her throat until she felt the cart begin moving again. They rolled onwards for perhaps twenty minutes until she heard the merchant steady his horse, the animal nickering gently as they came to a halt.

"You can come out now," the man said, tugging back the canvas.

The lights of the city were distant as Tallin counted out the money to pay the man who had driven them to relative safety. An extra three jade pieces purchased them some bags of fruit and nuts. They were not quite the hearty supplies Tallin had hoped to buy from the city market, but it was better than returning to camp empty handed.

They walked through the night, finally reaching the place where the others had set camp as the sun began to push fingers of light into the morning sky. Tallin was exhausted, and Ithal was limping, his feet blistered and sore.

Cearul was sitting beside a guttering fire, warming his hands over the embers. He looked up as they crashed through the underbrush towards him, his eyes widening when he saw Fianna's bruised face.

"What happened to you?" he said, rising to his feet and hurrying over to Fianna.

"Short version," Tallin said, "The emperor doesn't believe us and thinks we have something to do with the undead. He threw us in jail."

"I got them out," Ystril said, smiling at Cearul's goggle-eyed expression as the elf looked him up and down.

"Who are you?"

"My name is Ystril. I am – was, I suppose – one of the emperor's dungeon keepers."

"He's come to help us find the necromancer," Tallin said.

"Not quite the army we hoped for," Fianna said with a snort.

"At least we got out," Tallin said. "Being imprisoned is not something I want to repeat in a hurry."

"I'm just glad you're safe," Cearul said, wrapping his arms around Fianna and pulling her tightly against him. "We were all set to come after you at dawn. I should have been there."

Fianna shook her head. "You were needed here to watch over the others."

Cearul inhaled. "Of course. You wouldn't know."

"Know what?" Fianna asked.

"The aulin has woken. Fychan, her name is, apparently. Though she doesn't say much."

"Where is she?" Tallin asked.

"Oh, she's asleep again now. In the tent, under a blanket, with that damned culai wrapped around her."

Tallin laughed. "Well, it never gave up, you've got to give it that. We could all do with a bit of that perseverance."

"I'd much prefer we'd persevered with killing the thing," Ithal said.

"He's just tired," Tallin said. "We all are. Now, if you don't mind, I'm going to grab a blanket myself and try to get a little bit of sleep before we move on."

"So we're still going on then, even without an army?" Cearul asked.

"I don't see that we have any choice," Tallin said. "There are people coming up out of their graves all over, and nobody else knows what to do."

"And we do?"

"Not really, but we have a better idea than most."

"Encouraging," Cearul piled a few more sticks on to the fire. "Sleep well then. We'll wake you in a few hours."

"Thank you," Tallin said, looking around for a sheltered spot to lay down.

NINE

The aulin was a fascinating creature. She hadn't seemed at all perturbed by the sudden arrival of three more people, and limped between them all solemnly as they gathered around the fire eating a scanty meal before they packed up camp. The culai trotted at her heels, panting like a fireside dog.

She stood proud and upright in front of Tallin, who was seated cross-legged by the fire. The top of the aulin's head was level with Tallin's shoulder. "Fychan," she said, pushing a thumb into her own chest. Then she pointed at the culai. "Faolain."

Tallin pointed at herself, said her name, and named Ithal and Fianna, who nodded at the aulin as they were introduced.

"Are you staying with us, then?" Fianna asked her.

Fychan nodded, her violet eyes sparkling and a wide smile across her face. "You helped Fychan. Fychan will stay. Fychan will help. And Faolain. He will stay too."

"Great," Ithal muttered.

"So where are we headed?" Cearul asked.

Kirian looked at Tallin. "Did you find any information from the city?"

Tallin shook her head. "Sorry."

"My instinct is that the necromancer dwells in the north," Kirian said, "somewhere cold, and abandoned for years."

"That sounds like my dreams," Tallin said. "I always dream of an old, damp castle with a broken down roof, and the sky is always grey and gloomy."

"Then I propose that we continue to travel in that direction. We will need more supplies, so we will need to find a town or village to replenish before long," Kirian said.

"We'll need to be careful not to be recognised," Ithal said. "I don't think we ought to stop until we are well clear of the city. They'll probably have a price on our heads by now."

"I agree." Tallin said. "We go north for as long as we can before we need to stop."

"We should head towards the village of Wyley," Kirian said. "It is about four days travel, but we will be able to rest there a while. It is large enough to hide there, but small enough for the villagers not to know of us."

"It's probably best that we travel off the road, too," Ithal said.

"Agreed," Kirian said.

They packed up what was left of their belongings.

Now that Ystril was coming with them, the horse that had carried the tent had to be commandeered as a riding animal. The tent was rolled up as small as possible and strapped to Cearul's back.

"I'm going to have sore muscles by the time we stop," the elf grumbled.

"I'll give you a nice massage, my love," Fianna said, instantly cheering him.

Fychan travelled with Fianna and Ruari continued to ride with Kirian, as the now well-rested horses began their slow trek towards Wyley. They found themselves following the trail of a thin yet fast flowing river, winding its way along a gorge thick with pale-leafed trees which kept them sheltered from the road. The horses splashed through the shallow water, kicking wet rocks out of the way as they walked.

When it began to rain as the sun sank over the horizon that night, Tallin sighed despondently. One tent would not keep them warm and dry, and it would be an unpleasant night ahead for most. An overhanging rock face beside the river would provide meagre shelter, but it was the best they could find.

It was too wet for a fire, so she huddled beneath the stone and chewed on dried fruit, pulling her sodden blanket around her shoulders.

"That will only make you colder," Kirian said, gesturing at the blanket.

"I'm trying to convince myself that it's a fluffy, newly-washed woollen bedspread," Tallin said.

"Is that working?"

"No." She shivered violently and coughed.

"Come on," Fianna said. "We need to share our warmth."

It was not going to be a comfortable night's sleep, Tallin thought, as she tried to settle with somebody's elbow digging into her hip and a cold foot pressing against her shin.

The next few nights were long and quiet, except in sleep. The rain had stopped, at least, but Tallin's dreams continued to plague her. Twice she woke screaming, bringing the others rushing to her side.

"Your nightmares are getting worse." Kirian's tone was matter-of-fact, but his expression was one of worry.

Tallin sighed and nodded. "Yes. I can see all of it, what the necromancer is planning. I don't know how my magic can stop him."

"Tell us about it," Fianna said. "We need to know what we are up against."

Tallin's brows drew together. "He's using the souls to build an army. They're crude, he's made them out of what looks like scrap, but each of them is alive. Somehow, he's put the soul in them to animate them, and he has complete control over them."

Fianna frowned. "But what is he planning? War?"

"Why else would he be doing this?" Tallin rubbed at her eyes and sighed. "I don't know his motives, but I do know the souls are suffering. We need to stop him before his army gets too strong."

As they closed in upon their destination, they began to see more evidence of civilisation. A fisherman saluted them as they rode through the shallows, following the trail of the river, a basket of silver-scaled fish piled wetly in a basket beside him. On impulse, Tallin offered him a coin for his catch, which he happily agreed to, turning the copper piece in the sun and watching it sparkle. Later that day, they baked the fish over a fire, the flesh pale and tender. It was the best meal they had eaten since they left Clestead many days ago.

It wasn't always easy to travel without using the roads, although it often made for a lively journey. They found themselves galloping through a wheat field as a farmer shouted angrily behind them, fists waving at the destruction of his crop; shortly after that, they had to wade through the knee-deep mud of a woodland swamp, unable to sit on the horses in case they sank too far. Tallin imagined that the smell was still clinging to her as the lights of Wyley appeared in the distance.

The village was small and spread-out, and the very first building they came to was the tavern. *The Rocking Boat*, read the old wooden sign outside swinging from a red-painted beam. It was a large, ancient looking building made of green-tinged grey stone, a large, covered stable block attached on one side.

"I say we stop here," Ithal said hopefully.

"I need a bath," Tallin said, "so if they can provide hot water, I agree."

"Never mind water," Fianna said. "I could murder an

ale."

They pushed the door open hesitantly. They were a strange group, they knew – covered in mud and sweat, carrying weapons and travelling with an aulin. Yet the horses would enjoy the shelter and, gods knew, Tallin would do anything for a proper bed, if only for a night.

The bartender was a rotund, sweaty man with glasses and strangely coiffured facial hair which seemed to stick out in all directions. He looked over at them with an expression which was only mildly curious.

"If ye're after food, the kitchen's closed. Rose went off home early, she did, 'cause her ma took sick this morn. Bread an' cheese is all I could do for ye."

The man's accent was broad and flat; a true Middle-lander, Tallin thought. She had not met many people from Yarrow, and she found the thickness of his voice hard to decipher.

"We were hoping for some rooms for the night," Tallin said.

"Although bread and cheese would go down well, I'm sure," Ithal said, his stomach rumbling at the thought of dinner.

"Two jade pieces fer each room," the man said. "Show me yer coin.". He bent over the small pile of coins Tallin offered him, sorting them and testing them between his teeth.

"Up the stairs," he said eventually, "first doors on the right."

"May we leave our horses in your stable?" Kirian asked.

"Another silver piece fer hay," the man said, "an' ye'll have to see to 'em yerself."

Tallin counted out another coin on to the bar as Ystril and Ruari went outside to put the horses away.

There were three rooms with two beds in each, spare wooden frames with a thin feather mattress. Even so, Tallin thought, they were a welcome sight. She sank down on the edge of one of the beds and began to pull off her boots. The leather was crusted with swamp mud, and she wrinkled her nose at the smell.

A large iron jug hung over the fireplace, and Tallin wasted no time in heating up some water for the copper tub which stood underneath the room's only window. Bolting the door, she took a brief but satisfying bath, scrubbing the grime from her skin and the sweat from her hair. She used a length of string to tie her dark hair in a loose pile atop her head, rubbing herself down with a threadbare towel found in a tatty wooden cupboard before slipping on the thin lemon-yellow cotton robe dug out from the bottom of her backpack and leaving her gold tunic to soak in a fresh tub of cold water.

She pulled on her filthy boots – a strange combination, she thought, and was grateful for the lack of a mirror – and made her way downstairs to enquire about the bread and cheese.

Tallin snorted, giggled, and smacked Ithal on the back, making him choke on his ale.

"And then," she said, swaying slightly on her stool, "and then he sneezed right in the High Cleric's face."

"It was the spices," Ithal protested.

"It was disgusting," Tallin said, her eyes shining. "You should have seen his expression."

Fianna laughed. "I always wondered what went on at those banquets."

"Not much," Tallin said. "They were boring. Not even anything decent to drink."

"That was probably a good thing," Ithal said, looking pointedly at Tallin. She belched and grinned.

Empty mugs littered the table, drops of spilled beer soaking into the crumbs which were all that was left of the large, white loaf the bartender had brought them two hours earlier. The man returned to the table now, bearing another flagon of ale.

Tallin drained her mug and held it out for a refill.

"Are you sure you should be drinking more?" Ithal asked.

"'m fine," Tallin said. "One more won't hurt."

Three mugs later and Tallin was singing a song, slightly out of tune and very loudly. Cearul and Fianna had gone to bed, joining Ruari and Fychan who had been in their room all evening. Ystril had decided to bed down with the horses in the stable, unaccustomed to sleeping on a mattress.

"I think you've had enough," Ithal said as she leaned over the table to grab the flagon. He slid the ale out of Tallin's reach as she grumbled and cursed. Tallin stretched out an arm, slipped from her stool and landed on the floor with a crash, laughing until tears ran down her cheeks.

"I will take her to her room," Kirian said, grabbing Tallin's arm and helping her to her feet. She leaned heavily against him, and he slid an arm around her waist to steady her.

Tallin lay her head on his shoulder as they staggered up the stairs. "You wanna nother song?"

"No, thank you," Kirian said. "You will have to be quiet soon, Ruari and Fychan will be asleep."

"I could come to your room?"

"No."

"Ithal won' mind."

"Ithal will need his sleep, the same as the rest of us. You included."

"Wanna sleep with you."

She felt Kirian tense beside her. "No."

They reached the door of the room she was sharing with Ruari and Fychan, and Kirian leaned over to tug on the handle.

"Sleep it off, Tallin. Good night," he said.

Tallin blinked up at him, his face swimming in her vision. Even so, she thought, even out of focus he looked handsome. She wondered if she had ever seen anyone quite so lovely in her life, and decided almost immediately that she had not.

"Lookit you," she said.

"What?"

"You're so pretty," she said, trying to smile seductively. It looked more like a grimace. "So pretty."

"Tallin," Kirian said slowly. "You are drunk."

"And you're still pretty," she said, pressing her body against him. "Kiss me?"

"We have already had this discussion," he said, shaking his head and attempting to pull away.

"And I don't care," Tallin said. "Just wanna kiss you."

She stretched up and pressed her lips against his cheek. He flinched.

"We will talk about this in the morning," he said, pushing open the door. Tallin stumbled through it, almost falling on to the bed.

"Goodnight, Tallin," Kirian said, closing the door softly behind him.

Tallin cracked open one eye and groaned at the morning sunlight which appeared to be stabbing her in the brain. Fychan stood beside the bed grinning at her.

"What do you want," Tallin tried to say, although the words came out in a jumbled blur. Her tongue felt as if it was made from wool, and her throat was dry and scratchy.

Silently, Fychan handed her a cup of water. Tallin took a deep draught.

"Thank you," she said. "Perhaps that ale wasn't such a good idea after all."

Fychan shook her head violently, still smiling.

Everyone else was already awake and they had congregated in the bar, heads bowed over plates of smoked bacon and potatoes. It seemed that Rose was back on duty, her presence heralded by the smell of crispy fat which permeated the air and made Tallin's stomach rumble.

Ithal looked over at her. "Wasn't expecting to see you at all this morning. Breakfast?"

She perched on the bench beside him and eyed his plate. "Yes, please."

A young woman, long, dark curls cascading almost to her waist, took Tallin's order and soon an enormous plate of fried bacon, egg, potato and tomato sat in front of her, heat rising from it in curling tendrils. She cut into the bright yellow yolk of an egg, suddenly ravenous.

"This is amazing," she said through a mouthful of

food.

"We know," Ithal said. "We don't need to see it."

"We've been talking," Fianna said. "We thought we would stay another night, get ourselves ready to hit the road again. Clean clothes, full bellies, give the horses a rest. What do you think?"

"I'm not going to argue," Tallin said, "but I don't think I'll be joining you in the bar again tonight."

"From what I hear, that's a wise decision," Fianna said.

"And what do you hear?" Tallin raised an eyebrow.

"What I hear is that someone can't handle their drink," Fianna said, breaking into a wide smile. "And perhaps that someone gets a little handsy when they're drunk and gets a bit carried away with our handsome herbalist here."

Ithal put his head in his hands and groaned.

"Handsome?" Cearul nudged Fianna in the side with his elbow. "Careful, or you'll make me jealous."

"You wouldn't," Fianna winked at him. "Besides, nobody is more handsome than you."

Ruari made a loud retching sound and everyone turned to look at him. He mimed putting his fingers down his throat and throwing up on to the straw-covered floorboards.

"Kid's got a point," Ithal said.

"Yeah, yeah," Fianna said, rolling her eyes.

"I wasn't handsy," Tallin protested, though she had a horrible feeling that she had been.

Kirian coughed.

Tallin busied herself that day cleaning up her boots and drying her tunic and leggings. Mid-afternoon, she joined Ithal and Fianna for a game of keruti, the game pieces provided by the bartender.

"My mother taught me to play this," Fianna said, a huge pile of tokens sitting on the table before her.

"What was she, a professional?" Ithal said, pushing over another token as he lost the next round.

"Hardly," Fianna said. "She was a miner. I think she used to play this with the other miners during their breaks."

"A miner?" Tallin asked.

"Yeah, she'd do shifts down the silver mines in Skiffield," Fianna said. "Probably why I remember the rules of this game so well. One of the few memories I have of her from when I was little."

"So who looked after you?" Tallin asked.

Fianna snorted. "My da, when he wasn't soaked in whisky at least. Truth be told, I was pretty self-sufficient. Had to be."

"Sounds like you had a rough time," Ithal said.

Fianna looked at him in surprise. "No. Why would you think that?"

"Dad a drinker, mum never around, doesn't sound idyllic to me."

"Not going to lie, it wasn't all happy and perfect, but they loved me, you know? I always had a soft bed to sleep in and food on the table, and whenever I saw my ma, I had what felt like years of love packed in to a few days, so it wasn't bad by any means. Plenty of kids had it worse than me."

Tallin nodded. "I feel the same way."

Ithal looked at Tallin. "You don't talk about your parents much."

She shrugged. "Not much to say."

"How old were you when you went to the monastery?" Fianna asked.

"Nine summers," Tallin said. "My ma caught me doing magic out in the garden, and she called the priest, and the next thing I remember, there were some men on horses come to take me away."

Fianna frowned. "Being taken away from home, just like that. Confusing for a child. You must have been angry."

Tallin nodded. "Most people don't seem to understand that. I don't know what they expected. Yes, I was furious for a long time. Still am, really."

"Do you still see your ma?" Fianna asked.

"Not often. Perhaps at Brumalia, or on my name day, but never for very long. It's hard, to be honest. I can see the sadness in her eyes, and it never goes away."

"What about your other family?"

Tallin sighed. "There is nobody else."

Fianna stretched over and squeezed her arm. "You're my family now."

"Thank you."

Tallin felt as if there was a knot in her throat. Perhaps it was the effects of last night's beer or the result of talking too much about her loved ones, but after the next round of keruti was finished, she made her excuses and redistributed her tokens. She remembered seeing a wooden swing in the small meadow behind the inn and took herself off to be alone for a while.

Her skin was warming in the sun and she was dozing on the swing when she sensed she was being watched. Blearily, she opened her eyes and swallowed hard when she noticed Kirian standing at the edge of the meadow, his eyes on her.

"Kirian," she said hesitantly. "I need to apologise for my behaviour last night."

"I did not realise that ale would have that effect on

you," Kirian said. "Perhaps I should have stopped you earlier."

"I wouldn't have listened. I didn't listen to Ithal."

"True."

Kirian crossed the meadow and sank down in the grass near the swing, pulling idly at the petals of the tiny, yellow flowers that grew abundantly around them. There was a long, tense silence as Tallin watched him intently, waiting for him to speak. She scraped her toes along the ground as the swing rocked slowly back and forth.

Eventually, Kirian cleared his throat. "You called me pretty."

Tallin blushed and closed her eyes. The memory of the previous night was returning rapidly.

"And Fianna said today that I was handsome. Am I?"

"Are you fishing for compliments, Kirian?" Tallin asked, her face still aflame.

He frowned. "I am not sure what you mean. I was simply asking a question."

Tallin exhaled and dragged her heels in the dirt, drawing the swing to a standstill. "You must know you are."

"How am I to know these things?" Kirian asked, perplexed.

"Well, you are," Tallin said, not meeting his gaze. "I might have been drunk but I didn't say anything that wasn't true."

"You also said that you wanted to kiss me."

Tallin made a strangled noise in the back of her throat and wished that Kirian would go away. She had no desire to revisit the embarrassment of the ale-soaked evening before. Kirian, however, continued to look at her expectantly. She sighed.

"I suppose I did, at the time," she said. "Beer does that to people sometimes."

"Why do people drink it, then?"

Tallin blinked and smiled. "No idea. I don't think I'll bother again."

"It had no effect on me," he said, frowning down at his fingers.

"Lucky you."

Tallin pushed herself off the swing and headed back towards the tavern. Kirian opened his mouth as she passed, as if he was going to say something to her, but when she paused and looked at him, he turned away.

A handful of coins bought them all dinner that night, a hearty venison casserole with root vegetables and herb dumplings. The meat was tender and juicy, the gravy peppery and thick. Tallin ate so much of it that she thought she might not be able to move. She slouched back on the bench and watched Kirian as he walked up to the bar to buy himself a drink.

The young woman who had brought their breakfasts earlier was behind the bar, and she smiled widely at Kirian as she began to pour an ale from a large, wooden cask. Tallin watched the woman stare at him from under long eyelashes, leaning over to touch his arm as she passed him his drink.

"Why don't you do something about it?" Cearul whispered into Tallin's ear, making her jump.

"What?" she hissed.

"You know. You like him. It's obvious," Cearul said with a sly grin, "so why don't you just tell him?"

"He isn't interested."

Her fists clenched involuntarily as the barmaid leaned over to whisper something in Kirian's ear, and his cheeks flushed pink.

Cearul chuckled. "I might not be the best at spotting these things, but even I can see that's not true."

"Just leave it, Cearul," she said with a sigh. "It isn't going to happen."

The elf shrugged and smiled. "We'll see."

Tallin was about to respond when the door of the tavern crashed open and a man virtually fell through it. The barmaid looked up, releasing her grasp on Kirian's arm.

"Sebeo," she said, "what in the gods is the matter?"

Sebeo stood with his hands on his knees, trying to catch his breath.

"Summat weird's up, Rose, summat wrong. At the lake," he said between gasps.

"Wrong? What d'you mean?" Rose said.

"Steffan was down there fishing, he was. He came running back shouting about the lake getting warm. I jus' bin down there now, and all the water is glowing like candles," Sebeo said all in a rush. "Tis all these weird lights doing it, under the water and in the air."

Kirian looked up at the man. "Souls," he said, sounding as if his voice was coming from far away.

"What're ye on about?" Sebeo demanded.

"I have to see them to be certain, but it is likely nothing for you to be worried about," Kirian said. "Which lake is it?"

"Lake Lutoria, down by them woods just south of the road," Sebeo said.

"I should go," Kirian said, turning from the bar and pushing away his mug of ale. Rose pouted at him prettily, but he did not seem to notice.

"Wait," Tallin said, standing up. "You can't go by yourself. What if it's dangerous?"

"I am certain the lights are harmless," Kirian said. "I will be fine. I expect I will be back within an hour."

"If you're going, we're coming with you," Tallin said.

"Speak for yourself, girl," Ithal said. "I've got a full mug of ale from a fresh cask, and I don't intend to let it go to waste."

"We should be sticking together," Tallin protested.

"Ithal will stay here to look after our things," Fianna said, raising her own mug. "And our beer. I'm keen to get a look at these underwater candles, myself."

"Good," Tallin said. "We can't let anyone take risks, not with things the way they are at the moment."

Kirian rolled his eyes but was smiling as Tallin and the others followed him out of the inn.

Tallin stood on the sandy bank, feeling the water wash over her toes. Her eyes were wide as she swung her head from side to side, taking in the sight before her. A haze of steam rose from the surface of the lake where the warmth of the water met the cold night air, and all around them were tiny, glittering sparks which danced through the mists.

Her heart seemed to beat faster with the beauty of what she was seeing and she turned to Kirian with a childlike expression of wonder.

"These lights are, what, souls that have been drawn back through?"

Kirian nodded. "They were nymphs, a long time ago. They are exquisite, are they not?"

She looked up at him, the shimmering water reflecting across his face like a veil.

"Yes," she said simply.

They stood in silence for a long time, watching the little wisps bounce and play across the azure surface. Tallin's eyes itched and filled with tears. For a brief moment, she regretted what they had to do, knowing that, should their mission succeed, this would once again be just another cold, muddy lake.

She gazed up at Kirian again, noting the dark circles under his eyes and his serious expression. This journey had been hard on all of them, and she wondered if she looked as strained as he did.

"Come on," she said, glancing round at the rest of the group. "I'm going in."

"What?" Kirian frowned, his head tilting to one side as he weighed up whether she was serious.

Fianna laughed. "Swimming isn't my strong point."

"Mine either." Cearul grinned at her and winked. "If there's no danger here, we'll be off and leave you to it."

Kirian pursed his lips. "I have not swum for a long time. Perhaps we should all just go back to the inn."

Tallin pouted. "Don't be such a killjoy. The water's warm. Race you to the other side?"

She didn't give him a chance to respond. Tugging him behind her, she ran into the water, feeling it splash and soak into her leggings. Her skin prickled in the sudden heat, and with a laugh, she threw herself down and began to swim.

Ten minutes later, she pulled herself out on to the opposite bank and watched Kirian make his way towards her. He was an ungainly swimmer, all limbs and splashing, his normal poise and grace nowhere to be seen. She couldn't help but smirk at him as he reached her, his dark brows knitted together in a scowl.

They sat on the bank beside each other, their clothes clinging damply and hair plastered to their cheeks, shivering as the water cooled in droplets on their skin. It was peaceful and quiet, and Tallin was struck by the realisation that this was the first time they had been truly alone together. Her cheeks heated despite the chill in the air.

Kirian stared into the water, his face set in a stony expression.

"Come on, it was fun," she chided, nudging his arm.

He turned to her and a slow smile broke across his face, making him look instantly younger and more carefree. She wished he could look that way all the time.

"I am not good at fun," he said, "but you make me want to try. Thank you."

He leaned forward and brushed a wet strand of hair away from her face with one finger. She caught her breath as her eyes met his, the expression in them almost painful to connect with. For just a moment, she saw a powerful, raw need, burning like a white-hot flame in the depths of his gaze. Then he looked away, his throat working as he swallowed deep breaths.

"I did not know this would happen," he said.

"What do you mean?" Tallin asked, her voice shaky.

"You," he said, turning to face her again. The passion in his eyes had been replaced with a desperate sadness. "When this started, I knew that I had to help, and I sensed that you were the one who had the power to do what was needed. I was doing my duty, as I always have. I never knew what it was like to really live. I am just beginning to understand."

"You've never done something just because you wanted to?" Tallin asked.

"No," Kirian said, "never. But I might try it, now."

She felt his stuttering breath against her skin as he moved forward and pressed his lips against hers, hesitantly and inexpertly. Tallin inhaled sharply through her nose and closed her eyes.

"Is this all right?" Kirian asked shyly.

"More than all right," Tallin said and kissed him again. He sighed softly into her mouth and she tasted the sweetness of his breath as he opened to her. His beautiful eyes fluttered closed, and their bodies swayed together as they both sank deeper into the kiss, droplets of water from his hair falling on to her face and trailing in opaque rivulets along her skin. She shivered gently as his hand skipped down her spine and curled around her waist, pulling her closer.

She wrapped her arms around him, tilting her head as her tongue twined with his, blood running molten through her veins and her skin sizzling with lively magic as tendrils of desire took root in her abdomen. She could hear her heartbeat pulsing in her ears as his fingers traced light circles across her back.

When they finally broke apart, she was stunned and breathless and her bones felt as if they had liquefied in her body. They stared at each other in silence, lips puffy and pink, the lights of the wisps glittering over their skin. Tallin watched as the astonished adoration in Kirian's eyes slowly turned to uncertainty.

"I am sorry," he said eventually. "I lost control of myself."

"Don't you dare," she said, feeling chilly fingers of dread replace the languid heat of arousal.

Kirian looked down, biting his lip. "You would want this, even knowing that I must leave you?"

Tallin took his hand, feeling it tremble in her grasp. "We could all die before this is over. If it's ever over. We could all end up like that man we had to burn back at the cathedral."

Kirian nodded solemnly.

"If I die, if my last moments in this world are going to be as a mindless shambling horror, then I want to take as much good as I can from living," Tallin said.

"I suppose I can understand," Kirian said.

"So are you going to kiss me again, then, or what?"

Kirian swallowed hard and nodded, his mouth

descending upon hers once more.

By the time they returned to the tavern, the others were sinking ale with gusto and playing a card game with several villagers.

Fianna glanced over at them. "We explained to everyone that there was no danger. I'm glad it stayed that way. How was the water?"

"Warm," Tallin said, "then cold. But it was amazing."

"You took a while," Fianna said with a wink. Tallin blushed scarlet and Kirian shuffled his feet and stared at the floor.

"Told you so," Cearul said, his lips twitching as he held back his grin.

"About time," Ithal said. "Suppose you'll want me to move in with Ruari and Fychan later then?"

Tallin's eyes widened. "No. It's not like that."

"Not yet, at least," Cearul said.

There was a loud thump as Rose slammed down another pitcher of ale on to the table, foam spilling over the sides and soaking into the wood.

"I'm going to bed," Tallin said, "and I suggest you do the same. We should be leaving early tomorrow morning; we need to keep pressing northwards."

"Ah, it's not even full dark yet," Ithal said.

"Well, don't complain when I wake you at dawn, then," Tallin said, heading towards the stairs. Kirian followed her, ignoring the catcalls from Fianna and Cearul.

"Good night, Tallin," he said, as they stood outside her bedroom door. "Sleep sweetly."

"I will," she said, and kissed him one more time before creeping into her room, careful not to wake Ruari and Fychan who were asleep draped horizontally over the bed beneath the window. She sank down upon the other bed, pulled off her boots and damp tunic, and lay back on the scratchy blanket thinking about the way Kirian's eyes lit up when he looked at her, the scent of lilies on his skin and the surprising softness of his lips on hers. Sleep came easy to her that night, and she did not dream.

TEN

They were right on the border of Yarrow, and within thirty minutes of setting off the next morning, they were crossing the boundary. Yarrow was a dry, cool country full of quarries and industry, the landscape into which they rode quickly turning from lush fields to muddy patches of grey shale. They kept off the main roads, travelling across a barren land where little grew, the chill of the wind cutting into their skin.

They were approaching a rocky outcrop when an arrow rushed through the air beside them, narrowly missing Fianna's horse, which immediately reared up. Fianna let out a shout and grabbed the horse's neck, clinging on tightly until his hooves were once more back on the ground.

"Bandits," she cried, sliding from the horse's back and pulling her sword out of its scabbard. Raising her shield, she began to advance upon the boulders, a second arrow missing her by a whisker. Tallin quickly dismounted, handing her horse to Ruari to hold as she ran behind Fianna, her fingers twitching as she coated the warrior in a protective sheen of light.

There were three men and a woman crouched atop the stones, scrawny and dirty-looking in ragged leathers. They looked as if they had not eaten for days, and they lashed out clumsily and hastily. Fianna stabbed the oldest man through the throat, and he went down gracelessly, feet drumming against the floor as he bled out into the earth.

Ithal was wrestling with the woman, half his weight but armed with a sharp-looking dagger which she was desperately trying to sink into his chest. Tallin threw another spell towards them, lifting the weapon right out of the woman's hand. She squealed and tried to surrender, but Faolain was already at her ankles, sinking his teeth through her leggings. The poison would kill her slowly.

The second man was beardless and young, perhaps only a teenager. His hands shook as he tried to aim an arrow at Fianna's head, and it flew well wide of its mark. Tallin sent tendrils of pale lilac light to wrap around him and hold his arms against his body. He screamed, the magic hot and blistering against his skin, but she focused and held him firmly in the grip of the spell.

That was all it took for the last of the bandits to drop his sword and run, stumbling, into the desert, his hands above his head.

Tallin walked over to the boy and removed his bow and quiver before loosening her magic's hold. He wailed and curled up into a ball on the ground, trembling and sobbing.

"Wants his mother," Ruari said.

Ithal looked down at the woman lying at his feet, already paralysed by Faolain's poison, pale green foam forming on her lips. She had brown skin and olive eyes just like the boy, and they both had the same slightly hooked nose.

"Guess he's out of luck there," he said.

"What are we going to do with them?" Cearul asked.

"Look at them," Ystril said. "They're desperate, not criminals."

"They shot an arrow right at me," Fianna said.

"Wouldn't you, if you were starving to death in the desert?" Ystril asked.

"Not at people, I wouldn't," Fianna said.

Ystril pursed his lips. "I don't know. I reckon most people would do whatever it took, when it's a matter of life or death."

"I've got his weapon now," Tallin said, "and I think he's pretty harmless. Perhaps we should let him go."

"What about her?" Ithal poked the woman in the hip with the toe of his boot.

"Well, she's going to die, isn't she?" Ystril said.

"I didn't," Ithal said. "Maybe we can help her, too."

"She tried to stab you." Fianna shook her head.

"If I can travel the country with a gods damned culai, I'm sure I can live with saving her life," Ithal said.

"Please," the boy whispered. He was looking up at them with watery eyes which seemed too big for his gaunt face. Tallin sighed.

"Have you got the herbs, Kirian?"

"Yes. We need a fire," Kirian said, already digging in his pack.

"I just hope we don't need those herbs later," Fianna said with a snort.

Cearul touched her arm. "Come on, Fi. Look at the state of them. They need help."

"My heart weeps," she said, walking away and beginning to brush out her horse's tail.

Ruari created the poultice, with Kirian watching over him. The boy was becoming adept at handling the herbs, grinding them together confidently. He was able to recognise all of the leaves that were in Kirian's pack and was a quick learner when it came to mixing them for salves and teas. He applied the poultice carefully, tipping the remaining water into the bandit's mouth.

Some minutes later, the woman stopped drooling and her cheeks took on a pinker tone. She was not yet conscious, but her breathing was more steady.

"She will recover," Kirian told the young bandit, who wept and pressed his forehead against Kirian's boots. Kirian winced and stepped back.

Cearul crouched down beside the boy. "Here. We do not have much, but take this meat and biscuit. Be careful."

The boy took the food from Cearul almost

reverently. He stared at him in disbelief, then nodded his thanks before cramming one of the biscuits into his mouth.

"Thank you," he mumbled, crumbs decorating his lips.

"Remember the mercy we showed you today," Kirian said as he swung himself back into the saddle.

"And burn his body," Ystril said, kicking at the dead bandit. "Nobody is staying in their graves now, and trust me, that's not something you want to see."

The boy looked confused but nodded, and Tallin glanced back over her shoulder as they rode away to see him scuttling around searching for more wood for the fire.

"That was a good thing you did," Tallin said to Cearul, once the boy and his mother were out of sight.

"Nobody ever became a better person because of cruelty," the elf said.

The sun beat down on them relentlessly for days. Tallin felt as if she were being boiled alive. Her parents had originally been from Yarrow, so, she supposed, the warmth should be in her blood, but she had lived for too long in the wetter climes of the south. Fianna, a southerner to the bone, was struggling, the skin on her nose and cheeks pink and sore.

"Don't worry," Ystril said, "it'll get cold soon enough, and then you'll be wishing for the heat again."

"I doubt that," Fianna said. "I'm sweating so much that I could drown a boar."

"I'll remember that if we meet one," Cearul said.

"You'd have to give it a good wash before you ate it," Fianna said cheerfully.

"Think it's you who could do with the wash, my love," he said.

Fianna elbowed him in the ribs. "Hey, watch it."

"Love you really."

Ruari rolled his eyes. "You two."

"Sorry," Fianna said. She didn't look sorry.

After seventeen days on the road, stopping only briefly in small hamlets and villages to restock their supplies, the paved stone of the roads gave way to shingle and mud. The burning heat had turned into fresh, breezy days and cold, bitter nights. It would not be long before they passed through the last vestiges of civilisation and headed into the northern countries, renowned as being inhospitable and barren. Tallin thought Ystril was right. She was already missing the searing rays of the sun.

"We are near the border," Kirian said one morning as Ithal heated up some water for the bean soup Tallin was beginning to hate more than the cold. "We should cross into Tir Liath before middle-light tomorrow."

"How will we know?" Ithal asked.

"We will not until we reach the old villages," Kirian said. "The roads all look the same around here."

"What old villages?" Fianna asked.

"Tir Liath was once home to the Jotunn," Kirian said, "before they were fought to extinction hundreds of years ago. Their villages and military defences still stand. The castle we are trying to reach was once a Jotunn palace, probably the home of the leaders of their ruling class."

"How do you know all this?" Ithal asked.

"I like to think that I am something of a scholar," Kirian said. "Books and history are important to me."

"We shouldn't forget the past," Tallin said. "It's good that people care enough to learn about it."

"Knowledge is never useless," Kirian said.

"What about the knowledge that a boar's orgasm lasts for half an hour?" Ithal asked.

Nobody graced him with an answer.

ELEVEN

The old tower of Tulach Túr had once been used as a lookout and as the first line of defence for the ancient communities of the Jotunn people centuries before. Unlike the Jotunn villages, it still stood, smooth, grey sides mostly unmarked by the passing years. It would be a good place to stop and shelter, Tallin thought. The staircase was narrow, and it would be cramped, but it was easy to keep watch from the top of the tower, and it was safer and drier than sleeping under the bare and scrubby bushes on the ground outside. They tied up the horses and began to climb the stairs, dark and slippery with moss.

Whatever had once been in the tower had long since gone, decayed or stolen by looters. The room at the top of the stairs was now a plain stone circle, dark and cold, and they knew they would have to huddle together for warmth. They all agreed a fire was out of the question; it could draw too much attention. It was well known throughout Glendoran that Tir Liath was home to the last descendants of the Jotunn, those known as mountain elves, and that they were a rough and vicious people who cared little for any who were not their kind.

"I met a mountain elf, once," Ystril said.

Cearul made a dismissive sound. "They're not real elves, you know."

"They are half elven," Kirian said. "Their ancient matriarchs were elven just as you are, Cearul."

"Hard to believe," Ystril said. "This one looked nowt like him."

"They look more like the Jotunn in appearance," Kirian said.

"So the Jotunn fathered the first mountain elves, then?" Tallin asked.

"Yes," Kirian said. "The Jotunn were immortal, unless killed in battle. They were wiped out by humans hundreds of years ago, but before they became extinct, they kidnapped elven women in large numbers and got children upon them to continue their blood. The half-elf babies were ignored by humans as they appeared elven at birth. Elves were not seen as a threat."

"Why did the humans kill the Jotunn?" Tallin asked.

"Greed," Cearul said. "They wanted the land for themselves."

"Yet when they won it, they decided it was too cold to survive here," Kirian said. "A whole race, made extinct, for what?"

"That's terrible," Tallin said.

"That's humans," Ithal said.

"No wonder the guy I met hated humans so much," Ystril said.

"Where did you meet him?" Cearul asked.

"He was in the gibbet in the middle of Harrintown," Ystril said. "Guards caught him stealing sheep from a small farm just outside the city walls. No idea why he'd travelled so far south. Hung up in that gibbet for all of Febrin, he did, before he died. Shouting and cursing near the whole time."

"That might have had something to do with him hating humans, too," Fianna said.

"It probably didn't help," Ystril agreed.

"Is it true they're as tall as two horses?" Tallin asked.

"Taller than me," Ystril said, "and stocky, too. Brown skin a bit like yours, Tallin, not dark like Cearul's. Long yellow hair, this one had, all done up in braids, and a big braided beard to go with it. Quite a sight."

"Elf with beard?" Ruari asked, puzzled.

"That's the Jotunn blood in them," Cearul said. "Elves would not normally grow hair anywhere except their heads."

"If not for their ears, nobody would know they had elven blood at all," Kirian said.

It was cold atop the tower, and they had to curl up close together under the remaining blankets. Tallin slept little, and when she did, she had nightmares about towering half-elves with glowing eyes and wild hair. Even the warmth and soft pillow of Kirian's chest, where she lay curled so that her own breath heated her cheeks, did not comfort her.

The light of the dawn was harsh and bathed the tower in pale blue rays. It drew Tallin out of her drowsy haze, and she was soon wide awake, rubbing her hands against her skin to try to chase away the chill. Nobody looked rested, Tallin thought, but they had no choice but to move onward.

They rode on through the remains of the centuries-old villages where the Jotunn used to live. The tower may have survived the passing of the years, but the same could not be said for the remaining buildings. The horses stepped carefully over broken-up rubble and old foundations, the occasional pillar or partially-collapsed wall the only sign that taller structures used to stand in this place.

They stopped for a while on the outskirts of a small wood, the first shade they had found since dawn. The trees were poor shelter from the biting wind, and Tallin shivered as she picked burrs out of Bridget's tail.

"Ironpine grows near here," Kirian said, "and it will be a valuable healing herb. I will go and harvest some with Ruari while the horses rest."

"Do you need help?" Fianna asked. "You never know what might be in these woods."

Kirian shook his head. "There are no native species in this area which would be any danger to us. The herbs are not far. We will be fine. Thank you."

They disappeared off into the trees as Tallin and Cearul mixed up the last of the oats they'd purchased from the innkeeper in Wyley for the horses. The animals were looking a little footsore and ragged, and Tallin wondered how much longer they would be able to keep pushing them. She ran her hands down their legs in turn, searching for any heat or swelling in their tendons. Still sound, she thought, and hoped they would stay that way.

Fianna had lit a small fire to heat up some porridge for themselves, and Tallin took a deep draught from her waterskin, pulling a face at the warm, stale taste. By the time the porridge was ready, Kirian and Ruari were still not back.

Tallin frowned. "How far away could this ironpine have been?"

"You know what the boy's like for wandering off," Ithal said.

"I think we should go and look for them," Tallin said.

"If you want me to come with you, I will," Ystril said. "I'm sure the horses are in no rush to get going again."

"Thank you, Ystril," Tallin said.

"You'd better not get yourself lost so when Kirian and Ruari get back we end up having to come and look for you," Ithal said.

"We'll be fine."

Tallin and Ystril headed off into the undergrowth, Tallin fighting off the urge to call Kirian's name.

It turned out she didn't need to. They hadn't walked far when she heard a scrabbling sound and a groan.

Kirian lay on the ground, bleeding from wounds in his chest, two arrows still protruding from his flesh. Blood bubbled from his lips as he stretched out a hand towards her.

Tallin flung herself to the ground beside him, her fingers pushing his hair from his face. He was damp with sweat, cold and clammy to the touch, shivering and gritting his teeth through pain.

"Kirian," Tallin whispered, "oh gods, Kirian, please be all right."

Ystril crouched down and peeled back the man's tunic. "He's lost a lot of blood."

"Will he live?"

"I don't know," Ystril said.

Tallin swallowed down air as sharp daggers of panic sliced through her chest. "We need to get him back to the others."

"But where's Ruari?" Ystril looked around. There was no sign of the boy.

Tallin swore, wishing that someone had stopped them from wandering off, or that Fianna had insisted on going with them. Kirian always seemed so self-assured, and nobody had thought to question him. *Stupid.* She stared, almost in a trance, at the blood staining his tunic and soaking into the earth beneath him.

"We will have to look for Ruari later. Come on, help me move him," Tallin said, curling her arm around Kirian's shoulders and lifting him from the ground.

Kirian moaned, his eyelids fluttering, and another lance of fear shot through Tallin's body.

Ystril was strong and scooped Kirian up as if he weighed nothing. He strode back through the trees as Tallin buzzed around him, her hands shaking and her knees barely holding her upright.

"Gods, what happened?" she heard Fianna call, and then there were arms around her, supporting her as Ystril lay Kirian down on the ground, Cearul bending over him and frowning.

"Probably mountain elves," Ystril said, his voice sounding far away. "Looks like Ruari ran off, unless they got him too."

"We're going to have to make camp here and hope the elves don't come back," Fianna said. "He's in no shape to move, and we can't leave without the child."

Fychan tugged at Fianna's leathers. "Faolain will find."

"What are you saying?" Fianna looked down at the aulin.

"Faolain will smell," Fychan crinkled up her nose and made sniffing sounds. "Faolain will find Ruari."

The culai tilted his head as if he were listening. He whined.

"You think he can track the boy?" Ithal said, looking suspiciously at the animal.

"Yes."

Fianna nodded. "Then let him go. Please find the lad, Faolain. We must return him safe to his mother."

The culai whined again, licked Fychan's face and disappeared into the trees.

The rest of them turned their attention back to the wounded man on the grass in front of them. Pale at the best of times, Kirian was now almost chalk-white, his black hair standing out in stark contrast to his skin. His eyes were closed and his lips set in a tight line.

"I don't know what to do," Tallin said.

"None of us are healers," Ithal said, "but at the least we can remove these arrows and get the wounds clean."

"He's going to die, isn't he?" Tallin was pacing, her fists clenched.

Ithal looked her in the eye. "Don't say that. We will do our best, all of us."

Fianna gripped one of the arrows in her fist. "Hold on, now," she said, and pulled. Kirian let out a gasp and his body tensed, rising from the ground. Fresh blood bubbled from the open wound, and Fianna immediately tore off a piece of her own tunic and pressed it against Kirian's chest. "Press on this," she instructed Tallin, who did so, her hands shaking.

Fianna removed the second arrow and applied another pad to the wound. Kirian was semi-conscious, making whimpering sounds as Cearul gently removed his tunic, soaked some cloth in water and began to clean his inflamed skin.

"We need to hope for no infection," Fianna said. Her expression was grim, and Tallin noticed the look that passed between her and Cearul. It was clear they expected the worst.

Ystril gently carried Kirian into the tent, laying him down on a bedroll and covering him with blankets.

"You go and lie with him, Tallin, and we will keep watch," Fianna said, wrapping an arm around Tallin's shoulders.

"I can help with the watch," Tallin said, feeling guilty that they would have to sit out in the cold. "We can take turns in the tent."

Fianna shook her head. "I know how I'd feel if it was Cearul in there. I'd be no good for anything. You need to be with him."

"It's not the same," Tallin said.

"Nonsense," Fianna said. "I've seen the way you look at him. It's exactly the same, whether you know it or not."

Tallin looked at Fianna for a moment then gave her a quick hard hug before pushing through the tent flaps and dropping to her knees beside Kirian. His breath rattled in his throat, and she lay a hand on his forehead. He was cold, too cold, and the skin around his eyes was darkening as if bruised. Hot, salty tears began to roll down her cheeks, and once the dam broke she was sobbing, clinging to the blankets which covered him and repeating, over and over, "Please, Afallach, do not take him. Please, let him live."

As her tears subsided and she lay beside him, her hand covering his, she thought about what Fianna had said and realised she had been right. She watched Kirian's eyes twitch beneath his closed lids, felt the hitch of his breath in his chest and leaned over to press a kiss on his cheek.

"Please don't die," she whispered into his ear. "You got me into this. You can't leave me now."

She watched over him as the day turned dark outside the tent, long into the night even when she could see only the paleness of his skin in the darkness. Her eyes stung with the tears she had cried and felt swollen and sore.

All through the night she sat beside him, telling him stories in a broken, hushed voice. She made up wild and wonderful tales of warrior women fighting dragons and saving the handsome prince, she invented ridiculous stories of goblins and mermaids falling in love, and she told him more about her own past. About how she had always longed to be a noblewoman so she could wear the dresses that her mother would sit up all night stitching, but how now she wanted nothing more than a quiet life on a farm, somewhere safe and peaceful where nobody would expect anything of her. Somewhere she could wake up in the morning next to the man she loved, somewhere she could have children and watch them grow.

"And I won't have magic at all," she said, "and my children will be called Yolanda and Irin, and they will grow up with their parents around them knowing nothing but love."

"A good life," Kirian said, his voice cracked and hoarse.

Tallin yelped and looked down at him, his eyes shining in the darkness. He smiled tightly and winced, and she felt her heart trying to escape her chest.

"Oh gods, Kirian," she said, her voice choked and strained. "Oh, gods."

"Just me," he said, letting out a long, shaky sigh. "It is good to see you."

"I was so scared," Tallin said, tears thick in her throat.

"Me too," he said with a laugh which turned into a cough. He hissed in pain and Tallin hovered over him, a concerned look on her face.

"How can I help you?"

"We were ambushed before we reached the ironpine," Kirian said, "but there should be some lamis in my bag still. Look for a purple coloured herb with a thick, waxy leaf in the shape of spikes. It may help with the pain."

Tallin dug around in his pack and found the herb wrapped in a dark cloth. She handed a sprig of it to him, and he put it in his mouth and began to chew.

"I can't believe you're awake," Tallin said, gazing down at him. "I thought you were going to die."

"That will not happen," Kirian said, reaching over to squeeze her hand. "I will be fine."

167

He frowned suddenly and looked around. "Where is Ruari?"

Tallin shook her head. "We don't know. He wasn't with you. Faolain is trying to pick up his scent."

Kirian lay back on the bedroll and closed his eyes with a loud exhalation of breath. "They have got him."

"Who are they? Who attacked you?"

"Mountain elves. Three of them," Kirian said. "I presume you did not see them, so they did not come this way. They have taken Ruari."

"Perhaps he just ran off?"

"No," Kirian said. "He is a brave child and would not have left me. He is with the elves."

Tallin chewed on her lip, trying to make sense of the situation. "Why would they want a human child?"

"I have no idea," Kirian said, "but it cannot be good."

"Let's hope Faolain finds him."

"Culai have good noses," Kirian said. "There is reason to hope."

"You've shown me that much," Tallin said.

Kirian smiled. "Always have hope. Now, could you get me a drink of water? My throat is dry."

Tallin brought him a waterskin, and he drank deeply

before sighing and closing his eyes. She curled up beside him, feeling his hand rake through her hair as she fell into a light doze. As her breathing became regular and even, she heard his voice as if from a long distance. "Yolanda and Irin," he whispered, a sadness in his tone. That was all she heard before the darkness of sleep slipped over her.

She woke to find Kirian sitting up, propped against his pack. He was still pale, his lips dry and cracked, but his eyes were bright, and he smiled at her as she gazed up at him.

"I am glad you slept," he said.

"How are you feeling?"

"Much better," he said, "thank you. I should be up on my feet in no time."

"There is no rush," Tallin said. "We need to wait for Faolain to come back."

"I hope he returns soon."

"So do I. Now, are you hungry?"

Kirian nodded. "Ravenous."

Tallin went to fetch some breakfast and found the others huddled around the fire, looking cold and miserable.

Fianna looked up at her. "Everything OK? How is he?"

"He's awake," Tallin said, "and he says he'll be fine."

"Oh, thank the gods."

"I've been doing that for half the night," Tallin said with a smile. "I've just come to get him something to eat."

Cearul passed her a small pot which had a ball of sticky porridge clumped in the bottom of it. "Sorry. That's all that's left."

"We're going to need to hunt, if we're to stay here," Ystril said.

"I'll come with you," Cearul said.

"Be careful," Fianna said. "Be on your guard."

"We will be," Ystril said, and they began to gather their weapons and strap on their armour. Tallin wished them luck and took what was left of the porridge in to Kirian, who had fallen asleep again.

She watched him in the muted light which filtered through the canvas, his face drawn yet peaceful. His long eyelashes fluttered as he dreamed, his lips slightly parted as he snored gently. The blankets had fallen away from his chest and Tallin looked in surprise at the already-healing wounds on his torso, pale pink and knitting together at a rapid rate. The herb he had taken had clearly had powerful restorative properties.

When he woke, Tallin offered him the cold porridge. "I can heat it up again, if you prefer?"

He shook his head. "This is fine. I just need to eat something to help regain my strength."

"You seem to be healing up well," Tallin said.

Kirian looked down at his wounds. "I am feeling a lot better. I am sure I will be well again in a day or two."

Tallin leaned in and touched his cheek. "I can hardly believe it. I honestly thought we'd be lighting a pyre."

"Obviously it was not as serious as you thought," he said, catching her wrist in his hand and pressing his lips against her palm.

"Obviously not," she echoed, then looked down at the ground. "I was a bit of a mess, I have to say. The thought of losing you was worse than any of my nightmares."

Kirian tightened his grip on her wrist

"Do not become too enamoured of me," he said, his voice husky. A heavy silence hung in the air as Tallin slowly raised her head to meet his gaze. His eyes were intense, his expression bleak and full of pain – this time not from his injuries.

"You are going to lose me," he said. "I cannot give you what you want. Perhaps ... perhaps it would be better if we kept apart from now on."

"You don't mean that," Tallin said, her heart leaping into her throat.

"I do not see another way," he said. "It will only hurt us more if we continue."

"How do you know what I want?" Tallin's tone was sharp.

"A quiet life with a quiet man, two children, a lovely little farmhouse," Kirian said. "That is not me. It will never be me."

"That was just a story," Tallin said. "I was keeping myself occupied, trying to chase my fear away. It'll never happen."

"But you've dreamed of it, nonetheless."

Tallin twisted her fingers in her lap. She could not deny his words.

"Once, perhaps. But that is all it is. Just a dream. It's you I want," she said, an edge of desperation creeping into her voice.

"I know," he said. "But it would not be fair."

"Who are you to say what is fair?" she spat.

Kirian looked at her sadly. "A man who is growing to care for you," he said, "and who knows where this path is leading us. That is who I am."

Tallin stared at him, disbelieving. Eventually, he looked away.

"I am sorry," he said. "I wish it could be different."

"You're sorry? Well, so am I," she said, her voice cracking as tears welled in her eyes. "I'm sorry I ever kissed you. You're right. This was a bad idea all along."

She stood and left the tent, feeling like walking until she vanished into the woods. Fianna stopped her.

"Everything all right?"

"Fine," she said, allowing herself to be led over to the fire. "He's going to be fine."

TWELVE

Ystril and Cearul returned, struggling to carry a young deer shot cleanly through the eye with an arrow. Tallin sighed softly when she looked at the beautiful dead creature, but she knew it would feed them well for some days to come. They had not had any fresh meat since Ruari killed a raftan with a slingshot before they left Yarrow, and the deer would fill their bellies better than the vegetables, grain and dried garlic sausage they had been surviving on.

Fianna greeted Cearul with a hug and immediately began to butcher the deer with her dagger. Tallin turned away, suddenly queasy after recent events. She did not need to see more blood and be reminded of what she had nearly lost. She sighed. Lost him anyway, she thought, just in a different way.

"Don't like the sight of blood?" Ystril said from behind her. "You're going to struggle if we get into a proper fight, then."

"I'm fine," Tallin snapped. "Seen plenty of blood over the last weeks, thank you very much. I'm quite used to it by now."

"No need to rip my head off," Ystril said, raising his hands.

"Sorry," Tallin said. "I'm just not in a very good mood."

"Thought you'd be dancing for joy, what with your fella on the mend and all," Ystril said.

Tallin laughed sourly. "He's not my fella."

"That's not the impression I got," Ystril said. "Heh. Does that mean he's available?"

Tallin glared at him.

"Sorry, was meant to be a joke. Not funny."

"No. Not funny."

"What went on between you two?"

Tallin narrowed her eyes. "Don't take this the wrong way, but it's really none of your business."

"Received loud and clear," Ystril said, pulling off a snappy salute. "For what it's worth, I'm sorry. You would have made a good couple."

"Yeah, well, we're not," Tallin said. "Didn't figure you as the kind of person who would care either way."

"You wound me," Ystril said dramatically. "Really, I'm an old romantic at heart."

"What about you, then? Got anyone special?" Tallin asked.

Ystril stopped smiling. "Not anymore."

"I guess it's my turn to be sorry," Tallin said.

"No need for that," Ystril said. "Been ten years this year, so it's not as if I haven't had time to get used to it. Still feels like yesterday, though."

"What happened?"

"The plague, in Tramante," Ystril said. "We had only been married two years."

Tallin didn't know what to say. She settled for, "That's awful."

"It was. He was the most wonderful man I'd ever met. I still miss him every day."

"What was his name?"

"Fedlia," Ystril said. "He was five years younger than me and a lot more handsome. A much better person than me, too."

"I find that hard to believe."

"Flatterer." Ystril waved his hand dismissively. "It's true, anyway. Should have been me who died."

"You're making it count," Tallin said. "I'm sure he would be very proud of you."

"I don't know about that."

Tallin patted him on the arm. "I'm proud of you, anyway. You've been a huge help. We wouldn't even be here if it weren't for you."

Ystril inclined his head solemnly. "Thank you."

The sun was beginning to sink over the horizon when Fychan jumped to her feet, scanning the forest.

"Faolain?" she called. "Faolain?"

There was an answering whine, and the culai bounded through the bushes and began to leap around the aulin, wagging his tail.

Fychan wrapped her arms around the animal's neck and kissed his nose. "Faolain. Good boy."

"Does he know where Ruari is?" Cearul asked.

"Wait," Fychan said. "I will ask him."

Tallin wondered how anyone would be able to understand the culai, but the aulin didn't seem to have a problem. She sat with Faolain on the floor, whispering into his ear as the culai whimpered. After about ten minutes, she got to her feet.

"The boy is northwest. A stone fort. Elves keeping him in a dungeon. He is well."

"Can Faolain lead us there?" Fianna asked.

"Yes."

"We will go at first light, then, if Kirian is healed enough." Ithal said.

"I will be healed enough," Kirian said, stepping out

of the tent. He had dressed again in his ragged and stained tunic, but his face was smooth and unlined with the pain that had overcome him that morning. He was less pale, and the dark circles beneath his eyes had dissipated.

"I don't know how you recovered so quickly," Fianna said. "I removed those arrows myself, and they were deep. You're very lucky."

"The herbs helped," Kirian said. "But yes, I have been fortunate."

"You should take the tent tonight," Tallin said to Ithal, pointedly ignoring Kirian. "You must have been freezing out here last night. I will sit on watch."

The night passed slowly and without incident. Tallin regretted her offer as the temperatures dropped below freezing. She wrapped a blanket around herself and got as close to the fire as she dared. Even so, she thought, it would probably be less chilly than being in the tent with Kirian. She replayed their conversation over and over in her mind. Growing to care for her, he had said. He had an unusual way of showing it.

She sighed and rubbed her hands together. Perhaps Isbel had been right all along. Kirian was the strangest man she had ever met. She wished she didn't find that so oddly compelling.

They set off early the next morning, the horses nickering restlessly at being loaded up once more. Faolain ran ahead, dashing through the woods until he was almost out of sight before turning and circling back excitably. The going was slow over the stony ground, the sharp, bare twigs of the trees catching in Tallin's hair as they rode beneath them. A branch cut her face, and she winced and touched her cheek, her finger coming away coated in blood.

"We must be heading to Madûn Stronghold," Kirian said. "We are going in the right direction."

"You would know it," Tallin said.

"Like a walking map of Glendoran," Ithal chuckled.

"Is it far?" Cearul asked.

"At this speed, we should get there tomorrow morning, if we stop overnight," Kirian said. "We will need to be careful. The stronghold is exposed, and they will be able to see us coming. It is an old Jotunn army fort."

"How are we going to get near them then? They'll outnumber us, and they've got the defensible position," Fianna said.

"We aren't going to be able to just ride up to it," Ystril said. "We're going to need a plan."

"I can create a shield for us, to hold back arrows," Tallin said.

"How long will it hold for?" Ystril asked. "It's possible that there are many elves there, and they will all be ready for us."

Tallin shrugged. "It takes a lot of power to maintain it. It will hold until I'm drained, and that depends on

179

how many there are. It's a risk, but what choice do we have?"

"Fychan is small," Fychan said. "Fychan can sneak in to the fort."

"And then what?" Fianna asked.

"Fychan will poison the elves."

"Have we got any herbs that would work as poison?" Ithal asked Kirian.

"No," Kirian said. "Most of the herbs I carry are for healing."

"Fychan will use Faolain," the aulin said.

"What do you mean?" Tallin asked.

"Of course," Ithal said, "I know as well as any how dangerous those culai glands can be. Is it possible to extract the poison?"

Fychan nodded. "Will be painful for Faolain. But Faolain will do it for Fychan."

"Will it even work?" Cearul asked. "Elves are immune."

"Plains elves are immune," Kirian said. "Mountain elves have Jotunn blood, so they may not be."

"It has to be worth the risk," Tallin said. "We have nothing else."

In camp that night, Faolain's piteous wails filled the

air as Fychan reached inside his mouth and squeezed the glands which were tucked into the animal's cheek. The culai was clearly in agonising pain, but remained in full submission to the little aulin, even feebly wagging his tail through the guttural growls and whimpers. The poison ran down the animal's teeth and into the small bowl that Fychan held beneath Faolain's mouth, glutinous and grey. Ithal shuddered.

"I almost feel sorry for the poor thing," he said.

"Good boy," Fychan said, "Good boy, Faolain."

"What are you going to do with the poison?" Tallin asked.

"Fychan will sneak into kitchen. Fychan will put poison into food."

"And then when the elves are paralysed, we can enter the stronghold," Fianna said. "Let's hope it works."

"Let's hope that Ruari doesn't eat the food," Cearul said.

Tallin shivered at the thought. "We have no choice."

"Fychan will tell Faolain when it is safe. Faolain will tell you."

"This is very brave, Fychan," Tallin said.

"Fychan is brave," the aulin said, grinning widely.

"Yes," Cearul said. "You are."

THIRTEEN

They did not have to ride for long the next morning until the stronghold came into view in the distance, looming on the horizon like an enormous black tooth. It was an imposing structure, and Tallin shivered to think of what Fychan had to do.

"Are you ready?" she said to the aulin.

"Fychan is ready."

With the poison safely decanted into a small bottle taken from Kirian's backpack, Fychan set off, Faolain on her heels. It would be a long walk for the little aulin, so the horses were hobbled and Cearul and Fianna went to hunt and gather food for the ongoing journey.

"Do you think she'll make it?" Ithal asked.

Tallin shrugged. "It's a huge task. I know aulin are good at hiding, but even so, we have no idea how many elves are in there. I just hope she doesn't get killed."

"She would not be alive if we had not helped her," Kirian said.

"That doesn't mean her life belongs to us," Tallin said.

"Of course not," Kirian said. "But for her, there will be a debt to repay. This is her way of doing that."

"There is no debt," Tallin said. "I don't help people for what I can get out of them."

"I know," Kirian said, "and that is admirable. But she is not doing this for you. She is doing it for her own sense of honour. To deny that would be considered a slight."

Tallin nodded. "I see. I might not agree, but I understand."

Cearul and Fianna established a little camp in a clearing amid the trees, and they all settled in to wait for news.

It was to be a long wait. After another cold night, Tallin's muscles had seized up and she felt as if she would never be warm again. It was painful to sit, painful to walk. She remembered how sometimes her mother would complain about her hands after sewing for hours and how she had likened her fingers to knotted tree branches. Tallin's entire body felt like that. Not even sitting by the fire helped to ease the aching.

"I feel as if I am ninety years old," she grumbled, stretching out her fingers to toast them on the open flames.

"How do you think I feel?" Ithal moaned. He had been miserable for days, and Tallin was not surprised. His face was drawn, and new lines had appeared around his mouth and eyes.

"I did warn you," she said. "You could have stayed at the abbey."

"Bit late now," he said. "Besides which, I'd be even more worried about you if I hadn't come."

"Better to be worried than cold, surely?"

"Nope," he said. "I'll warm up, some day. Worry doesn't go away as easy as cold."

Tallin shook her head. "You worry too much."

"You're out here in the middle of nowhere, freezing cold, trying to save a child from enormous men with swords, on your way to challenge a man you tell me is the most powerful mage seen in the land for centuries, and you think I worry too much."

"Yes," Tallin said. "It doesn't help."

"Remember when we went out to look for Kirian and the boy?" Ithal asked.

Tallin remembered how anxious she had been and her constant fretting over how long they were taking.

"Shut up, Ithal."

Close to middle-light of the next day, Faolain shot out of the undergrowth like a furry cannonball and bounded up to them, tail wagging. He barked.

"Does that mean the plan worked?" Ithal said to him.

The culai whimpered and hopped up and down on the spot, tongue hanging out, before turning tail and racing back towards the stronghold.

"I guess it does," Fianna said.

They saddled up the horses and, hearts in mouths, began to canter towards the fort. They had to trust the animal, Tallin thought, although she half expected to be shot down by an arrow before they got to the walls. As they drew nearer, they could see the battlements were empty.

"Looks like she's done it," Ithal said. "Arse of the gods. Who'd have thought it?"

"You're going to have to be nice to Faolain now," Tallin said.

Ithal groaned. "We'll see about that."

The fort was even more imposing up close, the walls damp and running with water and the stone underneath almost black with mould. Large, strange insects scurried about, darting in and out of cracks in the surface.

"Looks like this place is a death trap without the elves," Fianna said.

"It is centuries old. You will need to watch your step in some places," Kirian said.

They tied the horses up around the side of the fort, and Ystril forced open a door with little effort, the wood rotting and soft.

"Not much of a defence now, then," Tallin said.

"If you can get here, no," Cearul said. "The strength of a place like this is in its location. They will always see you long before you see them."

Inside the stronghold, the conditions were little improved. Torches guttered on the walls, spitting out dark smoke which stained the walls further, the heat creating drops of moisture which coursed along the bricks in slimy trails. They turned the first corner and Fianna nearly tripped over the body of the first elf, lying prone on the floor with a kitchen knife protruding from his throat.

"Gods," Fianna said. "The little one is more bloodthirsty than she looks."

"Don't mess with an aulin," Cearul said.

"I figured."

The next door opened into the main hall, and the only word Tallin could think of when she peered in was carnage. Bodies littered the room, and their deaths had clearly been agonising. Many of the elves had bloody fingers where they had clawed at the floor and broken heels where their feet had drummed against the stone. A large tureen stood on the wooden table in the centre of the room, and the smell of vegetable soup still lingered in the air.

"Ah, the scent of death," remarked Ithal.

Faolain whined and tugged at Ithal's trousers. The man jumped back, cursing. "Get off me, vermin."

"I think he's trying to guide us" Cearul said.

"Well, he could do it with less teeth," Ithal said.

"Come on," Fianna said. "We need to find the boy."

They followed Faolain down an old stone staircase, slippery and narrow. Tallin's breath came quick and loud as she imagined her foot slipping and her body tumbling to the bottom of the steps, picturing what the fall would do to her bones. Her nails clawed into the walls as she pushed against them for support, one foot in front of the other, slowly but surely.

Two more elves lay in the mouth of the doorway below, one with a cut throat. Blood had slicked across the floor, thick, black and viscous. Tallin wrinkled her nose as she stepped over the bodies into a small, dark dungeon.

"Ruari?" Cearul called. There was no reply.

"What if he's eaten the soup?" Ystril whispered.

"Don't say that," Tallin hissed.

"Ruari?" Ithal had an edge of panic in his voice.

"I thought I heard something," Ystril said as Faolain pricked his ears and trotted off through an archway to the right.

They called for the boy again, and this time, Tallin could hear a whimper. Muffled and weak, but definitely a response to their cries.

They found Ruari in a tiny, cramped cell right at the

end of the smallest, narrowest corridor of the dungeon. His hands and feet were bound with rope, and his mouth was taped shut. He looked dirty and ragged, his skin pale and bruised, but he was alive. Tallin sank to her knees in relief.

"Thank the gods. Get him out of there," she said.

"The cell is secured well," Ystril said. "This type of lock cannot be opened without the key."

"So speaks the expert on jailing people," Ithal said.

"And rescuing them," Tallin said. "Don't forget that part."

"Those elves back there must be the jailers," Fianna said. "They should have the keys."

"I'll go."

Ystril disappeared into the gloom of the dungeon, returning shortly after with a bunch of keys dripping sticky blood on to the floor.

"Sorry about the state of them."

"So long as they open the door, I don't think anyone cares," Fianna said, trying the first key in the lock.

It took seven tries before the right key turned in the lock with a click, and Cearul rushed through the door, falling on his knees to gather Ruari in his arms. He peeled the tape from the boy's mouth with tenderness and care. Ruari winced and cried out, his lips bleeding.

"Cearul?"

"Shh," the elf said, "you're fine. You'll be fine now. We're here."

Ruari blinked and began to cry. Cearul cradled him gently as Tallin picked at the knots in the rope holding his wrists and ankles.

"Did they hurt you?" Cearul asked softly. Ruari shook his head, and Tallin let out a rush of breath that she had not realised she had been holding.

There was a scuffling noise and Fychan swung around the door, clinging to the bars like a monkey.

"Fychan saved the boy. Fychan made everyone dead."

"Yes," Fianna said with a wry smile. "Fychan did. Well done."

"We should go," Tallin said, desperately wanting to leave the dank, gloomy fortress.

"Agreed," Ystril said. He bent over and lifted Ruari from Cearul's arms, carrying him from the cell as if he were made of glass. They made their way back through the macabre rooms, and Tallin tried hard not to look at the corpses. It had been the only way, she knew, but it was still unpleasant to see so much death.

"Should we set fire to the place?" Fianna said. "Before they come back?"

"I don't think it will burn," Kirian said.

"Then we need to get clear from this place as quickly

as we can," Ithal said. "Come on. Hurry."

They emerged blinking into the daylight and clambered on to the horses, setting off at a swift gallop heading north. It would not be long before they reached the soggy lands of the Blightwood, considered to be the most haunted place in Glendoran. Tallin felt sick at the thought. It seemed that their difficult day was nowhere near at an end.

When the stronghold was out of sight, Cearul reined his horse to a walk, and the others followed his lead.

"How are you feeling, Ruari?" Cearul asked.

"Better," the boy said. "I was scared."

"We were all scared," Cearul said soothingly. "You're safe now."

"Nobody safe." Ruari shook his head. "Nobody."

"What do you mean?" Tallin asked him.

"Mountain elves know about mission. Elves trying to stop us," Ruari said.

"What? They know why we are here?" Tallin frowned.

"Yes. Kept me as trap. Lure you in, kill you, stop you."

"But why?" Fianna asked.

"Elves want to live forever," Ruari said. "Helping Gwion."

"Who's Gwion?" Fianna asked.

"Necromancer. Gwion. Wants for his people to be immortal again."

"Neither humans nor elves have ever been immortal," Cearul said.

"No," Kirian agreed, "but Jotunn were."

"Yes," Ruari said. "Think they can be again. Elves protecting Gwion, helping Gwion. But we can get him. He is in Caer Gwynfor, far north."

"How do you know all this?" Kirian asked.

"Elves speak elven around me. Think I human," Ruari said, a smile on his face for the first time since his rescue.

"Oh, you amazing boy," Fianna said, hugging him. "Now we know where we have to go."

"It's not that amazing," Ithal said. "We're going to have to go through Blightwood."

"Can we ride around it?" Cearul asked.

Kirian shook his head. "The boglands are the only way."

Tallin shivered. She had heard many tales of the wood and its dark history. No humans ever tried to cross it now, and Tir Diffaith – the northernmost region of Glendoran – was home only to the hardiest races.

"I think we should stop before we get to the boglands," Cearul said. "Once we travel into the Blightwood, we cannot stop or turn back. We should be fully rested before we get there."

Fianna and Ithal made noises of agreement.

They pulled their horses off the track and found a shabby little meadow, the grass almost grey with the lack of sunlight. The wild flowers were not pretty things, as they were in the south – the leaves spiky and the petals thick and dull. Despite their appearance, the horses immediately set about eating them.

"Have you been this far north before?" Tallin asked Kirian as he set kindling to the fire.

"Rarely," he said, "but from time to time I travel to these parts."

"What do you know of the Blightwood?"

"Only what the old tales say," Kirian said. "I have not spent much time there myself, but there seems to be some truth in the old stories which say how dangerous it is. Once, I passed through just after a traveller had died there. I found what was left of her body, sucked down into the mud until the pressure of it crushed her lungs. We will need to be very careful."

"That's comforting," Tallin said. "Why didn't this Gwion person set up his awful collection of souls in the south?"

"That would be too easy," Kirian said.

Tallin sighed. "It's like there's some kind of

unwritten rule to make sure saving the world is as difficult as possible."

"Try not to worry," Kirian said. "We are nearly at the castle now. The bog and forest will be the final part of our travels."

"Not that final, I hope," Tallin said. "I was thinking about going home afterwards."

"Of course," Kirian said. "And I am sure that you will."

"I wish I had your confidence."

"You should," Kirian said. "If anyone can do this, you can."

Ithal had said the same to her, weeks ago. As she curled up next to the fire and closed her eyes, Tallin thought that it wasn't any more true now than it had been then.

FOURTEEN

The ground began to soften underfoot as they neared the edge of the bogs which heralded the start of the Blightwood. Pale green steam rose from the soil and Tallin coughed at the stench of rotting moss.

"You'll get used to it," Ithal said as everyone scrambled for a handkerchief or piece of cloth to put across their faces.

"I'm not sure I want to," Tallin said, wrinkling her nose. Even the horses were beginning to appear restless, whickering and tossing their heads. Tallin hoped it was just the smell that was disturbing them.

"We are going to have to dismount," Kirian said. "The ground is weak here, and we do not want the horses to sink into the earth."

"Walk quickly, too," Cearul said. "Don't stand in the same spot for too long, or you'll start to get bogged down."

"Watch out for the wet parts of the ground," Kirian said. "Try to stay on the more solid areas. The grass is darker over the deeper parts, so avoid those areas, especially with the horses."

"If we do that, will we be safe?" Tallin asked. The steam made the bogland look ghostly, and a shiver trickled down her spine.

"I am not sure of the dangers," Kirian said. "Some people say that there are crocolins in the deeper parts of the Blightwood, and of course there are the old tales about restless spirits. We need to stay alert."

Tallin nodded, her hand tight around Bridget's bridle and her eyes firmly glued to the ground, watching every step she took. They walked forward swiftly and in silence, concentrating fully on their path. The only sounds were the sloshing of their feet in the mud and the horses' occasional whinnies.

Fychan and Faolain led the way, their slight frames seeming to glide over the sopping surface. Occasionally, Fychan would stop and poke at an area with a stick, checking how soft the mud was. Once or twice, she was able to warn them around a particularly sticky spot, and they followed her lead gratefully.

They had been walking for about forty minutes when they heard the bubbling noises for the first time. Ruari, with his keen hunter ears, noticed it first and tugged at Kirian's tunic to make him stop.

"It's coming from over there." Cearul pointed off to the right. "It sounds like mud boiling."

Tallin tilted her head. Sure enough, after a short pause, she heard the sound – faint, but unmistakeable.

"What could be causing it?" she asked.

"I don't know," Fianna said, "but I don't fancy

finding out."

"Agreed," Ithal said. "Let's keep moving."

Tallin tried hard not to look in the direction of the noises, focusing again on her feet as she stepped carefully over shallow puddles of filthy black water, her boots clogged with mud. They had not gone much farther before she froze, sensing movement in the corner of her eye.

"Cearul," she hissed to the elf, who stood just in front of her. "I think there's something over there."

The elf turned his head and went rigid, his hand on his bow. He cursed softly under his breath.

"Ghouls," he said.

Tallin turned slowly, her heart beating so hard she felt it would tear from her chest. In the distance, through the mist, she could see dark shapes rising from the mud and twisting into vaguely humanoid forms. As she watched them, they began to wail, a nightmarish pealing of agony and hatred which rang through her ears and burrowed under her skin, which prickled with fear.

She had never seen anything like this before. Not even the undead risen from their graves were as horrifying as the figures which began to glide towards them now. The ghouls were of the bog, that was clear from the mud which clung to them, hot and sizzling. Yet they were almost transparent, as if they were made of smoke. Their form wavered and swam, first that of a human, then a dog, then a dragon. What never changed were their eyes. Looking into their eyes was like looking into a beautiful crystal, Tallin thought, multi-faceted and shimmering with all the colours that could be seen in this world. Yet even as she was struck by their unearthly beauty, she could feel them burning into her mind, feel the terrible dark fingers of their gaze plucking at her thoughts.

At the edges of her vision, Tallin could see Cearul nocking his bow, but he wasn't pointing it at the ghouls. The arrow was aimed straight at Ithal, who in turn was bending to pick up a rock.

"They are turning us against each other," Kirian shouted. "Resist them. Look away."

A swell of hatred bubbled up inside Tallin at the sound of Kirian's voice and she gritted her teeth. She wondered what it would be like to take her dagger out of its scabbard and sink it into one of his oh-so-beautiful eyes. She giggled as she imagined how he would fall to the ground, and she pictured stamping on him with the heel of her boot, grinding the fine bones of his face into dust beneath her muddy foot. She grinned and felt her magic skitter beneath her skin, stretching out her palm to call up a ball of light with the power to set his hair afire and boil his blood within his veins.

Oh, he would be sorry. He would be sorry.

"Tallin, no," she heard him call out, panic in his voice. She watched the sphere form in her palm, bright and twinkling with energy. It became larger and larger, shimmering with iridescence, as beautiful as the crystal eyes of the ghouls. She lifted her arm to revel in her power and to ruin the man who had broken her heart.

What am I doing?

Tallin blinked. She pulled back her arm, looking in astonishment at the sizzling bright bubble barely leashed in her palm. Turning her eyes up to Kirian, she let out a small gasp of horror when she saw him cowering from her, shielding his eyes from the glare of her spell.

She became aware of the ghouls to her right, shrinking back into the mists at the sight of her magic. Ithal was standing stock still, rubbing his forehead as he stared in puzzlement at the stone in his hand. Cearul was on the ground, his cheek bruised and bleeding from a cut. He lay pinned beneath Ystril, who was looking in horror at his grazed knuckles. Fianna lay curled in a ball on the ground, her fists so tightly clenched that her nails had cut into her palms. Tallin could hear her muttering to herself but could not decipher the words.

"They are scared of the light," Kirian said. "No weapon will work against them, but your magic will."

Tallin stared at her hand, then at the ghouls. Their eyes still sparked with rage, but they were beginning to dissipate into the haze of the bog. With a yell, she released the magic from her palm, watching as the orb shattered into glittering shards which flew through the mists like arrowheads. The ghouls were drenched in the pale rays of her magic, shrieking and popping as if they were being seared in flame. Tallin stretched out her fingers and more magic poured out, beating at the creatures until they were reduced almost to nothing, the last tiny shreds of their being soaking back into the mud, their eyes winking out.

She collapsed on the wet earth, dizzy and gasping.

"They are gone," Kirian said. "You saved us."

"What were they?" Tallin asked, still breathless with the drain of her energy. "Were they souls, too?"

"No," Kirian said. "These creatures have always existed here in the bog. Nobody knows where they came from, but they were never anything else."

"You know a lot about this place," Ithal said.

"I have spent a long time studying," Kirian said. "I have always been interested in the land and, as I travel a lot, I need to know about the dangers I may face."

"Useful," Ithal said.

"I am glad to be of help wherever I can," Kirian said.

"You any good at laundry?" Fianna asked, picking at the mud which coated her breeches. They were all going to be a fair old sight by the time they got out of this place, Tallin thought.

"I do not think I have any soap," Kirian said with a smile.

"Tch," Fianna said. "This stuff is going to stain."

"I think we have bigger things to worry about, my love," Cearul said.

"You don't understand. These breeches cost a fortune," Fianna grumbled. "Best kid leather in the land."

"Your own fault, then, for wearing them on a journey like this," Ithal said mildly.

"I make new for you," Ruari said, "when we are

home."

Fianna raised an eyebrow. "You can sew?"

"Can sew. Can do lots of things."

"Then you have a deal," Fianna said.

"If everyone is well, we should move on," Kirian said, and there was a general mumble of agreement as everyone dusted themselves off and continued their careful path through the mud.

It was well past middle-light when the air around the bog began to clear and they saw the first trees which marked the edge of the forest of Blightwood. These trees were different to the grand, knotty old oaks and pale, elegant willows of the southern lands. They were tall and sturdy, their trunks bare of any bark and shiny smooth. They were so dark they looked black to Tallin's eyes, and she wondered if this was a result of them soaking up the rich, peaty earth beneath them. They stood in uniform rows, as if planted by Tiorme the forest god himself, their leaves equally dark and glossy and so abundant that Tallin could not see the tops of the trees. From her position beneath them, it seemed as if they could go on forever, right up into the realm of Everlasting.

"Trees are scary," Ruari said, his eyes wide.

"Why do you say that?" Cearul asked.

"Dark. Too dark," the boy said, shivering.

"The dark won't hurt you," Cearul said, patting Ruari on the shoulder.

Tallin wished she could be so certain. She, too, felt uneasy around the trees, as if they were somehow watching them. Ridiculous, she thought. They had no eyes with which to see them, but she couldn't suppress her own shudder as she looked up at the shiny, ebony leaves which swished in the light breeze overhead.

"The dark might not hurt," Tallin said, "but I still wouldn't want to be stuck in the forest come night time."

"We will have to hurry, then," Kirian said. "This forest is not small, and we may have to be prepared to set up camp if we do not make it through before it gets late."

"A cheerful thought," Ithal said, rolling his eyes.

The ground beneath them became more solid as they moved deeper into the forest, the trees perhaps sucking up the moisture of the earth. They still had to watch their step as thick roots rose above the surface of the ground in dark humps. They took turns to ride the horses and lead them, sparing them from carrying weight where possible but also taking the strain from their own aching feet. Tallin hadn't taken her boots off in days. She knew that when she did, her skin would scream with the rawness of blisters. Fine kid leather or not, there was only so much walking a person could take, especially one who was not used to anything more strenuous than a stroll around the gardens.

Cearul's headlong crash into the undergrowth happened without warning. Tallin didn't realise what had happened, thinking that he had simply tripped over a tree root and fallen over. She almost laughed, until seconds ticked by and he didn't get up, didn't dust himself off with a wry grin and a rebuke for being clumsy. At first, she didn't see the blood soaking into the ground, so dark was the earth beneath him. It wasn't until Fianna screamed – a raw, inhuman sound – and fell to her knees beside him that she realised – with a sudden, panicked thump of her heart – that he had been hurt.

"Shit," Ithal hissed, bending over the stricken man. An arrow flew through the air where he had been standing, disappearing into the trees behind him with a crack.

Kirian grabbed Cearul's bow, fallen by his side on to the earth.

"Mountain elves," he said, urgency and panic in his voice. "We must fight."

Fianna ignored him, her face buried into Cearul's shoulder as she sobbed. Tallin glanced at the man's face. His eyes were closed, and he lay unmoving, the broken shaft of the arrow that had pierced him sticking from his ribs. A white-hot tightness swelled painfully in her chest, panic and fear and rage building to a crescendo as her skin began to spark with power.

Ithal lifted Fianna's sword and shouted into the trees. "Face us, don't hide like cowards!"

"Take the shield," Ystril said, pushing Fianna's shield into Ithal's other hand and raising his own. "We need to hold the arrows off and attack. We're sitting targets here."

Fychan scurried down from one of the trees ahead of them. "Fychan see six elves. Faolain attack with you."

They advanced through the trees, leaving Cearul lying on the ground with Fianna and Ruari bending over him. Ruari was crushing some herbs and desperately trying to force them into Cearul's mouth.

"Where are they?" Ystril whispered to Fychan.

"To the east," Fychan pointed. "Two up trees with bows. Four on ground with sword."

"Go for the archers first," Ystril said, his voice low.

An arrow flew out of the branches of a tree and Ystril raised his shield, intercepting its path. It sank into the wooden shield with a loud thump. Tallin looked up at the tree, spotting a stocky elf balancing on one of the thicker branches. She felt the rage within her crystallise as she looked at the man who might have been responsible for Cearul's injury. She blinked and focused, raising her hands.

Blindingly bright rays burst in waves from her fingertips, the heat of the spell making her gasp. The magic crackled and burned through the air, wrapping itself around the archer like a cage. He opened his mouth, screaming, but no sound permeated the white ropes of light which surrounded him.

"He won't be able to hurt us now," Tallin said. "Find the others."

The second archer had tied himself to a branch a little lower, two trees behind the first man. Kirian raised Cearul's bow and took aim, letting an arrow fly at exactly the same time the elf released the string of his own bow. The elf's arrow hit Ithal in the knee, sending him tumbling to the ground with a shout. Kirian's arrow was more on target and the elven archer slumped from the branch, his body twisting, arms flopping above his head. The arrow had pierced his eye and killed him in an instant.

Ystril had pressed on through the forest and engaged two elves in a swordfight. He was outnumbered but strong enough to parry the blows they rained upon him. Another elf was advancing upon Ithal, his sword raised, and the fourth was lying on the floor convulsing. Tallin saw the grey, furry tail of Faolain scurrying away.

Tallin clapped her hands together, and it was as if the sky folded in on itself. All luminosity drained from the air, and she found herself holding a sword of pure radiance, burning with the power of sunlight.

She swung the sword with as much effort as she could muster. It weighed nothing and sailed through the air with a noise which reminded her of sausages cooking in too much oil. She braced herself for the impact when it hit the elf, but it cut through his spine like he was made of nothing more substantial than butter. He fell to the ground, his body almost severed at the waist, blood pouring out on to the damp earth.

Tallin retched at the sight, vomiting a pale, thin stream on to the ground as she bent over with her hands on her knees, the magical sword losing its energy and winking out. Behind her, Faolain and Ystril were finishing off the remaining two elves, Ystril driving his sword through their eyes as they lay on the ground thrashing from the culai's bites.

"Is that all of them?" Ystril asked, looking around.

"All are dead," Fychan said, swinging from a branch. "Except first one in magic cage."

"What should we do with him?" Kirian asked.

"I say we take him back to Cearul and Fianna," Ystril said, "and let them decide what to do with him."

"Agreed," Ithal said, "but I'm going to need a hand. I can't put any weight on my leg."

Ystril bent and gathered Ithal up in his arms, carrying him as if he were a small child, not a slightly overweight old man. Tallin and Kirian stood at the foot of the tree below the archer, who was still screaming, his eyes wild and unfocused.

"How are we to release him?" Kirian asked.

"We won't," Tallin said, her mouth set in a firm line. She narrowed her eyes and snaked out a hand, a long, thin rope of light curling from her fingers and joining with the magic which kept the elf trapped. It brought the man tumbling from the tree to land at Tallin's feet.

"Get up," she said, her voice oddly flat and emotionless. The elf stumbled upright, looking at her with a gaze which conveyed as much hatred as Tallin had ever seen.

"Move," she said, tugging at the rope and dragging the man back through the forest. He swayed along behind her, twitching and wincing all the way, the shackling spell clearly burning his skin. Tallin was glad of it. It was no less than he deserved.

It was not long before they could hear Fianna

shouting, begging the gods for help, her words broken up with tears. Tallin ran the rest of the way, barely breathing, fingers of fear squeezing her heart.

Cearul lay just as they had left him, a pale tinge to his lips. Kirian crouched beside him.

"I am sorry," Kirian said. "He is gone."

The words did not register at first and there was a hideous, weighted silence before Fianna began to wail, babbling almost incoherently as she pulled Cearul into her arms.

"No, no, no, come back, my love, I need you."

Tears rolled down Tallin's cheeks as she watched Fianna cradle her lover, her face crumpled in agony as if it were her own heart that had been run through.

"I'm so sorry," she sobbed into his hair. "I should have protected you. I failed you."

"You did not," Kirian said, placing his hand on her shoulder awkwardly. "None of us had any idea the elves were there."

"Elves," Fianna muttered as she looked around, her eyes flashing as they fell upon the ensorcelled mountain elf quivering behind Tallin. "Is this one of them?"

Tallin nodded. "Yes. The others are dead."

"As will he be, soon," Fianna said, her voice dangerously low. She stood up and stalked over to Ithal, holding her hand out for her sword. Ithal handed it to her solemnly.

She walked over to Tallin and fixed her with a hard stare. Tallin swallowed and forced herself to meet the woman's eyes, hard though it was to see the swollen redness, the pain reflected in their depths, and the smears of Cearul's blood across her cheek where she had laid her head on his chest.

"Will this pierce your magic?" Fianna asked, lifting her sword.

"Yes."

"Good."

Fianna seemed to grow ten feet taller as she stood in front of the mountain elf who had killed her lover. He fell to his knees, mouth still open in pain, and looked up at her, his eyes rolling.

"Can he hear me?" Fianna asked.

"Yes," Tallin said.

Fianna gave a curt nod and knelt on the ground, looming over the elf's prostrate body.

"You have taken from me the only person I have ever truly loved," she hissed, her voice sharp and barbed. "How dare you? Who in the name of all the gods of our world are you to take a life that is worth far more than your own? He was a good man, a good and honourable man, who would never have sought to do you harm. I ..."

Her voice cracked and she swiped a hand forcefully across her eyes.

"I never even had the chance to say goodbye," she continued, fury dissipating into raw anguish. "I'll never be able to hold him again, or kiss him, or wake up on a bedroll freezing cold and aching, and turn to see him sleeping beside me and know that, despite everything, I have a reason to smile."

The tears were coursing down her cheeks, her face almost collapsing inwards with the pain of her loss.

"I can't change what you did," she spat, "but I can make damn sure that anyone who loves you will feel the same way I do."

She raised her sword over the man's chest, holding the hilt with both hands.

"May Afallach abandon your soul to walk the empty wastelands of Idir for all eternity," she said, as she brought the blade down with all her strength.

Tallin watched silently as the man's body tensed, his mouth opening in one final agonised silent scream before his eyes glazed and the spark of life left them. Fianna remained kneeling beside him, her hands pressing down on the pommel of the sword as her shoulders shook with sobs.

"We will need to burn them," Kirian said. "There are five more, a little further on."

Fianna looked at him, her brow knotted. "Not Cearul."

"I am sorry," Kirian said. "We have to. You have seen what happens if we do not."

Fianna shook her head. "No, no. Perhaps he will come back. We might get him back."

"You saw the man in the graveyard in North Inwold," Tallin said gently. "If his soul comes back, it won't be him, not really. We need to let him be at peace."

"But what if there's a chance?" Fianna continued, her voice rising.

"Perhaps we should wait and see," Ystril said.

"Have you seen those who have risen from the dead?" Tallin asked. Ystril nodded. "Well, did they seem like they had come back to life to you? They might not be dead, but they're not alive either. We can't let that happen to Cearul, Fianna. I am so sorry."

"No," Fianna said, backing towards Cearul's body with her sword raised. "Nobody is touching him."

"Please," Ithal said, tears in his eyes. "We all loved him, Fi. But we need to let him go."

"Do what you must with those things," Fianna said, waving her blade in the direction of the dead elf, "but he deserves more."

"Come on," Kirian said softly, laying a hand on Tallin's forearm. "We should cut some branches for pyres."

Tallin looked up at him, her eyes pink and her expression resigned. "Yes. We should."

They left Fianna crouched over Cearul's body, Ithal sitting by her side, and began to strip branches from the nearby trees.

"Gather enough for two," Kirian said, his voice quiet. "We should build one for Cearul far away from these elves."

Soon, they had a large pile of wood, Fychan throwing sturdy twigs down from the tops of the trees while Ystril used his sword to hack through the thick lower branches. Tallin struck her flint and lit the pyre as Ystril and Kirian dragged the bodies into the growing flames.

Returning to Cearul's body, they built a second pyre – smaller than the first – between the trees. When it was done, Tallin put a hand on Fianna's back.

"Fianna," she said softly, "we need to say goodbye to him now."

Fianna looked up at her, the earlier fight gone from her eyes, replaced with a desolate grief which pained Tallin's heart to see. She nodded, slowly and hesitantly, Cearul's hand still clutched tightly in hers.

Ystril bent to lift the elf on to the pyre. Fianna shook her head.

"Let me," she said, standing unsteadily.

Fianna slid her arms beneath Cearul's body and gathered him up, his lithe frame light in her arms. She lay him reverently down upon the neatly-arranged wood, kissing his lips as her tears ran down his cold cheeks.

"Goodbye, my love. May we meet again in Everlasting," she whispered, her breath coming in long, shaky sighs.

Kirian moved to her side, wrapping an arm around her shoulders as he repeated the prayer Tallin had heard him speak to the old man back in the cathedral's graveyard. Through the blurring of her own sight, she could see Kirian was crying too, tears running in quick trails down his pale cheeks. He made no attempt to wipe them away.

"May your sleep be dreamless and may you forever be at peace."

Kirian knelt beside the pyre and pressed his lips to the back of Cearul's hand before setting fire to the branches. They caught light easily, and soon the flames were licking around the elf's body, their crackling and snapping the only sound in the silent forest.

FIFTEEN

Both pyres had burned down, the bodies reduced to ash and bone, before they took another step. By then, the sky was beginning to cloud and darken, the evening drawing in. It seemed they would be spending the night in the forest after all.

They helped Ithal on to one of the horses. Ruari had treated his wounded knee with a poultice and strapped it up, but he was still unable to bear weight. Barely speaking, they began to walk into the trees at a dawdling pace. Tallin didn't feel ready to leave Cearul behind and to accept that he was gone forever. She couldn't imagine what Fianna was going through, each small step taking her further away from her lover's resting place.

Tallin thought that, had she been in Fianna's boots, she would have felt like burning with him.

"Hey!" Ruari cried out from the front of the group. He patted at a cut on his forehead, which was already bleeding in thin stripes down his cheek.

"What happened?" Ystril asked.

"Tree hit me," Ruari said, frowning.

"What do you mean?" Tallin asked.

"Branch moved. Hit my head."

Tallin saw a shifting movement and turned her head to see another tree bend towards Ithal, knocking him from the horse. He tumbled to the ground with a yell, twisting his body in the air so he landed on his back.

"Are you hurt?" Tallin asked, rushing to his side.

Ithal sat up, shaking his head. "Just a little bruised."

"Gods," Ystril said. "What's happening?"

"Trees are angry," Fychan said.

Tallin looked around. The trees were shifting, their branches snaking towards them. She grabbed one and tried to push it away, but it was no use.

"They want us to turn back," Kirian said. "They do not want us here."

"This is ridiculous," Ithal said. "They're just trees."

"Apparently not," Ystril said.

"No," Kirian agreed, "Fychan is right. They are angry that we cut the branches."

"Told you," Ruari said. "Said trees were bad."

"Angry, not bad," Fychan said.

"How are we going to get through?" Tallin asked as the trees ahead of them twined their branches together to form a barrier, blocking the way between them.

"I do not know," Kirian said.

"Cut them down," Ystril said, sliding his sword from its scabbard.

"There are hundreds of trees here," Tallin said. "We cannot possibly fight our way through them all."

"What else can we do?" Ithal said.

"Tallin is right," Kirian said. "Every tree in this forest will try to stop us. We cannot pass."

"Please," Tallin called out, her voice echoing through the trees. "Please, we need to get through. We have to do something really important to help the dead souls. We are so sorry that we hurt you, really we are. Please, please let us through."

The trees remained knotted together. Fychan attempted to climb the barrier, but a branch whipped round and threw her back.

"Perhaps if we wait?" Ithal said.

"No," Kirian said. "They wish to drive us out. It will become dangerous if we try to stay."

"Then what are we supposed to do?" Ystril asked.

"We have to leave," Kirian said.

A tight ball of dread spooled low in Tallin's stomach. That would mean crossing the boglands again, this time at night.

"So what are you saying," Ithal said, "we're just

giving up? Going home?"

"We can't give up," Fianna said. "Not now. Cearul won't die for nothing."

"Fianna is right. We have to get to Caer Gwynfor. Is there another way?" Tallin asked.

Kirian sighed. "It will not be easy."

"Easier than trying to fight our way through hundreds of angry homicidal trees?" Ithal asked, raising an eyebrow.

"We will have to cross the ocean, from the isle of Tramante," Kirian said. "It is the only other possible way."

"We'd have to travel miles," Tallin said. Tramante was a wild island which could only be reached from a tiny number of port towns on the mainland, on account of the Altior Ocean being a notoriously treacherous body of water to cross. They would have to retrace their steps back as far as Yarrow, and she was certain they did not have enough coin left to purchase a boat crossing from an authorised ferrykeeper.

"And how do we do that?" Ithal asked. "To sail from Tramante to Tir Diffaith is impossible. Everyone knows what the waters are like in those parts."

"We can try it," Kirian said, "or we can stay here and deal with the homicidal trees."

Tallin kicked the ground and swore. She knew the old castle where Gwion was said to be was within a day's walk of the other side of the Blightwood. They were so close to their destination, so close to where they needed to be. It was ridiculous to think they would have to turn back, but she could think of no other way. The forest stretched from the coast up to the Silverpeaks, a cold, inhospitable mountain range which supported no life at all. The only other chance they had was the route Kirian suggested.

"Then we will have to try it," she said.

"What's wrong with you?" Ithal asked. "There's no chance we'll make it that way either. We may as well take our chances here."

"And all die in the trying?" Fianna snapped. "Only there'll be nobody left to burn us, so we'll all spend the rest of time wandering about as living corpses in this gods-forsaken place. I agree with Tallin. We have to sail to Tramante."

"Just like that," Ithal muttered.

"We will find a way," Tallin said. "We have to."

"Let's go, then," Ystril said, and turned the horses round.

By the time the trees thinned out and they stood once more upon the edge of the boglands, the sun was sinking over the horizon and the wet earth was bathed in a warm, rich glow which trickled through the mists in glittering rays. It would be breathtaking, Tallin thought, if it wasn't so dangerous.

"How will we know where to walk in the dark?" Ystril asked.

"We will have to go slowly and carefully," Kirian said. "And Ithal will have to get off his horse."

"But my leg," Ithal said, looking worried.

"You will have to hobble or crawl if you need to," Kirian said. "Your weight on the horse would be too much. We cannot risk losing you or the animal."

"Let me walk at the front," Tallin said. "I can try to light our way as best I can."

She didn't think her magic would hold up long enough to see them safely to the other side of the bog, but at least it was something. As before, Fychan and Faolain did their bit, skipping ahead to check for the safest path. They were in for a long night.

The sun disappeared from the sky and the air became even colder, a biting wind beginning to whip through their clothing. Tallin shivered, the pale light of her magic wavering as her body fought to conserve its energy. The steam that rose from the earth glowed in the darkness, an eerie luminescent green, and in its weak light Tallin could see tiny spores floating in the air around them.

"Don't touch those," Kirian warned. "If they break open on you, you will have a nasty rash."

They were about half way across the boglands when Tallin took a misstep. Perhaps she was not concentrating, exhausted and wrung-out after a gruelling and devastating day. Perhaps she simply wasn't looking where she was going, but within moments, she found herself up to her thighs in the mud, the wet, peaty soil making obscene squelching noises as it drew her down into its dark depths. She struggled, trying to kick her legs through the bog, but it only served to drag her down further.

"Help me," she cried, her voice high and piercing.

Fianna cursed, loud and long. "Hold on, Tal. I'm not losing you, too."

She and Kirian bent over, each of them grabbing one of Tallin's arms. She could feel them pulling at her, could feel her shoulders aching in their sockets as they tried to drag her out of the mud. The pull of the bog was stronger, though, and she could feel the heat of the mud covering her up to her waist. She looked at Kirian and felt tears threaten. His features were crumpled, his eyes wide and desperate, his arms shaking with the effort of holding her above the sucking peat.

"Use the horse," Ystril said.

"We need some rope," Fianna said.

"I think there's some in one of the backpacks," Ithal said.

"Mine," Kirian said. "Quickly."

Ruari ran over, a length of thin rope in his hands. Tallin thought it did not look thick enough to bear her weight. By now, the mud was nearly at her chest, and she couldn't feel her feet. Her skin was glowing with fear, sparks of light shooting from her body and flying into the night sky.

"Fychan can do this," Fychan said, grabbing the end of the rope and bravely balancing on the thick mud to wrap a loop of it under Tallin's bust, just as the black earth seeped over it. Ruari ran to take the other end to the horse, where he and Ystril fastened it to the pommel of the saddle.

"Walk him forward quickly," Ithal said. "Mind the bog. We don't want the horse going in, too."

The mud was at Tallin's neck. It almost covered her shoulders, although her arms were still pulled taut by Fianna and Kirian. Their faces were strained with the effort of keeping her from being sucked beneath the bog. She tilted her head to breathe, the fumes of the mist burning her lungs.

"Please hurry," she whispered.

The horse huffed as he walked forward and took up the tension in the rope, his muscles flexing.

"Come on boy," Ruari whispered into the horse's ear. "You help Tallin."

Tallin felt herself shift and slide forward almost imperceptibly.

"Keep going," she said, "I moved."

Kirian and Fianna were both breathing heavily as they continued to lean backwards, pulling at her arms. The horse nickered, blowing hard from his nostrils as he scrabbled against the soft earth, slowly moving forward.

"It's working," Tallin gasped, feeling the suction as her body began to be given up by the bog.

It took a final, considerable effort – everyone,

including the horse, running with sweat – but Tallin was finally released from the mud with a loud slurping noise which would have been funny, had she not been so close to a suffocating death. She lay on the ground, her clothes and skin saturated with black, stinking mud, tears running down her face as she sucked in great gulps of air.

She smelled revolting, like an unclean privy belonging to someone with chronic gut-rot. Her stomach was roiling with nausea, and she felt like screaming, but she was alive. Kirian's face leaning over her in that moment, framed by the glittering silver stars scattered across the night sky, was by far the most beautiful sight she had ever seen.

"I love you," she said wonderingly. She could always put it down to the intoxication of terror, later.

"Oh Tallin," he said, helping her to her feet. "I thought you were gone."

Before she could say anything else, he had pulled her into a tight hug, the filth of the bog smearing all over his tunic.

"This stuff reeks," Tallin said in his ear.

"Never mind," he said. "It will wash off."

"We aren't exactly going to be able to run a hot bath any time soon," Tallin said.

Kirian shrugged. "Better if we all have it on us then, so nobody is the fragrant pariah."

"I'm not hugging everyone," Tallin said.

"And I'm not getting that stink on me," Ystril said with a disdainful sniff.

"I'd chase you," Tallin said, "but I don't really want to fall in again."

"Talking of which," Ithal said, "do you really think we ought to carry on tonight? Wouldn't it be better just to huddle up here until the daylight comes?"

"I just want to get out of here," Fianna said, gazing into the distance.

"We nearly lost Tallin," Ithal said. "Look, we're all tired and distraught, and we don't want to make any more mistakes."

"He's right," Tallin said. "I wasn't concentrating, and we can't afford to do that in the dark."

And so they waited it out until morning, huddled together on what felt like a fairly stable piece of ground. Tallin didn't sleep at all, lying on her back staring at the sky and thinking about Cearul. She could hear Fianna snuffling beside her, trying and failing to cry silently. She felt the trickle of her own tears running down the side of her face into her hair.

The red eyes in the morning seemed to suggest that everyone had spent the night just as Tallin had. Everyone was drained and heavy hearted, lacking any real energy to go on. But go on they knew they must, and now they could see the pockets of loose ground, they managed to pick a steady path through to the other side of the bog without any further danger.

It was a strange experience, retracing their steps

towards Tulach Túr and the border of Yarrow. Tallin had hoped that the next time they would see these parts of the land, they would be jubilantly making their way home after defeating Gwion. Instead, she felt dispirited and subdued as they rode silently in single file across the barren, grey fields, Cearul's horse serving as a constant reminder of his absence.

She had always known they might not all make it back. She had known the danger they were riding into. Despite this, she had pretended that it would all be fine, had pictured the victory procession back through the gates of the abbey with all the villagers cheering. In her imagination, everybody was always there. Death didn't even seem possible. She had never in her worst nightmares dreamed that she would have to burn the body of someone who had become a close friend.

She never wanted to have to do that again. Yet she feared she would.

They spent another long, cold, silent night back at the old lookout tower. Fianna sat watch, staring mutely out into space. She was not eating, not sleeping. They were all worried about her, but she batted away any attempt to start a conversation.

"You're not going to be able to carry on if you don't sleep," Tallin said quietly as she folded herself down to the floor beside the warrior.

"Don't care," Fianna said, not even looking her way.

"Please, Fi. You can't give up. Cearul wouldn't want this for you."

"How the everlasting fuck do you know what Cearul

would want?" Fianna said, finally turning her head. Her eyes glittered with grief and yet more tears unshed, the skin beneath her eyes so dark that it looked bruised.

"I'm sorry," Tallin said. "I can't even begin to imagine how you feel. But you know I'm right."

"What if you are?" Fianna said. "It doesn't change anything."

Tallin squeezed Fianna's shoulder, and she flinched. "I'm here if you need me. We love you, Fi."

Fianna's jaw tightened and she blinked hard, but didn't respond.

SIXTEEN

"Where are we headed from here?" Ystril asked the next morning, as they looked out over the trees which marked the border back into Yarrow.

"We should stop at Chesterdale," Kirian said, "to stock up on supplies from the markets and some ointment for Ithal's knee. Then we need to go west, towards Port Antas. We need to find someone with a boat sturdy enough for us to cross."

"I'd do anything for a hot bath," Tallin said.

"I am not sure I can promise that," Kirian said.

Chesterdale was considered the main trading centre of Glendoran, set as it was in the heart of the country of Yarrow. Many of the more extravagant pedlars who arrived to hawk their wares in Clestead came from the city. They would sell anything from solid sticks of spicy perfume to exotic looking animals which the rich would keep as pets. Tallin had once saved all her coin for months to buy a tiny bright green bird in a cage from a travelling merchant. It had lived for three days.

It took three days to reach the outskirts.

"You should stay here," Kirian said to Tallin as they crested a hill, looking down on the sprawling buildings below them. "The emperor may still have a bounty on your heads. I will go into the market to purchase what we need."

"It makes sense for us all not to go," Tallin said. "But perhaps I could come, if I wore the hood up on my cloak. Nobody would make the connection then."

"There is no need for you to risk it," Kirian said. "I am perfectly capable of carrying what I buy."

Tallin pouted. "But I wanted to see the city."

She had been thinking about little coloured birds like the one the merchant had sold her. She'd never seen one in the wild and had fanciful ideas of whole parks full of wildlife within the city walls. She knew that if she did not take her chance to see it now, she would be wondering forever if Chesterdale was as unusual and eccentric as she imagined.

Kirian sighed. "Come on then."

She pulled the hood of her travelling cloak around her face as they passed into the city, following a stream of people who had queued at the gates to enter the busy markets. It was early morning and Chesterdale was just coming to life, farmers with heavily laden carts travelling in to the market square to offer their produce for sale.

Tallin had never seen so many people in one place. Even Harrintown had been quiet in comparison. It seemed that everything was for sale here, and Tallin wandered wide-eyed among the carts and stalls that were

225

crammed together around the outside of the square. She stopped to finger a soft, emerald-green silk tunic similar to the gold one she wore, except that one was by now irreparably stained and torn. The stallholder eyed her suspiciously. She supposed she did not look the type to spend money on fine fabrics, and she nodded to him and moved on.

She picked up a fruit from one rickety little stall, round and scarlet red, its skin thick and waxy. She had never seen anything like it before and wondered aloud where it grew.

"Only in the sandy soil of the west," Kirian said in her ear. "Have you never seen a misilin before?"

Tallin shook her head. "No. We never had anything like this in the monastery."

"Here," Kirian said, handing over a coin to the stallholder. "Hand me your dagger."

He took Tallin's dagger and cut the fruit cleanly in two, handing her one of the halves. Tallin gazed at the misilin in wonder. Inside, there was pale pink flesh and hundreds of small, glossy seeds, shining deep red like tiny rubies.

Kirian lifted his half of the fruit up to her mouth and she took a small bite, the flesh exploding in her mouth, soft and juicy, while the seeds crunched between her teeth. It was sweet and tart at the same time and she closed her eyes, humming in pleasure as she savoured the exotic flavour which seeped across her tongue.

"You have some juice," Kirian said, "here." He ran a finger along her chin, following a pale red sticky trail of fruit. Tallin opened her eyes and stared up at him, his eyes hooded and dark. She felt the air grow heavy around them, the fresh morning sunlight suddenly feeling too warm.

"Come on," she said, trying to break the sudden tension that grew between them. "We can't spend all day shopping. They'll worry if we take too long."

"You are right," Kirian said, his voice husky. "We can't shop all day. We should get what we need, and then we should go to the tavern."

"The tavern?" Tallin asked, her eyebrows raising.

"It is an unseasonably warm day," Kirian said. "I am in the mood for an ale."

Tallin regarded him with confusion. It was an unexpected request. She supposed, if they were quick enough in the market, they would have time to sit for a short while, but she never would have thought Kirian would suggest doing so. He always seemed to be thinking of what they had to do next, where they had to be, what task they would need to do when they got there.

Still, she nodded. "An ale, then. After we've bought the rice and meat."

Kirian hurried her through the market, past the stalls selling finely-stitched leather armour and shining steel helmets, past the wooden tables laden with fresh fruits and vegetables of all different kinds, past the small corrals holding spring lambs, just separated from their mothers and baaing plaintively. They stuffed sacks full of rice, dried peas, grain and sausage meat until the bags were so heavy that Tallin could barely carry them.

"I think we've earned this beer," she said, as they staggered through the narrow streets, arms full.

The tavern was called the Rolling Pony, the large sign beside the door intricately carved and painted to show a dapple grey horse on its back in a meadow. It was surprisingly quiet inside, dark and cool, low tables scattered indiscriminately around the large room. Tallin perched on a stool while Kirian went to purchase drinks from the bartender.

After some time, he returned carrying two small, pewter tankards foaming with dark ale. Tallin sniffed it. The beer smelled smoky and roasted and she smiled. Stout was her favourite type of brew, reminding her of long winter nights in front of the fire in the monastery library. She took a sip and sighed.

"Thank you, Kirian," she said. "This was a nice idea."

"Afterwards, I would like you to come with me," he said. "I have a surprise for you."

"What is it?"

"If I told you, it would not be a surprise," Kirian said with a smile.

Tallin downed her ale in three large gulps, sitting back and wiping foam from her lips before belching lightly. "Sorry."

Kirian rolled his eyes.

"I couldn't wait for the surprise," she said.

"Well, you will have to wait until I have finished my drink," Kirian said, lifting his still-full mug.

Tallin stuck out her lip. "Oh come on. You can't just say that and not show me."

"I can." Kirian took a leisurely sip of his stout.

"You're cruel," Tallin said. She was itching to know what the surprise could possibly be, and she had never been the most patient person.

"I could be even more cruel and change my mind," Kirian said.

"Don't you dare."

Kirian smirked into his beer.

The bartender came over to them then, a tall, lanky woman with mousy hair tied back in a loose plait and dark freckles across her nose and cheeks. She leaned over and dropped a key on to the table, grinning a wide smile showing crooked brown teeth.

"Room's at top of stairs on th'left," she said. "All ready for yer wife."

Tallin felt as if her eyebrows had disappeared into her hairline.

"Wife?" she hissed, after the woman had left.

"I wanted to avoid any speculation," Kirian said. "You will see."

He drained the rest of his ale, rose to his feet and

offered Tallin his hand. She took it and followed him up the stairs, ever more curious about what might lie in wait.

Kirian turned the key in the lock, and the door swung open to reveal a small bedroom, sparsely furnished with a low wooden bed and a large copper tub, which was sending thin spirals of steam up towards the ceiling.

"Gods, Kirian, I can't believe it," Tallin said, her eyes dancing with delight as she walked over to the tub to breathe in the floral scent of the water. "This is amazing."

Kirian looked at her solemnly. "Now you can get rid of that lingering bog stench."

Tallin stared at him open-mouthed before he laughed and she realised he was teasing her. She didn't know what to think of Kirian today. As wonderful and thoughtful as this surprise was, the biggest surprise of all was how he was acting, almost as if he didn't have a care in the world. It was so unlike him that she had to ask.

"Why have you done this for me?"

"You said you wanted a bath," Kirian said. "I wanted to make you happy."

"But why?"

"Do you not like it?" Kirian frowned, suddenly hesitant.

"No, no, I love it," Tallin said. "It was a lovely thing for you to do. Thank you. I just wasn't expecting it."

"That is generally the idea of a surprise."

"I suppose I'm confused," Tallin said. "You care about me."

"Yes."

"Yet you say we can't be together."

"I don't know."

Tallin sighed. "You need to make up your mind, Kirian. I can't keep on being pushed away."

"I know," Kirian said, his brows drawn together and mouth downturned. "I thought I could stop caring about you, just like I started. I have found it is not that simple."

"Gods," Tallin said, running her hand through her fringe. "No, it's not that simple. I have feelings for you, you fool, and you say you care about me. Can we not just try and make something of our time together, even if it's going to be short?"

"It will be," Kirian said.

"You go and ask Fianna if she'd still love Cearul even knowing what she knows now about how it ended. I would bet you all the coin I have that she would say yes without even having to think about it."

"You do not have much coin."

"That's not the point," Tallin said, resting her head in her hands. "It's worse to regret what you never had than to sorrow over what you've lost."

"That is wise," Kirian said.

"I'm glad you agree," Tallin said. "Now, I am going to have my bath before it goes cold."

"Very well," Kirian said, his hand reaching out for the door handle. "I will wait for you downstairs."

"What, and leave your wife to struggle to scrub her own back?"

Kirian hesitated, staring at Tallin in confusion.

"What are you saying?"

"I'm asking if you want to stay," Tallin said. "Don't make me feel even more embarrassed than I am by having to explain it."

Kirian thought for a moment, then nodded and pushed the door closed. "This time, I will not leave. I promise."

"There will not be any more chances," Tallin said.

"I understand."

"Good. Now, come here," she said, holding out her hand.

She drew him close to her and trailed a finger across a small healing scar above his eyebrow. "How did this happen?"

"I think it was the trees," Kirian said.

Tallin dragged her finger lightly across the soft skin

of his cheek, skating over his lips and chin before alighting on a small, fading bruise on his jaw.

"And this?"

"I cannot remember."

She slid her palm slowly down his neck, feeling him swallow hard.

"Your skin is always so warm," she said, "even when we're all freezing."

"I do not feel the cold like some people do," Kirian said.

"It makes you nice to sleep next to," she said, tracing around the collar of his tunic.

She heard him inhale sharply, a quick, shuddering breath which made her pulse speed up and a hot need spear through her body, the sudden urge to be touched taking her breath away. She pressed herself against his chest, feeling the thump of his heart racing against hers.

Her hands felt heavy as she fumbled with the straps of her armour, feeling as if she were seventeen again and doing this for the first time. Kirian's eyes blazed into hers as she began to slide her tunic from her shoulders, her dark caramel skin pebbling in the chill of the room. She let out a shaky breath as his hands dug into her hair, unwrapping the binding and letting the loose black waves fall over her shoulders.

"You are so beautiful," he said, his voice barely above a whisper.

Tallin's throat seemed to swell, and tears pricked at her eyes. Nobody else had ever said that to her and nobody had ever looked at her the way Kirian was now. Knowing how he felt about her filled her with warmth and made her feel as beautiful as his words.

"I love you," she said, blinking in the intensity of his gaze.

"So this is what love is," he said quietly, bending towards her like a sapling in the wind.

"Yes."

"It is not what I expected."

Tallin looked at him, a question in her eyes.

"Do not misunderstand," Kirian said. "I did not realise how powerful it was, to feel this way. It could take you over."

"Perhaps we could let it, just for today," Tallin said.

"Perhaps we could."

She kissed him then, tasting the sweet tang of his breath and the heat of his mouth against hers. Her hands continued to work at her tunic, dropping the soiled scrap of fabric to the floor. Her stomach fluttered as his fingers quested hesitantly over her skin, cresting over the soft swell of her breasts.

"The water is getting cold," he murmured, as her breast binding fell to the floor, baring her to him from the waist up. She smiled and hooked her fingers into the waistband of her leggings, tugging them down and stepping out of them. She saw him blink slowly, his lips parting as he stared at her standing naked before him.

"Will you wash my hair?" she asked.

Kirian nodded, speechless.

She stepped into the tub, the water no longer boiling but still warm enough for her to feel her muscles loosen, feel the sweat and grime begin to lift from her body as she rolled her shoulders and closed her eyes.

Kirian knelt beside the tub, a sliver of pale green soap in his hand. Tallin shivered as she felt him drizzle water over her scalp, untangling the thick knots in the ends of her hair with his fingers. She heard the bubbles from the soap fizz and pop next to her ears as he began to rub the scented foam through the lengths of her hair, gently separating her curls and pressing the pads of his fingers into the sensitive skin of her temples, making her sigh as she felt the tension of their seemingly never-ending journey leave her body.

She cracked one eye open. "There's plenty of room in this tub for two," she said, as he cupped his hands to pour water over her head and rinse out the soap.

"I..." he said, stopping and shaking his head. "I would like that."

Tallin watched him as he stood and began to clumsily unbutton his tunic. He was all thick fingers, stumbling over the fastenings as if they were a complicated puzzle. She smiled.

"Slow down," she said, "there's no rush."

"Sorry."

"No need. I'm not going anywhere."

He smiled at her then, a bright, genuine smile that she thought she had not seen for a long while. It lit up his face and took away the exhaustion and anxiety that was so often written in the depths of his eyes. At that moment, he looked almost like a young man just out of his studies, the world laid before him like a feast, instead of a weary traveller with the weight of expectation heavy and crushing on his shoulders.

Tallin's throat went dry as she watched him strip off his tunic and breeches, a pink blush colouring his cheeks as he became aware of her gaze. He was pale all over, a dusting of tan freckles speckling his chest. The scars from his arrow wounds had almost disappeared, faint pink lines the only clue he had ever been hurt. He was like a sculpture, she thought, lean and sharp. She could not look away.

Kirian ducked his head nervously, his shyness only making her heart leap even more in her chest. She had no idea how he couldn't know how magnetic he was, how lovely he looked. Yet she had seen how oblivious he had been to the stares he received from the shoppers in the marketplace earlier that day. People looked at him wherever they went, and he never noticed.

"I'm going to wake up soon, aren't I?" Tallin asked as Kirian stepped into the tub behind her.

"You think this is one of your nightmares?" Kirian asked as he sat down in the water, his legs curling around her hips. She leaned back and put her head on his shoulder.

"Quite the opposite."

Kirian toyed with her hair, flattening it out against her wet back. "You have wonderful hair. It is a shame that you have to keep it tied up."

"It gets caught on things," Tallin said. "And I wouldn't be much use in a fight with my hair in my eyes."

"True."

Tallin sighed as she rested against Kirian's chest. He ran his hand over her shoulder and stroked along the downy softness of her inner arm, making her skin prickle. She pressed her legs together and felt heat building between them.

"Touch me, Kirian," she said, her voice sounding as if it was coming from a long way away.

"Show me," he murmured into her ear.

She guided his hand to her collarbone, and he traced the raised ridge, drawing slow, twisting patterns across her torso. Leaning back into him, Tallin felt his chest hitch as his fingers moved over her breast, his thumb circling her dark nipple. She jolted with the sensation.

"Is that all right?" Kirian asked.

"More than that," Tallin said. "Don't stop."

Kirian stroked her all over like a cat as she lay in his arms, his fingertips skating over her damp skin, dragging in trails across her breasts, through the curve of her waist and settling on the flare of her hips. She wriggled against him, feeling him surge against her and gasp in her ear.

"Here," she said in a quick breath, taking his hand and pulling it down between her thighs.

He moaned and swore softly as his fingers dipped into her, a word she had never heard him use. It sent sparks fizzing down her spine, and she let her knees fall to the sides of the bath, opening herself to his hesitant explorations.

She watched him touch her, his hands pale against her skin, the water forming glistening droplets across the top of her breasts which quivered as she breathed. Kirian was gentle yet attentive, watching her closely for every reaction she gave him. She writhed against him, feeling the familiar ache building deep within her, and yielded completely to his touch. Her entire world in that moment shrunk to that tub, his hands upon her, the warmth of the water and the shallow pants of his breath ruffling her hair.

"Gods," she said, her voice catching in her throat. "Gods, Kirian, I..."

The sentence was never finished. She arched her back, her body wracked with tremors, feeling the magic inside her bubble and skitter through her veins. Shimmering orbs of light formed in the room around them and spun slowly through the air. They reflected in the globes of water on her skin, making her look as if she was adorned with tiny crystals. Her breath left her in one long, hard rush, the muscles in her legs feeling as if they had liquefied.

Kirian kissed her neck below her ear. She could feel

the smile on his lips.

"I didn't say it before," he said softly, "but I love you too."

Tallin wished she could stop time and never have to leave this little room. She suddenly wanted desperately for everything in the world to be normal, wanted to pretend that they were just lovers stealing an afternoon together before going back to their ordinary daily lives.

This was nothing like ordinary, she thought, but it was still a moment in time. One that she intended to make the most of.

She stood up in the tub and held out her hand.

"Come with me," she said.

She led Kirian across the room, trailing dark footprints across the wooden floorboards. Her damp skin tightened in the chill of the room, adding to the feeling of tension inside her, as if she was balancing on a rope. There were several small, thin towels on the bed and she picked one up, rubbing it over her hair to soak up some of the heaviness of the water.

"Let me," Kirian said, running a towel over her shoulders, down her arms, along her back. She smiled and turned to face him.

There was a softness in his gaze that she had never seen before. Kirian had always been sharp and focused, everything about him from his words to his movement economical and purposeful. This was the first time he had ever looked relaxed and open. She saw something else new in his eyes too, the darkening of desire and astonishment at the power of his awakening emotions.

"Your turn now," she whispered into his ear, and stepped slowly backwards until she felt her knees hit the frame of the bed. He followed her silently, solemn, trembling visibly as she drew him down to lay beside her on the soft mattress.

She ran the pads of her fingers over his chest, making him shiver even more violently and clench his jaw. She could sense that he was painfully unused to human touch, and she was gentle as she stroked his cheek, his neck, his shoulder, mapping out the shape of him with her hands in a slow dance of discovery. When she moved her palms along the inside of his thighs and touched him lightly between them, he cried out and bucked his hips from the bed, his face crumpling in an expression which was halfway between pleasure and pain.

"Too much?" Tallin asked softly.

"No," Kirian said, and pulled her hand back down.

Tallin followed the path of her fingers with hot kisses, her lips and tongue moving over the warmth of Kirian's skin and pulling sounds from his throat that she never imagined he could make. He was coming apart beneath her, his taciturn demeanour nowhere to be seen as he writhed and whimpered and said her name over and over again.

By the time she pulled him towards her and settled him between her thighs, he was flushed and ragged, damp hair falling over his face, his eyes half-glazed and barely able to focus.

"Ready?" she asked, brushing a dark lock away from his cheek.

Kirian couldn't speak. He nodded his head faintly, his fingers twisted in the sheets beside him. She touched his cheek and kissed him, then slid her hands down to his hips, guiding him forwards.

He stilled once he was inside her, his face buried in her shoulder, eyelashes fluttering rapidly against her neck. She felt him swallow hard and tense his muscles, struggling for control as she tightened around him.

Eventually, he raised his head and looked at her, full of wonderment.

"I love you," he said again, and kissed her hard as he began to move.

She gazed into the topaz depths of his eyes as he shifted his hips, his expression intense and dark. He was glorious and beautiful, and he created sensations within her which made her feel as if she was dancing on the edge of an endless chasm.

Her pulse thrummed in time with the rhythm of his movements, beating a tempo which threatened to unravel her and put her back together in entirely the wrong places. She surrendered herself to the undulations of his body, his warm breath on her face, the smoothness of his back as she dug her nails into him and sobbed.

The small, bare room was filled with the sound of them moving, skin slick against skin, voices weaved together in a chorus of harsh sighs and gentle moans. She was luminous with magic, shimmering flecks of light dancing through her, bathing the room in a soft glow and reflecting in their eyes like jewels.

He gasped into her ear and said something that she didn't catch, his voice soft and low and broken. Then he tensed and shuddered, his hands on her face and his lips on hers as she wrapped her arms around him and held him close as he came, shaking and breathless.

They were silent for a long time, lying still in each other's arms as they waited for their heartbeats to slow. Tallin ached pleasantly and her muscles felt more relaxed than they had for many weeks. She could not remember the last time she had felt so close to someone or had experienced the heady rush of release. She sighed deeply.

Kirian pressed his lips to her ear. "How are you feeling?"

"Wonderful."

"Good."

"What about you?"

Kirian laughed softly. "Surprised. Amazed. I did not expect this."

"Oh come on," Tallin said, "you probably had this all planned out when you arranged the bath."

"I did not," Kirian said indignantly. "I had no idea this would happen."

Tallin smiled, then looked down shyly at her hands. "Do you regret it?"

He shook his head firmly. "No. Of course not. How could I? Being with you ... it was beyond anything I could ever have dreamed of."

She let out a deep breath. "Does that mean we can do it again?"

"Oh yes. But not now. The others will be wondering where we have got to."

Tallin made a noise of agreement. "We should probably head back."

"Maybe just ten more minutes," he said, kissing her again.

SEVENTEEN

It was well past middle-light when they made it back to where the others had set up camp.

"Busy in the market?" Ithal enquired, his expression saying that he knew, or at least had a very good idea, what they had been up to.

"More people than I've ever seen in my life before," Tallin said, dropping the heavy sack of grain to the floor. "We managed to get everything we need, though."

"Looks like you got what you needed, too," he said with a smirk. Tallin blushed.

"Dried sausage?" Kirian asked innocently, offering a stick of meat to Ithal.

Ithal choked and laughed aloud. "No, thank you."

"Are you sure? I heard it was delicious," Kirian said.

Ithal stared at him, his eyes boggling. "Well, that trip did you the world of good," he said. "You seem to have developed a sense of humour."

"So I did," Kirian said. "And you seem to have developed a terrible case of not minding your own business."

"Fine, fine," Ithal raised his hands in surrender. "Let's get everything packed up. We've got a long way to go still before we get to the port."

It took nearly six days of riding before they crested the hill which looked down on the town of Port Antas.

It was a grimy, industrial-looking town on the far western promontory of the country of Yarrow. Tallin wrinkled her nose as they rode down a muddy cobbled hill towards the ocean. She could smell fish, quite strongly, and it did not seem fresh.

"How are we going to get across the sea?" Ystril asked.

"We need to find a ferrykeeper," Ithal said, "and haggle. Hard."

"Or threaten them," Fianna said.

"Let's try it a different way first," Ithal said. "We don't want the whole town turning on us."

The docks were busy, men and women in thick, waterproof clothing unloading boats, bringing in hauls of silver-sheened fish and large, grey crabs. One fisherman had caught an enormous barracuda in a net, and Tallin winced as she watched him stab the fish through the head to kill it.

"Excuse me," Ithal called out to the man. He looked up, wiping his knife on a stained cloth which looked as if it had been used for the same purpose many times before.

"C'n I help you?" the man asked.

"I hope so," Ithal said. "We're looking for someone to take us across to Tramante."

The man shook his head. "I don' go that far. Only fish close to the shore, me. Too dangerous far out."

"Do you know anyone who will?"

"P'rhaps. Try askin' in the inn up the road. Ol' Deri's in there most days, deep in his cups even at this time o' morning. 'E might be soused enough to agree to such a flight o'fancy."

"Great," Fianna muttered. "A drunk. Just who we need to take us across the ocean."

"Beggars can't be choosers," Ithal said. "Besides which, I used to sail a bit in my youth. So long as we have a boat, we can manage."

"It's a bit different out there on the ocean to the Bay," Tallin said. Clestead had a large sailing community based around the sheltered inlet of Cappa Bay on the south coast. It was a gentle, secluded body of water where boats could race each other without much danger. The open sea would not be the same at all.

"At least I know how to sail," Ithal said. "Come on, let's go and find this Deri person."

Tallin didn't feel any more reassured when they walked in through the door of the Laughing Peasant.

There were only about six people in the tavern, but almost as one, their eyes shifted to the doorway and Tallin felt them looking her up and down. None of them seemed as if they were about to offer a warm welcome.

"We're looking for Deri," Fianna said.

A burly, bearded man sitting on a high stool at the bar turned and spat into the sawdust which coated the uneven floor tiles. "Looks like it's me lucky day, lads," he said to two men who sat playing cards at a low table in the back of the inn.

"Don't count on it," Fianna said, a warning note in her voice.

"Aw, c'mon, love, been a while since I had a woman," the man said. "Specially not one as pretty as you. Bet you're a right wild thing in the sack, eh?"

He laughed salaciously, and Tallin shivered as she saw his tongue swipe across his lips, leaving them wet and glistening through the coarse grey whiskers of his beard.

"Don't worry, darlin'," he said, winking at Tallin. "Plenty of room for you too. Wouldn't mind seein' the pair of you puttin' on a proper show, eh? What d'you reckon, lads?"

"What I reckon," Fianna said, stalking towards the man, "is that you ought to shut your mouth right now before I shut it for you."

"Ooh," Deri said. "Pretty thing's got a mouth on her, eh? Just means I'll enjoy it all the more when you put it where it should be, sweetheart."

He smirked and rubbed a hand over his crotch. Fianna grimaced and shoved him back against the wall.

"You're disgusting," she spat into his face.

"That's what they all say," Deri crowed, laughing. "Change their tune when I gets 'em down on the floor, though, don't they? They all beg, in the end."

He made a grab for Fianna's arm, his thick, meaty fingers closing around her wrist.

"And you'll be no different, pretty thing. Get on your knees," he said.

Ystril stepped forward, his mouth curling in a snarl. Tallin held up a hand.

"Wait," she said.

Fianna twisted her arm, her hand clenching as she pulled violently free of the man's grasp. Without any hesitation, she swung her fist and punched him full in the face, the crunch of his breaking nose audible throughout the tavern. Deri dropped to the ground, holding his face.

"Bidch," he mumbled, blood trickling through his fingers.

"I'm not finished," she said, punctuating each word with a sharp kick to his side with the point of her boot. The two men at the table had put down their cards and were beginning to get to their feet.

"Shit," Ithal muttered.

Fianna unsheathed her sword and held it to Deri's throat. The man lay on his back on the floor, bubbles of blood and snot forming over his nostrils. His eyes went wide as Fianna pressed the tip of the blade against his skin, nicking the flesh.

"One more step," she said to the two men, "and I'll run this sword straight through him."

They looked at each other, shrugged, and sat back down.

"I ought to cut your balls off," Fianna hissed at Deri, who whined and attempted to curl into the foetal position. She kicked him in the stomach.

"Where's your boat?" she asked, her blade still held tight against his skin.

"Far side of town," he said, his voice blurry and thick.

"What's it called?"

"The Grifter," he said. "But it won't get you far. It's in dry dock. Hole in the hull."

"You'd better not be lying," Fianna said.

"I'm not."

Fianna swore and kicked the man again. He wailed in pain as his ribs cracked, and tried to skate across the floor on his backside to get away from her.

"Who else in town can take us to Tramante?" she

asked.

The patrons in the tavern looked at each other, several of them shaking their heads.

"Ain't gonna find no-one here wanting to do that," one of them said. "Not this time of year."

"We need to get to the island. It's important," Fianna said.

"Can't do what can't be done," another of the men said, shaking his head. "Sorry."

"Tell me something," Kirian said from beside the doorway. "Have you been burying your dead here recently?"

There was a strained silence, the only sound Deri's heavy breathing as he pulled in air through his injured nose.

Eventually, an old man spoke up from the back of the tavern where he sat alone, nursing a pewter mug of ale. "Bin burning them, we have. Have to."

"Oh?" Kirian said. "Why is that?"

"Reckon you know, or you wouldn't have asked," the man said.

Kirian nodded. "That is why we need to sail to Tramante."

The old man nodded his head, chewing on a piece of straw. "An' even if I were thinking about it, what's it worth to me?" he asked.

"We don't have much," Tallin said. "A little coin, a tent, some grain. Horses."

"How many horses?" the man asked.

"Six."

"They hard workers?"

"Got us all the way here from South Inwold," Tallin said. "Toughest horses I ever knew."

The man twisted the straw between his fingers thoughtfully. "Right you are. My daughter'll have the horses for her farm, and I'll cross you over to the island. And you'll need to pay my crew a jade piece each, thass four pieces. Do we have a deal?"

"All of the horses?" Tallin asked.

"All of them. Or no deal."

Ithal nodded. "You have a deal."

Tallin looked at Ithal, her head tilted to one side. "Are you sure?"

"Doubt we have enough coin to stable them here," Ithal said, "and they're not going to be able to sail with us. Best solution all round."

"But what will we do when we land?"

"You have feet," Ithal said. "You'll have to use them."

"Right," Fianna said, "we have an agreement. Just

one last thing to deal with."

She rolled Deri over on to his back with the tip of her boot and kicked him again in the side. He groaned and closed his eyes as she crouched over him.

"How many women has he done this to before?" she said loudly. The patrons in the tavern shuffled their feet nervously, looking at her in silence.

"Come on," she said. "One? Two?"

A young man sitting by the door piped up. "Dunno, but I've seen him do it about four times. That's why we don't get no women in here now."

"He makes them beg, right?" Fianna asked.

"Yes."

"And do they beg?"

"Yes."

"And does it stop him?"

The young man flushed. "No."

"Shame on you all, then," Fianna said. "Those women could have been your mother, your sister, your daughter."

Nobody said anything. Deri whimpered on the floor as Fianna pressed the flat of her hand into his chest, grinding against his broken ribs.

"I'm going to make sure you never do this again,"

she said. The man began to sob.

"Don't," he said. "I'm sorry."

"Beg," Fianna said.

"Please stop," Deri said. "Please don't. I'll do anything. I'll never come here again. I promise, please."

Fianna's eyes were hard and cold. "Not good enough."

Deri was crying now, tears mingling with the drying blood on his cheeks. "Please, please don't hurt me."

"They all beg, in the end," she hissed, and drove the blade of her sword into the floor between his legs. He screamed, a tortured, terrible sound, as blood began to seep through his trousers.

Fianna stood up and sheathed her sword, looking around the room at the other men, who were white-faced and terrified.

"Let that be a lesson," she said, turning to stalk out of the tavern.

Ystril looked at the writhing man.

"Shit," he said. "Remind me not to cross her."

"I've never seen her like that," Tallin said. "I hope she's all right."

"She's doing better than him, anyway, that's for sure," Ystril said.

"Come on," Ithal said, "let's go before someone calls for the guards."

They went back out to the street where Ruari stood, holding the horses. The old man looked them up and down.

"Need a bit o' feeding, but they'll do," he said. "The farm's just out of town a ways. Lead them there, and then we'll sail."

"Show us the boat, first," Ithal said.

The old man hobbled alongside them, leading them to a small but serviceable schooner moored beside a rickety wooden pier. *Silver Tiara*, the name on the outside read, rendered in cheap, flaking green paint.

"Here's my old gal," he said. "Nowt special, but she's sturdy enough."

"I'll wait here," Ithal said. "My old bones need a rest, and my knee is still too bad to walk back."

"Then I'll stay with you," Tallin said. She looked at Kirian. "Don't be long, will you."

"We'll be as quick as we can," Kirian said, mounting his grey gelding for the last time.

Tallin gave her mare a quick hug, kissing the velvety skin of her nose.

"Good girl," Tallin said. "You'll have a decent meal tonight and a barn to sleep in. Won't that be nice?"

Bridget nickered and blew hot, grassy breath into

Tallin's face. To her surprise, tears welled in her eyes and she blinked hard.

"Take care of them," she said to the old man. "They've been good to us."

"Don't you worry yourself," he said. "Jemima knows how to look after a horse, she does. Likes 'em better than people, I reckon."

"Don't blame her," Ithal said.

Tallin patted her horse's neck and stood back to watch them walk away, her eyes fixed on them until they rounded the corner at the top of the hill leading out of town.

"He'll be back before you've even had chance to miss him," Ithal said.

"I'm sure you're right," she said, turning to climb on to the boat.

Tallin had never sailed before. She sat on a small, wooden bench on the deck of the little vessel, looking out to sea and wondering what hazards might be out there. She knew that, no matter what had happened so far, this was more treacherous than any encounter on land. If they lost the ship, they were all lost. It was as simple as that.

"Fychan doesn't like water."

The aulin had followed them through the town with her culai, hiding in the shadows and behind barrels, bins and sacks. She and Faolain were on board the Silver Tiara now, but neither of them were looking particularly happy.

"You don't have to come, Fychan, if you don't want to. You've already more than paid us back," Tallin said.

"Can never repay saving life," Fychan said. "Fychan wants to help."

"If you're sure," Tallin said

"Fychan is sure."

Tallin closed her eyes and concentrated on the gentle rocking motion of the boat bobbing in the harbour. The only time she had sailed before, she had been sick, and that had been in calmer waters than the open sea. Hopefully there was a bucket on board somewhere.

EIGHTEEN

There was no bucket. Tallin held her head over the side of the boat, retching into the wind. The nausea had overcome her before the coastline was out of sight, and for the last thirty minutes, her stomach had been doing somersaults. Kirian sat beside her and rubbed her back.

"It'll settle once you get used to it," Ithal said, a sympathetic tone in his voice. Tallin paused in her heaving to swear at him before moaning pitifully and leaning over the edge once more.

"I have a herb which might help," Kirian said. "You will have to drink it in a tea, though."

"Doubt I'll be able to keep it down," Tallin said.

"I will try it. Come, Ruari, see how I brew the leaf," Kirian said, and led the boy down into the tiny kitchen of the ship, really just a metal barrel filled with coal with a grille on top. He reappeared several minutes later holding a chipped pottery mug which he handed to Tallin. She peered inside.

"It's brown," she said.

"It will help," Kirian assured her.

"It stinks."

"Hold your nose," Kirian said.

Tallin decided to trust him. She held her breath and downed the hot brew, feeling it burn through her chest and sit heavily in her stomach.

"Try not to be sick," Kirian said.

"I thought this was meant to stop me being sick," Tallin said. She felt her mouth water and swallowed hard to fight back the bile which was threatening to rise up her throat.

"It will," he said, "eventually."

"Oh, gods," she said, her hand over her mouth. "This was a bad idea."

"It wasn't my idea," Fergal, the old boat owner, said. "Bin happy to have stayed on shore today, I would."

"You seemed happy enough to make the deal," Ithal said.

"Before I knew you were bringing vermin on my boat, weren't it?"

Fergal had not been at all happy when he found Faolain aboard the Tiara. There had been a lot of threatening to turn back until Fianna had intervened.

"We had a deal," Fianna had said, "and I suggest if you don't want to end up like Deri, you honour it."

There had been no further argument.

Tallin grimaced and retched again. "I don't think Faolain wants to be here any more than I do," she said, wiping her mouth. The culai whined as if in agreement.

"You just wait," Fergal's voice cut across the boat. "We get further out to sea, often there's ocean-storms. This is flat and calm compared to that."

Tallin glared at him. "Thanks."

Fortunately, by the time the first dark clouds began to roll across the sky, the herbs had given Tallin a little respite from the sickness.

"Gonna be nasty," Fergal said. "Reckon you all wanna be below decks when this starts."

Nobody needed to be told twice. The air pressure had dropped dramatically, and where there had been a light breeze floating over the waves, there was now a biting wind whipping across their faces. Fat drops of rain began to fall as Tallin descended into the bowels of the boat.

It was designed for a crew of five, but more care had been given to cargo than living space, and they were cramped and uncomfortable. Tallin sat on the floor between Kirian's knees and tried not to think about throwing up. The movement of the sea seemed rougher from below deck, and the lack of air was not helping. Some of them had not had a proper bath for weeks, and the tiny room was beginning to cloy with the odour of unwashed bodies.

Tallin closed her eyes but found it only made things worse. She sighed heavily.

"How long does it take to get to Tramante?" she asked.

"Depends on the weather," Ithal said. "It's looking pretty bad, so we probably won't be there before dark."

A loud rumble of thunder echoed across the sky. Faolain whimpered and hid beneath one of the bunks.

"It's already dark," Ystril grumbled. "Bloody storm."

"I'm going to go and help the crew," Ithal said. "This weather is going to be filthy and they'll need all the hands they can get."

"You'll catch your death," Ystril said.

"I'll be fine," Ithal said. "Only a bit of rain."

"Looks like there's a spare oilskin on the back of the door," Tallin said. "You'd better take that, at least."

Ithal pulled the waterproof garment over his head. It was short and tight on his large frame, and Tallin wondered who it belonged to. Despite its small size, the boat was nicely painted inside and there were delicate tapestries pinned to the walls. They didn't seem like the sort of fripperies that the crew – a collection of rough-skinned deckhands - would indulge in.

The boat was rocking violently, and as Ithal pulled open the door to head up to the wheel, they could all hear the wind whistling through the mast and the sound of sea spray spattering across the boards of the deck. Tallin shivered.

"I feel sick," Ruari said.

"You're not the only one," Tallin said, feeling increasingly queasy again. "Have you got any more of that disgusting tea?"

Kirian dug around in his pack. "I have a few more leaves left."

Ruari braved the weather to make the tea, claiming that he wanted the fresh air. It didn't get much fresher than out on deck at that moment. Through the open door, Tallin could see thick streaks of lightning crackling through the swirling iron-grey clouds. She had never seen a sky so gloomy during the day, nor a storm so bright. The little boat was yawing violently from side to side in the waves, and each time it rolled, her stomach flipped and twisted. She supposed she should feel thankful that she felt too sick to concentrate on being scared.

"Is this boat sturdy enough for these waves?" Ystril wondered aloud. The expression on his face suggested that he would be quite pale, were he human. "It feels as if it's going to overturn."

"Think positively," Kirian said. "At least when the water is rough like this, the sharks will not be too near the surface."

"Sharks?" Ystril looked more nauseous than Tallin felt.

"No need to worry," Kirian said. "You would drown before they got to you."

"I'm supposed to feel comforted?"

Fychan was perched on the back of the bunk, and she patted Ystril's shoulder. "He is joking."

"I don't think he is," Ystril muttered.

There was a loud cracking sound from above, and they all felt the boat shudder as if it had been hit.

"Shit," Ystril said. "What was that?"

Ruari threw open the door and ran back inside, soaking wet with a panicked look on his face.

"Mast broke," he said. "Fell down. Lightning hit it."

"What does that mean?" Tallin asked.

Ithal appeared in the doorway behind the boy. "The main mast is down but the boat is safe for now. But the mast is dragging beside us, so we need to cut it free. Ystril, I need to borrow your blade."

"I'll help," Ystril said.

"Is there any sign of the storm passing?" Kirian asked.

"Not yet."

Tallin's stomach churned as the boat rolled again, tasting the too-familiar tang of vomit at the back of her throat.

"I can't take much more of this," she said.

"I make tea," Ruari said, offering her a mug of

rapidly cooling, rainwater-diluted brown sludge. She gazed into it pathetically.

"I might as well just puke," she sighed, before taking a large gulp of the fragrant liquid. Kirian squeezed her shoulder encouragingly.

"You will be fine," he said. "We will be through this soon enough."

She groaned and lay her head against his arm.

Both Tallin and Ruari had been colourfully sick before the storm eventually began to break. As the little schooner bobbed gently through the calming waves, Ithal opened the door.

"We seem to be through the worst," he said. "Though we are well off course. I don't know where we will end up landing."

The sky which framed him in the doorway was beginning to look more blue than grey, faint sunlight trying to push through the clouds.

"Any dry land will do," Tallin said.

"It'll be slow going," Ithal said. "We lost the main mast, with the sail and rigging. But it didn't damage the hull, and Ystril managed to cut it free before it dragged us all down with it."

"Can we still sail without the mast?"

"We only have the foremast," Ithal said. "It's better

than nothing, but it's not going to be easy."

Tallin followed him back out on to the deck, needing fresh air. The deck was soaked, runnels of sea water flowing over the wood and pooling beneath the benches. She perched on a low barrel, feeling the water soak into her leggings.

"How do you know where we are?" she asked Fergal, gazing out on to the horizon. All she could see was water, and it wasn't at all blue, like she remembered from children's books. It was grey and dark and she felt quite afraid looking at it.

"Compass and sextant," Fergal said, holding up two small copper instruments. They looked complicated to Tallin. "We need to be headin' due east. We do that, we'll get to Tramante eventually. Just mightn't be in the town we were aimin' for."

Tallin supposed she didn't much care where they landed, so long as she could stand without wobbling or throwing up.

The next few hours felt much like she imagined a slow death would. She felt constantly sick, despite the efforts of Kirian and Ruari with their herbs, and despite trying her hardest to take her mind from her stomach by joining in with several bawdy card games led by the crew.

She had never played these games before, and it seemed to her as if they had just made up the rules on the spot.

"So when you get the full one through five of cups, yeah, everyone else either gotta pay up, or run round deck with their arse out," said a swarthy woman named

Julima, grinning so that her gold tooth glinted in the lamplight of the cabin.

"I do not think those are the real rules," Kirian said.

"Got me there," Julima said with a wink. "Just wanted to see your arse, didn't I."

"Loser does have to drink a shot of this whisky though," an older man, Carn, said. He was the ship's boatswain. "Proper rough stuff, see if you can handle it."

"I don't think I could even handle water right now," Tallin said.

"You landlubbers, all so wet," Carn rolled his eyes.

"Not all of us," Ystril said. "Hand me the bottle then."

"You haven't even lost the game yet," Carn said.

"He's trying to prove a point," Julima said. "Don't make you no more manly though."

"I'm not really bothered about being manly," Ystril said. "Pass it over."

He took a swig from the bottle, brown and dusty as if it had been hanging around for dozens of years, and immediately coughed. Had he been human, Tallin was sure that tears would be streaming down his face.

Julima cackled. "Warned ya, didn't we?"

Ystril took several deep breaths. "Gods, that stuff is poison. What the hell is it?"

"Whisky. Kinda," Julima said. "Mebbe it might be mixed up with a bit o' extra alcohol to help it keep."

Ystril made a face, the scales on his cheeks bunching up. "Doesn't taste like that's worked."

"It wasn't much better before," Carn said.

"Know something funny?" Julima said. "You swore to the gods then. Thought your lot didn't go in for that kind of thing."

Ystril smiled. "Habit, I suppose. Been around humans for a good few years, now."

"Do you actually believe, though?"

"Can't say that I do," Ystril said. "Not sure I believe in anything, to be honest. I think it's more hope, these days, than belief."

"What you hoping for, then?"

Ystril shook his head. "I don't know. I guess the undead rising are some kind of proof that there is an Everlasting, after all. I suppose I just hoped that I would find out more."

"Yeah, well. I reckon the Everlasting is real enough, all right, but I don't much care for all these gods what people talk about," Julima said.

"I don't know," Ithal said. "I think it's comforting, to think that for every part of life there's someone watching over you."

"Creepy, more like." Julima wrinkled her nose.

"You would not be saying that if Pliusas were to save you from these dark waters," Kirian said.

"Where was she, then, when the storm was raging?" Carn asked archly.

"We survived, did we not?" Kirian said.

"Pah. That was down to skill and good fortune," Carn said. "Not some old water-god."

"Think what you will," Kirian said.

Julima sniffed audibly. "You believe, then?"

"Yes," Kirian said. "I do."

"So you reckon that all these gods, you know, Pliusas and Afallach and Ceremor and Samish and all the rest of them, what? Just hang around in the sky like faeries sprinkling magic dust over the world?"

"It is complicated," Kirian said. "I believe that they are simply people born to a particular role, and with that role comes the immortality needed to act as a god."

"What, like a job description?" Julima's expression was disparaging.

"It is just what I believe," Kirian said. "Many people think differently."

"Most people in the south think that the gods are not people at all," Ithal said. "We at the abbey teach that they are intangible, part of the fabric of the world around us.

That Tiorme is in every blade of grass, that Pliusas is in every drop of water."

"Well, I don't think it really matters," Tallin said. "People believe for themselves, in my opinion. So whatever works for them is just fine."

"Don't you ever wonder, though?" Julima asked. "You know, what the actual truth is, for real?"

"Since there's no way to find that out, no, not really," Tallin shrugged. "I just get on with life and don't really waste time thinking about such things."

"That's my philosophy, too," Julima said. "And I ain't wasting more time talking about it, neither. Who's up for another game of diamond dragon?"

She flicked the cards between her fingers and grinned.

Everyone was asleep except for the three members of the crew up on deck, and Tallin. She lay on the thin canvas bunk, staring into the washed-out grey light of the early morning and listening to Kirian snoring loudly into her hair behind her. She had never heard him make so much noise. Must have been the whisky.

Her stomach was still roiling, bile periodically rising sourly up her throat and making her too unsettled to even doze. She wriggled out from under Kirian's arm and padded lightly up the steps to the main deck.

Fergal greeted her with a raised hand. "Sure ye want to be out here? Ye'll catch yer death."

It was cold, too, out on the exposed upper deck. The wood was slick and chill under her bare feet, and she shivered.

"I'm fine," she said. "Just needed some fresh air."

"Don't get any fresher than this," he said.

Tallin nodded her silent agreement and leaned over the side of the boat, looking down at the ocean beneath her. It was much calmer than it had been, yet it still looked grey and foreboding.

"How much longer will we be sailing?" she asked.

"Hard to say," Fergal said. "We went right off course in the storm, and I'm no' sure where we are now."

She squinted at the horizon, hoping for a glimpse of land. There was nothing except an endless rolling expanse of dark water. She swallowed as her mouth began to water once more.

"I might die if we don't get there soon," she said pitifully.

Fergal chuckled. "Y'know, nobody ever died of seasick."

"There's a first time for everything."

"Ain't gonna be you," he said.

Tallin moaned softly. "I almost wish it would be."

"Buck up," Fergal said. "Kid's sick too, and he ain't

whining like a child."

She glared at him and pointedly turned her back, watching sea birds float through the sky, their beady eyes fixed on the boat as they waited for any sign of fish being brought aboard. The Tiara didn't have her nets out today, so they would be disappointed.

"Surely the birds can't fly too far from shore," Tallin said, "so doesn't that mean we are near to Tramante?"

"The island terns can fly for several days," Fergal said. "It's true, we may be only a day or two from land. We can but hope."

Nineteen

It was three days in the end. Three days of sickness and Tallin feeling as if her stomach was turning inside out. By the time Fergal shouted that he saw land in the distance, she was grey-skinned and permanently sweating.

It clearly wasn't the port they had hoped for. The beach was rocky and uninviting, the sand reminding Tallin of the iron filings which would scatter around the workbenches in the armoury back in the grounds of the abbey. There was a large sandbar stretching around the coast, stopping the boat from getting close enough to drop anchor beside the island.

"You're gonna have to get off and swim the rest of the way," Fergal said. "Can't get no closer than this or we'll run aground. Them rocks are pretty sharp."

"I can't swim," Ruari and Ithal said simultaneously.

"You got no choice," Fergal said.

"I will help Ruari," Tallin said. "I'm a pretty good swimmer, good enough to carry him with me."

"And you hold on to my belt," Ystril told Ithal. "Just keep your head out of the water, and I will do the rest."

"Faolain will help Fychan," Fychan said.

Fianna was first into the water, unstrapping her armour before diving gracefully into the lapping waves. She surfaced almost immediately and bobbed in the water as she waited for Ystril to follow. He threw himself into the sea with a loud splash of foam and held out his arms for Ithal to jump.

"What will you do?" Tallin asked Fergal, as she watched Ithal teeter on the edge of the deck.

"We will return to the mainland, as best we can without a mainsail," Fergal said. "I will pray to Pliusas that we have better weather on our journey."

"Thank you," Tallin said. She took the old man's calloused, dry hand in hers. "You did not want to sail with us, yet you did. If we succeed in our mission, it is in part owed to you."

Fergal looked down at his feet. Tallin thought his eyes looked wet.

"If you can stop this thing, 'twas worth it," he said. "My Verah, she died on the Tiara two months ago. Had a heart attack, she did, when we were too far out at sea to get her help. Turned back to shore, but she came back before we even got half way. Or summat did, at least. Wasn't her, no. Carn had to hit her over the head and throw her over the side. Won't never forget it. Married forty years, we was."

Tallin squeezed his hand. "We'll get justice for her."

"You be sure you do," Fergal said.

Tallin nodded and turned to jump into the sea. Fianna and Ystril were nearly at the sandbank, dragging Ithal between them as he spluttered and tried not to thrash. Faolain was coping best with the water, which was odd, she thought, as culai were animals of the plains. Yet his furry body was cutting easily through the waves as Fychan clung on to the ruff around his neck. They were almost at the shallows around the island.

She went in feet first, sinking beneath the waves before bobbing back up to the surface, blinking the salt water from her eyes.

The current was stronger than it looked, and she felt it tugging at her as she swam with Ruari clinging to her back. Her head was beneath the water, and she had to fling her neck back to gulp in heavy breaths as the foam went up her nose and down into her throat. She was a strong swimmer, but with the boy's weight on her, it was difficult to move with her usual grace and power. Kirian swam beside her, murmuring encouragement, but he was struggling himself as he splashed awkwardly towards the shore.

Gasping, she dragged herself on to the sandbar. Ruari let go of her neck, and she rubbed it absently.

"I need to rest," she said. She could feel her chest crackling, her breath coming in short, wheezy puffs.

"Sorry," Ruari said. "I hurt you."

She shook her head, listening to the boy sniffling beside her. "No," she said, "I'm fine, just tired. I've been ill for too long."

Tallin closed her eyes and rested her cheek against the coarse, gritty sand. It was warm, but dug into her skin sharply. She was too exhausted to care.

She heard the crunch of Kirian's knees sinking into the ground beside her and felt his fingers questing lightly through her fringe, tracing the line of her eyebrow.

"We should stop for a while, once we get to shore," he said, a note of concern clear in his voice.

"Mm," she said. She agreed with him completely. In fact, she didn't think she would be able to get very far until the exhaustion and nausea had lifted from her. She barely felt human.

The sun was bathing her with its bright rays; it warmed her skin and heated the grains of sand so that the aroma of summer beaches and salt water rose from them. She allowed herself to drift into a memory, back to a time when her mother had taken her to Cappa Bay to build sandcastles. She remembered digging a hole in the ocean-drenched shore as deep as her waist, squealing as she threw damp sand-balls at her laughing mother. It took days to get the stuff out of their hair, she remembered. Of course, that sand was soft and golden and looked nothing like the thick, iron-grey grains on which she lay, but the smell was the same.

She felt Kirian loosen her plait and drag his fingers through her hair, combing out the knots before re-braiding it, tucking in the tangled strands which had come loose in the water. That was something her mother used to do for her, too, although she used an old deer-bone comb instead of her fingers. Tallin felt the swell of nostalgia rising in her chest and, to her horror, she felt tears begin to push at her eyelids, her chin trembling with the effort of holding them back.

"Hey," Kirian said softly. "Are you still feeling unwell?"

Tallin nodded without opening her eyes. She didn't trust herself to speak.

"We will wait with you. There is no rush. The others have made it to shore," he said. His fingers continued to pet at her hair.

Time seemed to pass slowly in the haze of the heat and the weight of the exhaustion which pressed down on her like a heavy blanket. She sighed deeply, the press of air against her lungs stirring once again the nausea in the pit of her stomach. She focused on her breathing – in, out, in, out, until the sickness began to pass.

Maybe she even fell asleep before she was woken by a headache which pulsed within her skull. She had been lying in the sun for too long, and she mumbled a curse as she cracked open her eyes and tried to sit up.

"Take it easy," Kirian said, handing her his waterskin. "You need to be strong enough to make it over to the shore."

Tallin blinked, seeing lights explode behind her eyelids. She moaned softly.

"Not sure I can," she said, her voice rough and hoarse.

"I'll take Ruari," Fianna said. She crouched in front of Tallin and looked into her eyes. "Gods, you look like shit."

Tallin huffed a bitter laugh. "Thanks. I think."

"Don't mention it," Fianna said, waving a hand. "We've set up behind some dunes on the shore, it's pretty sheltered there, and I reckon we can get enough wood for a fire."

"Did anyone ever tell you you're amazing?" Tallin smiled at her.

Fianna's face froze. "Someone might have done, once," she said, her expression suddenly shuttered and closed. She turned and held out her hand to Ruari. "Come on, then, lad, let's get you over to safety. You've not had anything in your stomach for days; you must be hungry."

"Not really," Ruari said, wrapping his arms around Fianna's waist as she began to stride back into the water, his smaller feet scuffing through the sand behind her.

"Ready?" she asked him. He had barely squeaked out his affirmative response before she had pushed herself into the sea and was once again making for the island, her strong arms propelling her with apparent ease.

Tallin dragged her fingers through the hot, rough sand and watched it fall in dusty trails from her hand.

"You don't have to wait with me," she said, staring at the receding figures heading towards the shore.

Kirian was silent for a moment.

"You think I would leave you here?" he said finally.

"You must be hungry too, and Ystril had the packs," she said. "I'm fine here, I'm not in any danger, just a bit unwell."

"And I am fine here with you," Kirian said. "I am not in any rush. Besides, I am a poor swimmer. I would rather wait for you."

"And here I was thinking you were being all chivalrous." Tallin turned and squinted at him, framed by the sunlight which glimmered around his sea-tangled black hair.

"I am perfectly capable of it, if you wish," Kirian said, "but I do not think it necessary to lie about my reasons."

"I hoped you might have other reasons, too," Tallin said.

Kirian smiled. "There is that."

"What?"

He blushed and looked down at his hands.

"We do not get much time alone," he said. "I wanted to just enjoy your company, for once."

"I'm not much company." Tallin tried to grin. "I'm sick and hot and grumpy. You're probably better off not sticking around to see what sort of a person I really am."

"None of us are perfect," Kirian said, reaching out to squeeze her hand.

"Pfeh." Tallin blew sour breath through her teeth. "Perfect is overrated."

She looked over at the shore where Fianna was on her hands and knees crawling out of the surf. Ruari was already skipping away up the beach, his youthful exuberance not dulled by sickness or fear. Tallin wished she could be like that again, then blanched as she remembered how long it had been since she really felt free of worry.

Tallin heard the rustle of the sand moving as Kirian shuffled through it on his knees to sit next to her and felt the warmth of his arm as he pulled her close against his hip. She rested her head on his shoulder and closed her eyes with a long sigh.

"I love you," she told him, her words hanging in the heat of the air. She felt his hand tighten on her waist, and then she dozed.

She felt a little better when she opened her eyes again, her mouth dry but her head clearer. Kirian passed her the waterskin soundlessly and she took a deep draught, pulling a face at the warm bitterness of the water.

"Okay," she said, rising slowly to her feet. "Let's go."

"Are you sure you will make it?" Kirian said, his brow knitting in concern. "I could try to signal the others to come back and help, if you like?"

Tallin shook her head. "No. They have done enough. I'll be fine."

This close to land, the water was slightly sun-warmed, and she submerged herself without a wince. That came when she began to push herself towards the mainland, her aching muscles sending tight, twisting pains through her limbs. Still, she gritted her teeth and pressed onwards. She could hear Kirian splashing alongside her, his ungainly movements a constant shifting in the corner of her eye.

She was more tired than she had realised, she thought, as she tried to suck in a deep breath but managed to swallow instead a mouthful of salty seawater. She coughed and her eyes ran, tears mingling with the spray on her face.

Yet the shore seemed almost as if it was getting farther away. Her legs felt heavy as she curled them through the water, feeling the resistance of the current pushing back against her. She began to count in her head each time she kicked out her feet.

One, two, three, four...

Fifty came and went, and she felt a cramp pulsing in her leg, her muscles knotting painfully. She felt something spongy and gelatinous brush past her ankles, making her redouble her efforts. Perhaps the shore was closer now, though she felt so light headed that she could barely focus on what was in front of her. She just kept on kicking her legs as if they were mechanical, trying her hardest to ignore the pain.

Just as her head went underneath a wave and she felt more sea water stinging her eyes, she felt a hand close around the top of her arm. Blinking through the salt, she saw Fianna swimming beside her.

"Hold on to my shoulders," Fianna said. "I'll get you back to safety."

Tallin gratefully rolled through the water and clutched at the other woman. She wondered how Fianna had found the strength to brave the water yet again to help her, but this thought soon drifted away as all of her remaining energy became focused on holding on. She could feel the flexing of muscles beneath her fingers and the slipperiness of skin as she dug her nails in and clung on tightly.

She had no idea how long it took Fianna to reach the shore, but there could have been no better feeling than when they finally crawled out of the sea and Tallin's feet – or her knees, truth be told – once again touched the ground. The sands shifted, hot under her hands, but dry land had never felt so good.

Tallin lifted her head and began to crawl towards the dunes, watching as Ystril strode across the sand towards her. He reached her before she had managed to move very far, gathering her up into his big arms and carrying her back to where they had created a makeshift camp.

It was fortunate that the weather was warm, as they had no real shelter. The tent was long gone, left behind on the boat with most of their pans and everything that was too bulky or heavy to stow in one of the three remaining backpacks. Ruari had shinned up one of the large, overhanging trees and stripped off some of the leaves, which he was busily weaving together with strips of stringy bark to make rough sunshades.

"We all need rest," Ystril said, pulling a canopy of leaves over their heads. "We should stay here at least overnight."

"It's not even past middle-light yet," Fianna said.

Ithal gestured towards Tallin, who had closed her
eyes once more. "Look at her, does she look ready to
move on?"

"I suppose not," Fianna said. "You know, we don't
have much fresh water left though."

"Never thought I'd say it," Ithal said, "but I miss
those damn horses."

When Tallin next woke, she was so dehydrated that
even her eyeballs felt dry and scratchy, her tongue thickly
stuck to the roof of her mouth.

"Drink," she croaked, stretching out a hand to Ithal
who sat beside her whittling a piece of wood with his old
penknife.

Ithal peered down at her and handed over a
waterskin. It was saggy and only about a third full.

"Take only what you must," he said. "We are running
low, and we can't boil fresh as we can't seem to get this
wood to light."

Tallin wet her lips and took a small mouthful of the
warm water, swirling it around her mouth to coat her
teeth and tongue. Swallowing hurt, her throat was so dry,
but she stopped after two sips and put the stopper back
into the skin.

"Enough for now," she said, her voice still scraping through her throat like a broken blade. "Where are we going to find more?"

Ithal shrugged. "Ystril apparently thinks he knows where we are and says there may be a village two days from here."

"Two days?"

"Tell me about it," Ithal muttered. "We only have this waterskin and one more full one left."

"Gods," Tallin said. "We cannot tarry long then. I need to pull myself together."

"We're not going anywhere now, at least," Ithal said. "We will lose the light soon. Rest while you can."

"Is it safe here?" she asked.

"Ystril says that it is," Ithal said. "Think his exact words were 'only thing likely to get you in these parts is sandcrawlers.'"

"Not scared of those," Tallin said with a smile. "Besides, they make good eating."

"True."

They lapsed into silence, watching the sun sink slowly over the horizon, painting the sea with fingers of red and gold. It was peaceful here, Tallin thought, and she wished that she felt it inside.

True to Ystril's word, the night passed quietly. Once the sun had set, the heat of the day seeped out of the sand beneath them, and Tallin slept peacefully in the fresh sea-scented night air. She awoke in the pale dawn light with a raging thirst, but the churning in her stomach had settled and she finally felt as if she was getting better.

She wandered down to the water's edge where Kirian stood in the shallows using a stick to try to spear the small fish which gathered in shoals close to the shore. He was not having any success, the slippery silver creatures far too swift for his feeble efforts.

"I never liked fish much anyway," she said, wrapping an arm around his waist and laying her head on his shoulder. "Too many small bones."

"You need to eat," Kirian said, dropping his arm so that the tip of the spear dragged through the surface of the water.

"I need to get my arse in gear so we can go and find some fresh water," Tallin said. "Everyone has pandered to me enough. We should keep moving."

Kirian regarded her solemnly. She knew she must look a sight, her hair greasy and heavy with salt from the sea, her skin sallow despite the sunlight. She felt as if her eyes were sinking into her skull, and her lips were cracked and sore.

"I know, I know, I look like something crawled from the grave," she said.

"I am worried about you," Kirian said. "I do not think you are ready to travel."

"We can't sit around here forever, slowly dying of thirst," she said. "Look, it could be worse. I'm still here, still kicking, and still ready to do what I need to do."

"If you are sure," he said, frowning. "I would prefer you to get better, first."

"We don't have time," Tallin said. "I'll tell the others that we will be moving on before middle-light."

Kirian nodded and turned away, making several more perfunctory stabs at the shoal of fish with his spear.

TWENTY

They packed up the few belongings that remained with them, and the last of the waterskins, and began their trek inland. The sand was deep and hot under their feet, and Tallin felt as if she was wading through jelly. It was a relief when they reached the cliffs which surrounded the bay. There was a rough pathway cut into the stone, and although it was steep and exhausting in the heat, at least the ground was solid.

Before the sun had reached the middle point of the sky, they had come across a road. It was overgrown with weeds which broke through the dark stone surface, and it was deeply grooved from old cart wheels. It was still enough to make Ystril exclaim with joy and dance from foot to foot.

"We just need to follow this road," Ystril said, "and it is bound to lead us to a village. These are the old market routes."

"Which way?" Tallin asked, her eyes following the curve of the road which stretched into the distance like a dark, loose ribbon.

"Away from the coast, I'd say," Ystril said. "East."

The road was uneven and Tallin had to watch her

feet, focusing on each step and trying to ignore how long they had been walking for and how dry her mouth was. She felt light headed but knew she would have to hold on for as long as she could. They barely had enough water to get through the night, even used sparingly.

It was Fychan who noticed the cart first.

"Look," she called. "Horses."

Squinting, Tallin could see, through a haze of afternoon heat, two large, heavy horses plodding slowly towards them, drawing a long, flat-bedded cart. On the bench seat of the cart, driving the horses, sat a man, strong and wide-shouldered like Ystril.

Ystril swore softly. "By the gods. I didn't think these roads were used any more."

As they drew nearer, Ystril raised his hand and waved.

"Hey," he called, breaking into an ungainly run. Tallin watched the driver rein in the horses and step down from the cart, greeting Ystril with a touch of foreheads.

Tallin half walked, half limped towards them. She was surprised to see that the driver was a woman, a tall, slender koroni, her skin rich shades of turquoise and gold. Thick, dark blue scales rose in clusters above her eyes, giving her an intimidating look.

"This is Philis," Ystril said. "She's agreed to help us."

"Whoa, hold on," the woman said, grinning. "I said I'd hear you out."

"But I've told you what we're trying to do," Ystril said.

"And I've told you I think you're delusional," Philis replied, her tone sharp.

"We cannot all be delusional," Kirian said. "What he has told you is true."

"If what he's told you is that the shroud between the living and the dead is damaged and we're on some kind of bizarre mission to repair it," Ithal said.

"And even if you are, how am I supposed to help?" Philis asked.

"We need to reach the northern point of the island and find a boat so we can sail over to the mainland there," Tallin said, "and, more urgently, we are nearly out of water."

"Water I can help you with," Philis said. "As for sailing, I'd forget that idea. It is impossible."

"We have no choice," Tallin said.

The koroni woman made a dismissive noise in her throat. "You'll die."

"We are all doomed if we do not try," Kirian said.

"Nobody will sell you a perfectly good boat for such a pointless voyage," Philis shook her head. "You may as well give up now."

"Actually, we were hoping to barter for someone to

sail us," Tallin said. "We haven't got the money to buy a boat."

Philis stared at her for a heartbeat, then roared with laughter until she was wheezing to catch her breath.

"You people have made my day," she said, shaking her head. "Totally off this world, the lot of you."

"Can you help us or not?" Ithal asked, his tone sharp.

"Ach, you know, you've given me a good laugh," Philis said. "Best I can do is take you as far as Pettrick though. You're on your own from there."

"We'll take any help we can get," Tallin said. "Thank you."

They huddled together on the back of Philis's cart, squashed among the pumpkins, cabbages and crates of tomatoes that she was taking to market in Pettrick which was, as Ystril had told them, the largest town in southern Tramante.

"From there we can make our way north," Ystril had said. "We need to get to Glanthoe. That's the capital of the island and our best chance of finding a way to cross to the mainland again."

They helped Philis set up her stall when they reached Pettrick. The market square was bustling and busy. Most of the throng of people were koroni, and more than a dozen were young children.

"I've not seen so many of my people since the plague began," Ystril said, surveying the scene with a smile.

"Perhaps we are recovering, after all."

"Where are you from?" Philis asked him.

"Originally, my family were wine merchants from a village called Rinn on the west coast," Ystril said. "We had our own vineyards. Of course, those were the days before the plague when export was still free and people weren't terrified of contamination. Lost the whole lot twelve years back, and most of our staff too. I don't even think the village still exists."

"Not seen much business coming from that way," Philis said.

"The fact that there's business at all is an improvement," Ystril said. "When I left, nobody was going to market at all. People could barely grow enough for themselves, and if there were four of you left in a village you were doing well."

"It's taken a while," Philis said, "and most of the people here live in the townships, but we've survived."

"It gladdens my heart to see it," Ystril said.

"Hmph," Philis said. "Shame you didn't stay around to help with the regeneration. There weren't too many of breeding age left once the plague burnt itself out."

Ystril laughed aloud. "If breeding is what you were wanting, you wouldn't have been any better off with me here."

"Even so," Philis said, "you left."

"I had to get away. Too many memories."

"If we all thought like that," Philis said, "the island would be empty except for the ghosts. Make new memories. We have to go on."

"I guess some find that easier than others," Ystril said. "I don't regret my choice."

"We should restock our supplies and move on," Kirian interjected. "We are already well past middle-light."

Philis sighed. "I might be able to help you out. I've a friend who lives in the north who comes to Pettrick to sell boar. He usually comes every twenty days. If you can wait, and if you are prepared to offer him something in return, I am sure he would take you with him on his return journey."

So it was that they ended up crammed in the back of a covered wagon, pressed up against cages of unsold young boar who had already endured one long journey and three days on a market stall in the cloying heat and who were not at all happy to be there. One of them spent all its time trying to bite them through the bars of its pen. They smelled ripe and musky in the humid space of the wagon, and Tallin felt her newly-settled stomach begin to complain again.

"It's lucky we're going in this direction," Ithal said when Tallin complained. "At least he's sold most of them. Imagine what it would have been like on the outward trip."

"Even noisier," Ruari said. Tallin grimaced.

The pigs squealed and grumbled for the entire three day journey. From time to time, Philis's friend Klissald would pull the wagon over to the side of the road and come back to feed and water the animals. He never offered anything to Tallin or the others.

By the time they finally arrived at Klissald's farm on the outskirts of Glanthoe, Tallin was convinced they would never get the smell of pig out of their clothes. She was almost pathetically grateful to be out of the wagon and breathing the air of the farm, even though it could hardly be called fresh.

"Five days," Klissald said. "You start work at sunup and finish when it gets dark. I'll provide a basic meal, and water, but that's all. You will clean my farm."

That had been their price for the journey. Over the next days, Tallin reflected on their long trek and the hardships they had encountered on the way. None of them – not even the bog – had smelled as bad as this. They cleaned muck from the barns and pens that seemed as if it had lain there for months, gathering more layers. Ystril was bitten by a boar, and it went septic. Kirian had to clean the wound and bind it with a poultice.

"Why didn't we just walk?" Ithal grumbled on the last day. "It can't have been any worse than this."

"It's nearly over now," Tallin said, secretly agreeing with him. "And we've done something nice. These pigs will be much cleaner and more comfortable now."

"They don't seem very grateful," Ystril muttered.

"They are pigs," Fychan said.

The next morning, Klissald came out to the barn where they were sleeping and presented them with a basket of dried boar meat and pickles.

"You worked hard," he said, "and I thank you for your assistance. I hope you find what you are seeking on your journey."

"Thank you, Klissald," Ystril said, and pressed his forehead to the other koroni man. "I wish you prosperity for the future."

They followed the road north, and when the sun was just past the middle point of the sky, they saw signs of civilisation. Small shacks at first, clustered in groups at the side of the road. As they approached the town, the wooden huts turned into stone houses, which became larger and finer as they neared the city centre.

It was an impressive city, architecturally. Tallin gazed in awe at the tiled mosaics which decorated the mansion houses surrounding the main city square. They wove patterns in bright, vibrant ceramics and no two houses looked the same. Once, this area would have been home to the richest people on the island, according to Ystril. It was much less affluent after the plague, when those who could afford to leave did so before the borders were closed.

"Most came home after the dead were all buried," Ystril said, "but their passage off the island took much of their wealth, so they don't live the indulgent life as they used to."

"At least they're alive," Fianna said. "Pity about the poor souls who couldn't pay their way out of the exclusion zone."

"Money saves lives," Ystril said.

"Don't we know it," Ithal said. "Talking of which, how exactly are we planning on finding the coin to pay for a boat for our next little trip?"

"We have enough for supplies for a few more days and perhaps a night in a tavern," Kirian said, "but nowhere near enough to buy a boat."

"You heard what Philis said," Ystril said, "nobody will take us. We have to have our own boat."

"Well, I can't magic one up," Tallin said. "Perhaps we need to start asking around for work."

"No pigs," Ithal muttered.

"We can't afford to be choosy," Tallin said. "We'll have to do whatever it takes."

They had stopped in a little tavern for a mug of cheap ale and a pork pie when Ithal saw the poster.

"Monster Melee," it read in large, crimson letters drawn in such a way that it looked as if they were dripping blood down the page. "Think you're the finest fighter Tramante has seen? Prove it by entering the annual melee tournament and defeat all comers. Last year's Champion was Plisken Breyfus. Will you be able to beat him this time?"

There was a hand-drawn picture of a ferocious-looking koroni man raising a double-edged greatsword with thick hands and grimacing.

"There's a prize," Ithal said, pushing the poster across the table.

"And?" Tallin asked, raising an eyebrow. "Fancy your chances?"

Ithal snorted. "Don't be ridiculous. I was thinking more of Fianna or Ystril."

Ystril read through the poster, chewing his lip. "You know, people spend all year training for these things."

"Doubt they'd have been through what we have in the last few months though, eh?" Ithal said. "You two, both of you, at the peak of your physical strength. Has to be worth a try."

"I'm up for it," Fianna said.

"Well, if she is," Ystril said with a sigh.

"It costs four jade pieces to enter," Kirian said. "We only have perhaps a dozen left."

"If it'll earn us enough to get our boat, I think we need to give it a try," Tallin said.

TWENTY-ONE

The tournament was held in a large arena on the edge of the city on a hill overlooking the bay. They had spent their last coin on a bed in a tavern the night before in the hope that both Ystril and Fianna would be fresh and well-rested for the event. Fianna had spent hours cleaning and whetting her sword.

There were hundreds of people on the street. Many koroni men and women, some with children in tow, but also humans and the occasional elf made up the throng. Tallin moved with the crowds up the hill to the imposing, green-brick arena. Large, scarlet flags with yellow dragons sewn on them flew proudly at the top of tall poles which surrounded the building. Tallin could hear a lively bugle call being repeated over and over.

When they reached the tall, carved arches which were the entrance point to the arena, Ystril and Fianna – both wearing the yellow ribbons around their arms which identified them as competitors – were ushered away into a small room to receive their orders. Tallin shouted a good luck wish as she was borne away by the crowds into the main ring where the rest of them would be taking their seats to watch the spectacle.

The arena was larger than Tallin had expected. Rows of stone benches rose like the ribs of a giant in two large semi-circles each side of a sand-covered ring where the fighters would meet. Some spectators had brought cushions. They had obviously been before, Tallin thought, as she shuffled uncomfortably on her bench. An older-looking koroni man came into the arena, dressed in exuberant silks of fuchsia and gold which set off the shiny, dark green scales of his skin. The crowd fell silent as he walked in, waiting for him to speak.

"Welcome," he said, his voice a rich baritone which carried easily through the arena. "One and all, welcome to the annual Monster Melee. I am delighted to announce that this year we have a record number of entries, headed by last year's victor Plisken Breyfus!"

The crowd cheered dutifully. Some waved flags with the initials "PB" embroidered on to them in a violent shade of purple.

"As usual, the tournament will be in two stages," the man continued. "First, there will be duels until there are only twenty remaining fighters. Then we will have the Monster Melee!"

More cheering.

"The twenty best fighters will come into the arena together and fight until nineteen of them have surrendered," the man shouted. "Whoever is left standing will be our new champion."

Tallin glanced around her. People were starting to chant and sing, and the arena had a distinct party atmosphere. Tallin found it odd that people would want to celebrate fighting. It was not something that would ever happen in South Inwold.

A woman walked along the rows of seats, a deep tray around her neck.

"Rose petals?" she asked Tallin. "Only two silver coins."

Tallin frowned at her.

"To throw at your favourite fighter," the woman said and sighed theatrically, her hand fluttering against her chest. "Some of them are so handsome this year."

Tallin shook her head. "No, thank you."

"Can you imagine throwing rose petals at Fianna?" Ithal asked. Tallin sniggered.

"Almost wish I had the coin to buy some," she said.

They watched as the first two contestants were brought into the arena. They seemed mismatched – a huge, scarred koroni man, the leather straps of his armour painted silver so they stood out against his forest green skin, and a small, slight elven boy who looked no more than seventeen years old. The koroni was armed with a sword and shield. The elf appeared to have nothing but a slingshot and a bag of stones slung around his waist.

"Up first for your viewing pleasure," the announcer said in a cheerful sing-song tone, "we have our own Bourton Onis, who I am sure you will remember made it through to the final melee last year. Today he will be fighting a newcomer, Teren Brook. Let's hear your cheers for the first two fighters."

The crowd duly obliged.

It was soon apparent that the koroni man was slow and lumbering, and his strength was no match for the agility of the young elf. Teren danced around the ring, never within arm's length of his rival. He sent stones flying with perfect accuracy from his slingshot before skipping away.

Bourton bled from what appeared to be dozens of cuts to the face and scalp when he eventually sank to his knees and surrendered. Teren was announced as the winner, to yet more cheers, and both men were led away.

After three more fights, Ystril strode into the arena alongside a slender koroni woman, the muscles of her torso oiled up and shining in the sunlight. The scales of her skin were almost jet black, something Tallin had never seen before. She was strikingly beautiful and looked ferocious.

The announcer introduced her as Reilah, and the bout began.

She fought with a pair of daggers, quick and lithe, reminding Tallin of a wildcat. Ystril's reflexes were sharp, and he managed to block most of her thrusts, but he was unable to land a blow himself. Reilah seemed always two steps ahead of him, taunting him mercilessly, her bright white teeth gleaming in the sun.

Ten minutes into the fight, Ystril was beginning to tire. His opponent seemed to be toying with him now, like a panther with her prey. He parried a blow, stumbled, and almost fell. That was all Reilah needed. She spun behind him and leaped up on to his back, her arm around his neck, the sharp, glinting point of one dagger held to his jugular.

There was only one outcome.

"I surrender," Ystril said, frozen in position. "I surrender."

Reilah sheathed her daggers and dropped to the ground, shaking Ystril's hand with another wide grin.

"One down," Ithal said disconsolately.

"We still have a chance," Tallin said.

Several more pairs of fighters came into the arena, the winners triumphant, the losers hobbling away bleeding and bruised.

"Fianna's up next," Ithal said. "I can see her behind the gate."

In the ring were two women. One was an older human woman who looked about fifty years of age. She was lean and tanned from the sun and moved like someone who had fought battles all her life. Her opponent was a young koroni woman, a muscular fighter who wielded two fearsomely sharp swords. They had been circling each other for some minutes, neither willing to make the first move. The crowd were getting restless.

Tallin didn't know if it was the jeers that made the human woman lash out, her previous defensive stance all but forgotten, but she would never forget what came next.

The koroni parried the older woman's thrust with her own blade, swinging her other sword up in a defensive posture. The human woman kept moving forward, as if unbalanced by the sudden block, and the koroni's second sword went straight through her throat. The woman's white shirt almost immediately turned scarlet, blood fountaining from the wound. She dropped to the floor bonelessly.

Silence fell over the arena.

"I thought this was meant to be safe," Tallin hissed, looking at Kirian with panic in her eyes.

"People are fighting," Kirian said. "You cannot guarantee safety when there are swords."

Down in the arena, the koroni had dropped both her swords and fallen to her knees beside her stricken opponent.

"It was a mistake," she cried, cradling the woman's head in her lap. "I am sorry. May the gods forgive me. I did not mean to."

The announcer walked into the ring, raising his hands above his head as if he were trying to silence the already-mute crowd. Stretcher-bearers followed him, running over to remove the woman's body from view.

"A sorry sight," the announcer said, "but rest assured, her family will be compensated. Now, are we ready for the next fight?"

A few people murmured feeble agreements. One of the stretcher bearers returned to the arena with a sack of sand to cover up the bloodstains.

"Next up, we have the one you've all been waiting

for. Our reigning champion, fighter, lover and hero, Plisken Breyfus!"

The crowd perked up and more of them began to cheer, half-heartedly waving their flags and sending handfuls of rose petals showering down on to the sand.

Ithal groaned. "You have to be joking. Of all the opponents..."

The announcer continued. "Today he will face a warrior we haven't seen here before, Fianna Braden, all the way from Clestead."

Tallin cheered loudly, ignoring the disdainful looks thrown her way by a group of young koroni women sitting to their left. They all had "PB" flags in their hands.

"What?" she hissed, glaring at Ithal, who was shaking his head. "She can still do it."

"Have you seen the size of him?" Ithal asked.

Plisken was the tallest koroni Tallin had ever seen. Admittedly, she thought, she had not seen all that many, but he was almost a head taller than Ystril, and his shoulders were knotted with muscle. The scales of his skin, a vibrant violet colour, twisted and moved as he flexed his arms, and Tallin swore she could hear the collective sighs of hundreds of spectators, male and female.

He was impressive, she had to admit. The skin down his arms was pierced along the lines of his muscles and studded with deep purple gemstones which caught the light and sparkled. Around his waist, he wore the golden belt awarded to him last year for his victory, and he had the swagger to match.

Fianna stood quietly in comparison, deep in thought. She barely reached his shoulder, and Tallin felt her heart sink watching them shake hands.

The bell rang, signalling the start of the bout. Fianna raised her shield and waited.

Plisken fought with two swords, just like the woman who was in the ring before him. Tallin thought again about how that had ended, and shuddered. He advanced confidently, swinging one shining, curved blade. Fianna looked him straight in the eye.

"You don't scare me," she said, her voice carrying loud and clear across the arena. The crowd murmured their excitement at this challenge.

"I should," Plisken said, smiling widely.

He lunged at her, sweeping the blade down low beneath her shield. Fianna jumped back and blocked his attack before swinging her own sword. Her blow was parried by Plisken's blade.

It soon became clear that they were a match. Strong jabs from Plisken were met by Fianna's swiftly-moving shield. She was tenacious and stubborn, holding her ground against the man's increasingly urgent onslaughts.

"She is strong," Kirian said into Tallin's ear.

Tallin nodded. "I just hope she can outlast him."

The fight went on. Fianna was sweating in the heat, her hair plastered to her forehead, but her eyes had never once left her opponent. She was focused and calm. The koroni, on the other hand, was beginning to look flustered. It was clear that he had expected to win this duel a long time ago. Even the partisan crowd had started to cheer Fianna's blocks in admiration.

Tallin could see that Plisken was getting more and more wound up, tension clear in his stance. His emotions were broadcast loud and clear on his face: shock, frustration and anger. Fianna, on the other hand, was expressionless, fighting almost as if she were a machine. Block, parry, thrust.

Block, parry, thrust.

Tallin saw the koroni take a deep breath and take a massive swing, all his remaining energy being poured into his arms, his wrists, his blade. The sword curved round in an arc at speed, glittering silver as the sun caught the honed edge.

Fianna was still too quick. She turned on the balls of her feet, surging forward and pushing her solid iron shield into the arc of the koroni's sword.

There was a loud metallic clang, and the blade skittered away across the sand as Plisken roared in pain, his wrist bent at an unnatural angle. The crowd gasped in shock.

Plisken didn't surrender. Instead, he raised his remaining sword and advanced again.

This time Fianna blocked his attack easily and followed up with a lunge of her own blade. She caught the man across the chest, opening up a long, thin cut in his skin. Dark blood sprang from the wound and ran down Plisken's torso.

Still, he fought on, teeth gritted against the pain. Fianna kept her shield raised, advancing on the man slowly. He weaved from side to side, looking for an unprotected gap through which to strike. Fianna watched him as a hunter watches prey.

Tallin's heart leapt into her throat as Fianna shifted her shield to one side, leaving her opponent a clear view of her body. Plisken didn't hesitate, lunging forward with his remaining weapon. Quick as a flash, Fianna leapt sideways, leaving him stabbing into the air and stumbling forward. She swept her sword into the man's left boot, cutting through the leather into his tendons. He went over like a falling tree, shrieking into the dirt.

"Do you surrender?" Fianna asked calmly, standing over him with her blade pointing at his throat.

"I surrender," Plisken gasped, his face contorted with pain.

Fianna raised her blade and offered him her hand.

"Come on," she said, "you can stand."

The koroni man hobbled to his feet, leaning heavily on Fianna's shoulder. His damaged foot dragged along the ground as Fianna helped him from the arena, neither of them acknowledging the cheering crowd.

"Well, well," the announcer called cheerfully as he came back into the ring. "What a fight that was, and a quite unexpected result. Today we will see a new champion, that is now for certain. Will it be the fierce Fianna Braden? We will find out! Next up, we have a treat for you..."

Tallin tuned the man out. She was not interested in any more duels and felt she had seen enough violence for one day. She would be glad when the day was over, one way or another, and they were all safe.

Eventually, the forty fighters had all passed through the ring and twenty victors – in varying states of bloodied and bruised – were being primped and prepared for the final showdown.

The announcer had lost none of his enthusiasm throughout the long, hot day.

"And now, ladies and gentlemen," he said, "what we have all been waiting for. Our victors will return to the ring in one final monster skirmish to decide who our Champion will be. Each of them will, as usual, have a green ribbon tied around their right wrist. When they remove the ribbon, they are out of the fight. The last person to keep theirs will be declared the winner."

Twenty people lined up across the arena, their armour hastily cleaned, no trace of blood or dirt on their weapons. Fianna stood proud, looking directly ahead, not making eye contact with any of her opponents.

"On the first bell, competitors will have thirty seconds to get ready," the announcer said, "and on the second bell, let the fighting begin!"

The crowd were on their feet, shouting and whistling. The announcer bowed low and left the ring, and the first bell sounded.

Tallin closed her eyes as twenty people below began

to stake out their positions.

The second bell rang.

Tallin heard the clash of swords almost immediately. A man cried out, and the crowd rumbled in excitement. She squeezed Kirian's fingers and tried not to be sick.

"She is holding her own," Kirian murmured.

"It's only just begun," Tallin said, her eyes still squeezed shut.

"Maybe so," Kirian said, "but four have already surrendered."

Tallin cracked open an eyelid.

Fianna stood on the far side of the arena and was defending herself against two other fighters – a small, slight human man with two daggers who was trying to get past her defences, and a tall elven woman armed with a jagged spear. Clearly, her result against the reigning champion had marked her as a threat. The man was a clumsy fighter and, as Kirian had said, they were not troubling Fianna who looked calm and emotionless as she fended off their nervous attacks.

The woman suddenly sank to the ground unconscious, her spear clattering to the floor. Tallin frowned and looked around, spotting the young elven man with his slingshot. The elf was racing around the arena at speed, ducking and twisting to avoid the other fighters and taking any chance he could to send stones flying. One had caught the woman square on the temple and down she had gone.

The man with the daggers stared at the comatose woman beside him and made a catastrophic error of judgement. He dashed over to her and bent down to untie her ribbon and take her out of the contest.

Fianna didn't hesitate. She used her shield to knock the man over and raised her sword over his chest.

The man untied his ribbon, swearing, and made his retreat from the ring.

There were ten people left standing.

Fianna lifted her shield and stood, unmoving, her back to the wall. She waited for the fight to be brought to her. For a brief time, it seemed nobody had noticed that her former opponents had both been taken out of the contest, and the battle raged around her as if she were in the eye of the storm. Three more people removed their ribbons. Seven remained.

The young koroni who had killed the woman in the ring earlier moved over to Fianna. It was clear to Tallin that the koroni had no heart for the fight. She was going through the motions, lifting the sword and jabbing it without making Fianna break a sweat to defend against the tame blows. Sure enough, after only a couple of minutes the woman shook her head, stepped back and untied her ribbon.

Six.

Five. Four.

The only fighters who remained were Fianna, Reilah, the young elf with the slingshot – Teren, Tallin recalled – and a koroni man armed with a great axe.

Teren was the first to crack, the bag of stones around his waist empty. He tried to scrabble in the dirt to find them, but Reilah was too quick for him and she had him pinned to the ground before he could reload. She cut the ribbon from his wrist with a flick of one lethal dagger.

Three.

The koroni with the axe had swung at Fianna, who was skipping away from him like a dancer. Tallin couldn't help but feel impressed at the stamina of her friend. She couldn't ask for anyone better to watch her back, and she hoped that she would still be doing so after the day's event was over.

The three of them stood apart, staring at each other. There was a heavy silence, and Tallin saw a look pass between Fianna and the man. He nodded.

Reilah was in trouble. Fianna and the man advanced upon her as she backed away, shaking her head. As they drew nearer, she sprang at the man before he could lift his axe, cutting him across the torso with her daggers. He roared and stumbled backwards.

Fianna was nimble and strong, smashing bodily into Reilah before she had even drawn her daggers back from the blow she had landed. The woman fell to the ground and rolled, staggering to her feet. She had dropped a dagger in the dirt and eyed it warily, clearly weighing up whether it was worth trying to retrieve it.

She decided it wasn't and struck out at Fianna with a single blade. She was fast, much faster than Plisken had been, and she caught Fianna across the arm as she swung her shield round to meet her. Blood soaked through the arm of Fianna's tunic, and Tallin saw her flinch.

Fianna deflected the next blow, and that was enough time for the man to re-enter the fray. He swung his axe wildly, making Reilah leap away. As she did so, Fianna slashed at the woman with her sword, cutting a deep gash in her thigh. Reilah kept moving, her long, graceful strides turning into a slow, limping hobble. She dropped her other dagger and untied her ribbon, spitting into the dirt.

Fianna faced down the koroni man, allies turned enemy.

He lifted his axe, blood running in rivulets down his pale yellow skin, breaths coming in loud, rattling puffs. They stood for a full minute, neither of them moving, weapons raised.

The koroni cracked first, leaping forward with a yell, his axe swinging through the air. Fianna was ready for him, ducking to one side, the blade cutting past her harmlessly. She jabbed her sword towards him, and it sank into his hip. Her arm trembled as the blade ground against bone, and the man let out a high-pitched yelp. Fianna withdrew her sword and he staggered to one side, limping painfully, his axe dragging in the sand.

For a moment, they stared each other down again, blood running down the man's thigh. Then he smiled, a wide white grin, and untied his ribbon with a sigh.

"I surrender," he said. "It's yours. You've bested me, and I'm not in the mood for dying."

A bell sounded, and the announcer bounded back

into the ring.

"Halvar has untied his ribbon," the man said, "and so the tournament is declared officially over. I proudly announce the winner and your new Champion, Fianna Braden!"

He grabbed Fianna's sword arm and raised it into the air. Rose petals rained down, and the audience screamed their appreciation. Fianna looked bewildered.

"They'll all want to marry her now," Ithal said.

"She will say no," Ruari said.

"Of course," Tallin said, "and they won't dare ask again."

TWENTY-TWO

They ate well that night in the tavern, with plenty of ale. All on the house, as the elderly barkeep was delighted to have the new Champion staying in his rooms. The bar was packed with people wanting to shake Fianna's hand and, as predicted, there were several proposals of marriage.

Fianna bore it stoically, if uncomfortably. She looked exhausted when she finally escaped the crowds, well past middle-dark.

"You owe me," she hissed at Tallin as they walked up the stairs to their rooms.

"I know," Tallin said. "You risked everything today. I know I'll never be able to repay you."

"Not for that," Fianna said. "Fighting is no problem. It's having to smile and be nice to people all night that was the painful part."

"We'll have to do it again tomorrow when we try to find someone who'll sell us a boat," Tallin said.

"What do you mean we?" Fianna asked, an incredulous look on her face. "That's your job. I've done my bit."

"Fair enough," Tallin said, patting the other woman's shoulder. "I'll do the talking, you just look impressive. Good night, Fianna. And thank you."

"Don't mention it," Fianna said, "if only because I'd rather not think about it ever again."

Later that night, Tallin lay in the cocoon of Kirian's arms, contented and warm, her belly full of roast suckling pig and beer.

"We're going to be all right, aren't we?" she murmured drowsily.

Kirian stroked her hair back from her face and kissed her forehead.

"I think we are."

The next morning found them down at the docks, trying to find someone willing to part with their ship.

Glanthoe was a coastal town but, unlike many similar places, fishing was not a big business. The small harbour held perhaps a dozen boats, most of which were small, rough-hewn vessels. This was not the way people here made a living.

"Too dangerous," one sailor, Justa, said when Tallin asked her about it. "I might bring in a small catch each week of shellfish, but only those that can be caught within a mile from the coast. I wouldn't dare go any farther out."

Her partner, Torni, agreed. "Everyone knows that once you're out of sight of land, you're as good as dead."

"What's so dangerous about it?" Fianna asked.

"Who knows?" Justa said. "Nobody ever comes back to tell us."

"Well then," Tallin said, "perhaps we will be the first."

"For your sake, I hope so," Justa said, shaking her head.

"We need a boat first," Ithal said.

Justa shook her head. "Sorry. I built this boat myself by hand. Took me half a year. Far too fond of her to even think of selling."

"Do you know anyone who would?" Tallin asked.

Justa could think of only one person. They had to travel to the other side of town to meet with him, in the market district where he worked as a bookmaker from a dark, dusty room behind the bakery. Through the gloom, they could see an old human man sitting behind piles of paperwork, thin-lensed spectacles perched half way down his nose.

"Well, well, if it isn't the Champion," the man said, getting up from behind an old brown leather-topped desk. He spat on his palm and offered it to Fianna to shake. "Word'll spread, you know. Perhaps I can put your name on my sign? It'd look good, I reckon. Philp Tiruss, Official Bookmaker to the Champion of Glanthoe."

313

"I don't bet," Fianna said.

"Worth a try," Philp said, wiping his hand on his backside. "How can I help you then?"

"We'd like you to sell us your boat," Ystril said.

"Interesting," Philp said. "You come all the way out here to ask about my boat. Why mine in particular?"

"You know why," Fianna said. "Now, are you willing to sell it or not?"

Philp laughed. "Lucky you won on skill and not charm, eh? As for your question, that depends."

"On what?" Tallin asked.

"On how much you're willing to offer me," he said. "Now, if I'm right, nobody else with a boat is willing to do business with you, and you look pretty desperate. How much did you win in that tournament yesterday?"

"Some of it's already gone," Tallin said. "We celebrated."

"Two hundred jade pieces," Philp said, slapping his hand down on his desk. "That's my price."

"That's the entire purse," Tallin said. "We only have a hundred and eighty pieces left."

That wasn't true; she knew they had spent very little during the previous evening, thanks to the barkeep's generosity. Still, she didn't know when they might need some coin.

"Shame, then," Philp said. "Perhaps you should've thought about your priorities."

"What else can we offer you?" Kirian asked.

"Two hundred jade pieces," Philp repeated. "By the gods, are you deaf? I thought I made myself clear."

"And I'm saying we don't have it," Tallin said. "Please, one hundred and eighty is a fine sum for a small sailboat."

"It's worth two hundred," the man said stubbornly.

"We're offering you a hundred and eighty," Tallin said.

"Maybe we could have a bet," Philp said. "That's what I do, after all."

"What on?" Ystril asked.

"Games," Philp said. "I challenge the Champion here to take me on in a straight-up game of keruti."

Philp looked smug. Fianna smiled.

"We would need to check the game pieces," Kirian said, "to eliminate cheating."

"Of course."

"Then I agree," Fianna said.

"One hundred jade pieces then," Philp said, "at even money."

"Let's start then," Fianna said.

The board was laid out, the pieces checked over and deemed fair by Fianna and Ithal. Philp took the first move.

"Let's see if you have brains to go with the brawn," Philp said with a grin.

Ten minutes later, Fianna had the man in trouble. He was sweating and frowning as he pored over the board. Fianna's red pieces had his green surrounded, and wherever he could move, it looked as if she had him covered.

"How have you done this?" he said petulantly.

"Played the game," Fianna said with a sweet smile. "Your move. We don't have all day."

Philp sighed and moved his smallest piece backwards.

"One more loss," Fianna said as she moved one of her pieces across his and removed it from the board.

The man swore.

"Fine, fine, I concede," he said, upending the board and sending the pieces scattering across the floor. "Damn you."

"One hundred pieces, was it, then?" Tallin said.

"We had a deal," Philp said. "I didn't know your woman here was a hustler, did I."

"That's the risk you take when you gamble," Ithal said.

Tallin dug in her pack and counted out a hundred jade pieces on to the desk.

"I want a contract of ownership," she said, "before I hand these over."

Grumbling, Philp drew up a document which clearly passed on ownership of his vessel, the Peaty Sandy, to Fianna.

"It's easy enough to spot at the dock," Philp said. "Big green sail. Oars are locked away in a box on deck, here's the key. Good luck to you."

"He says, through gritted teeth," Fianna commented.

"Sure I can't put your name on the sign?"

"Do what you want," Fianna said with a shrug.

The Peaty Sandy was a small single-masted boat, painted a shade of beige which was flaking off to show the dark wood underneath. There were several sets of heavy wooden oars on board, each of which fitted neatly into the rowlocks beside the bench seats. Tallin hoped that between them, they would have the strength to keep the little craft on course.

For nearly half a day, they moved onward through the waters without incident. There was a sharp, chill breeze which bit through their clothes and made them shiver, yet they were thankful for it nonetheless as it helped to guide them through the gentle waves, the sails billowing softly as they filled with the wind. Tallin sat back against the side of the boat, watching Ithal guide Ystril and Fianna through the tasks of sailing. Her stomach was beginning to roil again, even though she must have drunk eight cups of the disgusting tea Kirian had made for her.

At least it was nicer out here in these waters. The sea was clear and blue, and sometimes she noticed large green-grey fish swimming beneath the boat. One of them flipped over on to its side and stared at her as she gazed down at it, its thick lips moving as if it was trying to talk. There was something innately peaceful about being out here, despite her sickness, the only sound the occasional slap-crack of the sail and the swish of the boat through the waves.

TWENTY-THREE

Ruari saw it first.

"Horse," he shouted. "Horse."

Tallin briefly thought of Bridget back in Port Antas.
There was no way a horse could be out here in the middle
of the ocean. The idea was unthinkable. And yet...

"By the gods," Ithal said, his voice full of awe. "The
boy's right."

Tallin followed his gaze to the west of the boat. The
figure was in the distance, gliding over the surface of the
water, but there was no doubting the shape of it. No
matter how many times she blinked and shook her head,
the horse remained, moving towards them at a speed
which would be considered a gallop on land.

Ystril's eyes were wide.

"A kelpie," he said. "I thought they were just an old
legend of our people."

"Looks like a horse to me," Fianna said.

Tallin watched Ystril's jaw tense, his throat

bobbling.

"We need to look away now," he said, though his eyes seemed glued to the animal. "This is dangerous."

Tallin closed her eyes, fighting an almost irresistible urge to stare. She could sense the animal drawing closer, could almost feel its presence. Perhaps she could just have a quick peek. After all, a horse galloping across the waves would be a sight she would never see again.

It was almost involuntary, the looking. And when she had looked once, she found she was unable to stop. Up close, the horse was simply the most incredible thing she had ever seen. It was tall and rangy, its long legs finely muscled and tapering into feathered hooves which appeared to merge with the water. Its skin shone in the light, shimmering with turquoise dapples over silver which seemed to reflect the movement of the sea. Its mane and tail were the shade of onyx, so glossy and dark that Tallin felt she had never truly seen the colour black before. Fine hairs flew wildly around the animal as if it were caught in a gale instead of a light breeze. It snorted, rolling a glittering eye at her as it drew alongside the boat.

Oh, it was beautiful. She wondered if its skin was as soft and velvety as it looked, wondered if the creature would be sun-warmed or if it would feel as cold as the depths of the ocean. She pushed forward, leaning over the side of the boat to get a closer look. Perhaps she would even be able to touch it.

Fianna jostled her arm and snapped at her.

"Get out of my way."

"Hey, don't push," Tallin retorted. "I was here first."

"I saw horse first," Ruari said. "Let me through."

The two women ignored him. Tallin cried out as Fianna wrapped her fist around her plaited hair and tugged.

"Get back," Fianna hissed. "Wait your turn."

"Don't touch me," Tallin said. She pushed Fianna's chest, making the other woman stumble back against the side of the boat. She lost her balance only for a moment, then she was back on her feet, grabbing Tallin around the throat. Tallin choked off a breath and scrabbled against Fianna's fingers.

Kirian grabbed Fianna around the waist, pulling her backwards.

"Let go," he said, "you're killing her."

Faolain whined, a plaintive sound which cut through the noise that was bubbling in Tallin's head. She glanced up from the floor of the boat as Fianna's grip loosened. Faolain had grabbed Fychan by the hair and was pulling her away from Ithal, who was kneeling across the edge of the boat, smiling as if he was eight years old and it was Brumalia morning. His hand was outstretched, and the great horse was nuzzling his palm, whickering softly.

"Look, it likes me," Ithal said, excitement bubbling in his voice.

"Oh wow," Ruari said, pushing past Tallin. "Let me."

Ystril picked Ruari up and wrapped his arms tightly

around the struggling boy.

"No," Ystril said. "I should be the one to touch it. They are from the legends of koroni people."

"It's pretty clear," Ithal said, "that this isn't a legend at all. It's as real as I am. I'll prove it."

Before anyone could object, Ithal twisted his fingers into the horse's flowing mane and leapt from the boat. He landed across the animal's wide back, scrabbling with his free arm and his legs to get into position. The horse stood patiently, turning its enormous head to one side to watch Ithal as he sat triumphantly upright astride it.

"This is amazing," he called, grinning wildly.

The horse shivered and made a noise like a bell. Coal-black strands of hair tangled around Ithal's hands, and Tallin realised with a rush of fear that the lively movement had not been the wind at all. Ithal yelled for help, tugging frantically in an attempt to free his fingers. More strands began to wind and weave their way around his arms, and his shouts turned into panicked, high pitched screams.

Tallin knew she was screaming too and felt Kirian's arms around her, holding her back as she tried to throw herself at Ithal and the horse. She watched helplessly as the animal reared up and plunged head first beneath the waves. There was a loud crack as the horse's tail disappeared under the water, and they could see the silver shimmer of it sinking rapidly into the depths of the ocean.

Screams subsided into choking wails, broken, inhuman sounds that Tallin had no control over. The boat was rocking with the efforts of Kirian and Ystril to restrain her as she fought them, her body twisting and kicking. Perhaps if she could dive in now it wouldn't be too late, she could still save him, cut him free and drag him to the surface.

"He is gone," Kirian said in her ear. "I am sorry, love. So sorry."

Slowly, she stopped thrashing and began to gulp in deep breaths of salty air, her chest feeling as if it were full of bubbles which pressed against her heart. The sensation physically hurt, and she retched. As the men let her sink to the floor of the boat, she looked up at Ystril angrily, her eyes flashing through tears.

"Why didn't you stop him? They're your legend, you said so. You should have known."

Ystril sighed. "I wish I could have. You saw what happened. We were all entranced the minute it got close enough."

"It's your fault," she spat, seeing the koroni man wince. "You should have done more. You should have stopped him from looking before it was too late."

"Don't you think I'm telling myself that?" Ystril snapped back. "I swear to you, if I could have, I would have."

"You should have known," Tallin repeated, her voice rising into a whine. Tears were streaming down her face, and she could hear Kirian sniffling quietly behind her as he ran the flat of his hand down her back over and over again.

"I don't need you to make me feel guilty," Ystril said, turning his back on her and walking away. Tallin buried her face in her hands and wept harder than she had since her Da died. In some ways, she thought, this felt worse. She barely remembered her Da, had never really understood who he was as a person. Ithal had been, in many ways, so much more. She still could not believe he was gone.

Ruari came over to them, his cheeks pink from the effort of holding back his tears.

"Ystril say kelpie unusual," the boy said. "Ystril say normally more than one. Normally in groups like a herd."

Kirian frowned. "He is worried that there may be more?"

Ruari nodded.

"Then we need to protect ourselves," Kirian said.

"How?" Tallin asked.

Kirian cleared his throat and looked at his hands. "The kelpie did not bewitch me. I thought it beautiful, of course, but I did not feel drawn like you say you all were."

Tallin drew back from him, pushing his hand away from her.

"Are you saying you could have stopped this too?"

"I was trying to stop you from being strangled. I am sorry. I could not do everything at once."

"I don't understand," Fianna said. "How come everyone else was sucked in but not you?"

Kirian shrugged. "I do not know. But it is an advantage. Other ships would be lost, if all aboard fell for the glamour. We do not have to be."

"What do you mean?" Fianna asked.

"You all need to blindfold yourselves," Kirian said, "and tie your hands to the oars. I will have to guide you and steer the boat myself."

"That's risky," Tallin said with a frown.

"What else can we do? If more kelpies come, I cannot save you all."

So it was that the little boat continued to sail north with all hands bar one sightless, rags and strips of sail tied tightly around their eyes. Tallin shifted uncomfortably. Her nose was stuffy and blocked from the crying, and the fabric over her eyes was damp and strange against her cheeks. Her wrists chafed against the rope, and she could feel the skin breaking and weeping painfully as she pulled on the oars. She still felt sick, made worse by the blindfold. For the first time in her life, she wondered if it would be easier if she just gave up and died. If it weren't for the knowledge that she would come back through, she might have considered it.

Then she felt Kirian's hand on her shoulder, squeezing softly, and his warm breath in her ear as he encouraged her to keep going, and she knew she would.

TWENTY-FOUR

The kelpies came. Tallin had lost track of time, but she thought it had not been very long. Perhaps the first of the creatures, the one who had taken Ithal, had raised a herd. Their song was powerful, and Tallin knew they were coming before Kirian shouted a warning.

Her head throbbed with the silent sounds of their enchantment. It felt like music in her mind, discordant yet beautiful. She had never experienced anything like it. It was as if the sounds the kelpies created were thin strands which weaved their way through her brain, pulling her towards them. She itched with the need to pull off her blindfold and look upon the creatures. Her fingers tingled and her eyes felt hot. Her wrists rubbed against their bonds as she strained towards the side of the boat where she could sense the beasts stood.

"Keep rowing," Kirian shouted. She realised that she had stopped, the oars slipping from her fingers which had gone weak as if they were made from sea water themselves. She tried to lift the oars again, but there was no strength in her grip and she let her fingers open limply, her palms resting loosely on the wood.

"I can't," she said, at the same time Fianna said the same words. The boat bobbed in the sea, drifting slowly in the light breeze.

The music of the kelpies echoed loudly inside her head, beautiful and horrible and seductive. She shook her head, desperately trying to free herself of the blindfold. Kirian had tied it tightly, and it did not move.

She could hear Kirian muttering, his voice low and monotonous and barely audible through the noise in her mind. She tried to focus on his words, but they were unclear. It sounded like he was speaking in another language, so strange were the sounds.

His voice was drowned out entirely when the air pressure around the ship seemed to drop suddenly, and her ears throbbed. Her body shook violently, and it felt like a steel cage was tightening around her chest. This was how it was going to end, she thought, sightless and scared in the middle of the ocean, sinking beneath the waves to the sound of her own heartbeat in her head and the magic of the sea-horses.

There was a thunderclap so loud that she felt her eardrums might burst, and then silence. She thought for one moment that she had gone completely deaf, then her ears began to ring and Kirian knelt beside her, untying her blindfold and telling her that everything was going to be fine.

The sunlight hurt her eyes. She blinked, tears welling, and watched Kirian as he made his way over to Fianna and began to pick at the knots holding her blindfold in place. The sea behind him was calm, and she followed the blue all the way to the horizon. There was not a single kelpie in sight.

"What happened?" Fianna asked, as she swept her gaze over the water.

"It was the strangest thing," Kirian said. "I was on my knees praying to Pliusas, asking her to help us, when the largest of the kelpies came right up to the boat, looked me in the eye and shook his mane, and not a moment later they all vanished beneath the waves."

"Why would they do that?" Tallin asked.

Kirian shrugged. "I have no idea."

"How do you know they're really gone?" Tallin asked. "Surely we should keep the blindfolds on."

Kirian hesitated, Ystril's blindfold in his hands. "Perhaps we should. I just got a sense that they were leaving us. I am rarely wrong."

"I'll risk it," Fianna said. "I've got enough rope burns to last me a lifetime."

"That might not be very long, if the kelpies come back," Ystril said.

Fianna looked at him, her eyes bleak. "I'm finding it harder and harder to care, to be honest."

Nobody had anything to say to that.

They rowed in silence until the sky began to darken and the temperature dropped sharply. Tallin shivered. It would be an uncomfortable night out here under the stars. She was sore and bleeding and, though it felt as if every muscle in her body was aching, she knew that rest would bring her no respite. Even when her eyes grew heavy and her lids slipped shut, all she could see was Ithal's face as the kelpie dragged him beneath the waves, and all she could hear were his screams.

She knew she would never forget them.

By the time the sun finally began to rise again on the horizon, Tallin's fingers and toes were almost blue with cold. She hadn't slept at all, having spent hours alternating between listless rowing and huddling up next to Kirian trying to share warmth. Looking around, she could see that the others all looked very much like she felt. Even Ystril, who did not tend to notice temperature, was hunched over under a thin sheet of plastic he had found under one of the benches.

She made a rumbling noise in the back of her throat, and Kirian cracked open an eye.

"What's the matter?" he asked blearily.

"Wish I was Fychan," Tallin said. "Got her own portable furry hot water bottle."

The aulin was curled in a ball underneath Faolain, the pair of them the only ones who had managed to get any sleep. Not that she looked any less tired than anyone else.

Tallin rowed on, almost mechanically. She was going through the motions, forward, back, forward, back, keeping the little boat cutting through the waves. It was as if nothing else was in her head except for that. Forward, back. Her eyes were glazed and a giant sea monster could have loomed up from the deep and she wouldn't have noticed.

She did notice the land when they finally drew near. For the first time in what felt like hours, her eyes focused and she felt something other than exhaustion in her mind.

The cliffs rose steeply from the sea, the grey stone so dark that it looked black in places. Near the waterline, the rock was worn almost smooth, and Tallin wondered if she would be able to see her face in it. For as far as they could see, the cliffs stretched into the distance.

"Do you know where we can get ashore?" Fianna asked Kirian, who was rubbing his chin and looking thoughtful.

He shook his head. "No. These cliffs, as far as I know, stretch all around this coast. We will have to look for a place where we can climb."

It felt like a hopeless task. They rowed slowly, the little boat skirting the rocks carefully. Hours passed, with no sign of any inlet or beach. When they came across a small hole burrowed into the sheer rock face about a third of the way up the cliffs, Tallin stopped rowing.

"What's that?" she asked.

Kirian glanced up. "It looks as if it was bored out by the wirry-dwarves who live in the crystal caves beneath Tir Diffaith. Probably for airflow."

"Crystal caves?" Tallin asked.

"Nobody really knows what is in the caves," Kirian said. "It is rumoured that they stretch for miles beneath the land and that coloured rocks can be mined there. The dwarves do a good job of keeping out those who do make it this far."

"Fychan go through hole," the aulin piped up. "Fychan see how wide tunnel is."

"It's a sheer cliff face," Tallin said. "You'll never get up there."

"Fychan climb."

"That's a beast of a fall," Ystril said, frowning. "It's too dangerous."

"How long do you think we can keep rowing out here before we all die of exhaustion, anyway?" Fianna said. "It's got to be worth a look."

Fychan was already cocking her head, looking intently at the cliff to gauge the best path for climbing.

"Fychan knows the risks," Kirian said. "We should let her try."

Tallin thought it was unlikely that they could have stopped the little aulin. She may be the smallest of them, but she was headstrong and stubborn. She didn't hesitate, and as the boat neared the rock, she readied herself like a cat and leapt at the cliff.

Her hands scrabbled for purchase on the water-smoothed surface and, for a brief heart stopping moment, she began to slide down towards the waves, her feet dipping briefly into the ocean. Then she seemed to catch her long nails against the rock and started to slither up towards the hole.

Tallin held her breath as she watched Fychan's undulating body rise slowly, her little hands reaching out for imperfections in the rock invisible to the eye. When she reached the hole and disappeared head first into the caves, Tallin let out an audible sigh.

"I wouldn't be too relieved yet," Ystril said. "We don't know what's in there."

"We know there are wirry-dwarves," Kirian said darkly.

"You aren't filling me with confidence," Tallin said.

"Wirry-dwarves are territorial creatures," Kirian said, "and they can be aggressive. If we manage to get into the tunnels, we will need to be very quiet to avoid being noticed."

Tallin sighed. "Nothing is ever easy, is it?"

"We might not be able to get in there, yet," Fianna said, "so let's worry about it when we are."

They waited quietly for Fychan to reappear. The only sound was Faolain's gentle whines as he stared at the cliff, as if he were willing her to come back.

Twenty minutes must have passed before they heard a scrabbling and the aulin's head poked back through the opening. She was grinning.

"Fychan sees tunnels get wider. Fychan thinks all will fit through. Maybe not Ithal, but he is dead."

Tallin felt as if the aulin had punched her in the stomach. "Why would you say that?" she asked, feeling herself beginning to shake.

Kirian steadied her with a hand on her arm. "Fychan

does not understand other people's grief."

"Surely she realises that she shouldn't speak about Ithal like that?"

"Why would she?" Kirian asked mildly. "Let it pass. She means no insult."

"So how are we all going to climb up there, then? Not all of us are agile like an aulin," Ystril said.

"We'll have to cut the sail down and use the rope to help us," Fianna said.

"Good plan," Ystril said.

Fychan scrambled back down the cliff and stood patiently while Fianna knotted the length of cord around her small waist. She was sure-footed in her return up the cliff face, as if she now knew exactly where to put her hands and feet. Once she had reached the opening to the caves, she tied the rope tightly around a sharp protrusion of rock at the cave mouth.

"Fychan done," she said. "Tie Faolain to the rope."

"In good time," Kirian said.

Fianna was the first to test the stability of the rope. She leaned back, feet against the cliff, resting her full weight against the cord. It held.

"I'm going up, then," she said, and began to haul herself up towards the hole. It took several long, laborious minutes for her to reach Fychan. Tallin watched her wriggle and twist to fit her body through the small gap. She looked like a worm struggling to find damp soil.

"Not sure I'm going to fit," Ystril said in her ear.

"We'll have to try it," Tallin said.

"Easy for you to say. You're not the one who's going to get trapped half way in and half way out of a cave mouth."

"Eventually, you lose weight, you fit through," Ruari grinned.

"Not helping."

His fears were realised a short time after. Tallin had gone up before him, leaving him the last person waiting on the small boat. She had managed to squirm through the hole without too much trouble and into the little hollow which lay behind it. It was dark and damp, and she felt as if she was being buried alive.

"I'm not going to make it," Ystril said from outside the cave. Tallin could see his face peering in as he blinked into the darkness. It was clear that his shoulders would be too wide to fit easily through the gap.

"We can't leave you," Fianna said. "There's no way I'm letting someone else die, not if I can help it."

Ystril looked miserable. "There's not much you can do about it. Perhaps I'll get lucky and be picked up by a passing ship."

Fianna snorted. "You know as well as I do that there aren't any ships around here. Best you can hope for is a swift death by kelpie."

"That's not making it any easier, Fi."

"I'm not trying to. It's a pointless argument anyway. I'm not leaving you there, and that's that."

"Must be something to help," Ruari said.

Tallin wriggled closer to the entrance and began to peer at the rock surrounding the hole.

"There might be," she said, jabbing at the edges with her finger. "This rock was hollowed out unnaturally and the job was a rough one. I might be able to widen the entrance."

"With those fingernails?" Ystril huffed.

"No," Tallin said. "Hang on to that rope. There might be some slight rock fall."

"Brilliant," Ystril said, but she saw his muscles tense as he gripped the rope tightly.

Tallin closed her eyes and thought about death, about the people she had lost. She thought about Ithal's face as he disappeared beneath the waves, remembered his screams. Her grief rose easily back to the surface of her mind, her chest tightening and her stomach feeling an emptiness which had nothing to do with lack of food.

It was enough to spark her magic into quick life, a golden glow suffusing her hands. She touched one finger to the edge of the rock, and the light began to seep slowly into the minute cracks in the stone.

Once she had poured enough light into the rock and

thin streaks of shimmering magic were visible around the entrance to the cave, she pulled her hands into fists and knocked them together.

With a shattering crack, the stone disintegrated around her, sharp shards raining down on her hair and slicing a thin gash across her eyebrow which immediately bubbled with scarlet blood. She ignored it and knocked her fists together again. Chunks of stone fell away from the cliff face, down past Ystril who swore as he swung on the rope, trying to weave away from the missiles. After several minutes, the stone had stopped snapping and sliding, and Tallin surveyed her handiwork.

The hole was much bigger now. Even Ithal would have fitted through, she thought.

Ystril pulled himself back up the rope, and Tallin helped him through into the tunnels.

"Thank you," he said. "I wouldn't have thought of that."

"You could've thought of it before any of us had to squeeze through there," Fianna said, trying to smile.

"We are all here now. That is the main thing," Kirian said. "Remember to be as quiet as you can. We do not want to attract unwanted attention from the wirry-dwarves."

"We were hardly quiet just then," Tallin pointed out with a wry smile.

"Hmm." Kirian rubbed his brow. "Then we wait here for a while. If we have already disturbed the dwarves, we will know soon enough."

"Dark in there," Ruari said.

"We will have to feel our way," Kirian said. "Tallin can use her light magic sparingly, but only as a brief flash to illuminate the way. We cannot risk a permanent light."

They huddled together on the edge of the cave, Tallin shooting occasional glances at the edge of the stone and the long drop to the sea below. She was torn between wanting to move on, away from the cliff face, and knowing that this would be the last daylight she would see for a while. She couldn't help but think of Ithal as she gazed out at the swelling of the ocean, the deep azure of the waves darkening to indigo in the distance. It was beautiful and serene, yet a graveyard for Ithal and many others, if the stories were anything to go by. The caves ahead looked like nothing more than what they were – dark and foreboding – but she knew that they would be no safer anywhere else right now.

TWENTY-FIVE

An hour passed, with no sign of danger. Kirian waved them forward, and they moved slowly on their hands and knees, except Fychan and Faolain who were small enough to walk. The stone was wet with a dark moss, which clung to their clothes and felt disgusting against Tallin's palms. It smelled salty and slightly fishy, and Tallin found herself wanting to retch again.

They were silent, crawling forward slowly, Kirian at the head of the line. He stopped regularly, listening for any sound from the depths of the tunnels. Each time, he moved them onward with a soft hum to signify all was well.

Tallin lost track of time. She had no clue whether the world outside the caves was day or night. It seemed that she had been in darkness forever, and each time she briefly sparked her magic into being to check the tunnels ahead, she was left with dancing specks across her vision. Her own magic was hurting her eyes. She wondered if she would ever see the daylight again.

She was sure there were worse places to die, but she couldn't think of any.

Rounding a corner, Tallin felt the stone above her head give way and the air around her become fresher.

She heard Kirian whisper her name, and called forth a spark of light.

In the heartbeats that the light glimmered around them, she saw that they were in what looked like a hollowed-out room within the network of tunnels. Crystals were dotted into the walls like cloves on a ham, and her magic sparkled off them. It was beautiful, the rainbow of colours almost too much for her eyes to bear. She waved her hand and killed the light show, though in her mind she could still see the glittering stones.

"This would have been sleeping quarters for the miners," Kirian whispered. "Looks as if it hasn't been used for a long time. Perhaps this part of the mine has been cleared."

"Maybe we should stop here for a time," Fianna whispered back. "We're all tired and thirsty."

Kirian exhaled softly. "If we must."

"I think we must," Ystril said. "We won't be any good if we don't rest."

"Wirry-dwarves come when Ystril snore," Ruari said.

"Hey," Ystril said. "That's rude."

"I'll prod you if you do," Fianna said.

He didn't; at least not to the extent that he would bring doom upon them. It seemed that everyone fell asleep easily, the small cavern filled with the soft sounds of shuffling and steady breathing. Tallin pressed her back against the wall, feeling the crystals digging into her skin, and sighed.

"Can you not sleep?"

Kirian shuffled over to her, his words soft in her ear. She shook her head, then realised he might not be able to see her in the pitch blackness.

"Too much on my mind," she said.

"It has been a difficult time."

She rubbed at her eyes. "Tell me about it."

"How are you feeling?"

"How do you think?" Tallin's words were sharp, though her voice remained soft.

"I am sorry about Ithal," Kirian said.

"Nothing for you to be sorry about," Tallin replied. "It was hardly your fault."

"If I could have done anything, I would have."

"I know."

They sat in silence for a time, Kirian so close that Tallin could feel the warmth of his body against her arm. She wondered if he had gone to sleep, until he spoke again.

"If it is any consolation, he will not be coming back as anything else. Not where the kelpie would have taken him."

Tallin felt angry tears spring to her eyes and she

swallowed hard, fighting to keep her tone low.

"That's no consolation at all," she said.

"I am not good at this," Kirian said plaintively.

"It's fine. I'll be fine," Tallin said.

"Is that true?"

"No."

Tallin felt Kirian's hand questing for hers, and she allowed him to wrap his fingers around her palm. She squeezed and he raised her hand to his lips and pressed a kiss to the tips of her fingers.

"I wish I could do more," he said.

"Kiss me," she murmured. "Make me want to be alive. Give me something to fight for."

She felt him tense and hesitate slightly, her words hanging heavily in the air between them, but then she felt his mouth against her cheek, seeking out her lips.

"I do love you," she whispered, and turned to him.

Kirian's lips were soft despite the harshness of the sea-salt air and the drying winds they had sailed through over the past days. He made a low noise in his throat as he kissed her, a sound of yearning which made Tallin glad she was sitting down. He kissed her urgently; he kissed her as if she was his life's breath and he needed her to survive. He kissed her in a way even he had never kissed her before, and she felt the familiar fire of need kindle in her belly.

She cupped his cheeks in her hands, tracing the fine bones of his face, feeling his long lashes flicker against her skin. She couldn't see his features, but by now she knew them so well that she could picture his expression, that heavy-lidded bliss that always showed on his face when she touched him.

In that moment, she felt the grief, horror and fear slide away from her, for there was no room for anything then but the love she had for the man in her arms.

"Be with me, please," she whispered in his ear, and he sighed softly.

Kirian slid her leggings down over her hips, his fingertips grazing her skin and making her shiver. He kissed her again as he ran his fingers up the inside of her thigh, swallowing any sound that she might have involuntarily made. They had to be quiet. Wirry-dwarves aside, their companions slept not thirty feet away on the other side of the carved-out room.

Silence was a challenge. She let out a small squeak when she felt him lift her legs and drape them over his shoulders. It took more effort to hold back a cry when she felt his tongue touch her lightly, tension spooling in her belly like a tightly wound spring.

She gritted her teeth as he explored her, his breath warm against her own heat, his mouth soft. She wanted to wail, wanted to say his name, and she sank her teeth into her own hand to swallow down the words that were in her throat, boiling to get free. When it all felt too much and she tried to wriggle away, he grabbed her hips and stilled her, lifting her into his mouth and closing his lips over her.

Her eyes were wild in the darkness, her hand sore where she bit into the soft flesh to contain her cries. Her entire body was taut and trembling, pressure building within her. She exhaled heavily, eyelashes fluttering as she shook her head from side to side, struggling to maintain her silence and to control her magic which slithered beneath her skin like an eel.

She felt the familiar sensations begin to shoot through her body as he continued to stroke her with his tongue, felt her muscles clench and her skin shiver. Her eyes rolled and her stomach tightened, and tears rolled down her cheeks as she came, shuddering and gasping.

There was no chance to catch her breath or to examine the row of indents in the flesh of her palm as, before the ripples of her climax even quieted, Kirian pushed himself inside her, pressing his mouth over hers so that she tasted herself on his lips. She sighed and scrabbled at his back with her fingers, pulling him deep as she clenched around him.

He set a furious pace, her shoulders scraping against the stone as her body moved with every thrust. It felt as if he was losing himself within her, losing control as his movements became rushed and erratic, his breath shaky and his muscles quivering as he struggled to hold himself back. It was a battle he lost, as he let out a soft moan and collapsed against her.

Eventually, he lifted his head from her chest.

"Sorry," he murmured. "I got carried away."

She threaded her fingers through his hair and smiled into the darkness. "You were gorgeous."

"I just wanted it to last forever," he said softly.

"It will," she said. "I'll never forget how you feel."

He buried his head in her shoulder, and she felt him sigh into her hair, his breath warm and sweet. It wasn't long before she realised that he was crying, his throat working furiously as he swallowed down his sobs. She felt the wetness of his tears against her skin.

"What's the matter?" she asked, frowning.

She felt Kirian shake his head. His voice, when it came, was soft and hesitant in her ear.

"I am not ready," he said.

She didn't know what to say, so she stayed quiet. Eventually, he spoke again.

"In all my life, in all these years, I never knew what it was to love somebody. I never expected to know. Yet, with you, I have found it. It is the greatest gift anyone could ever give me," he said. "And I am not ready to stop."

"Then don't," she said, stroking her fingers across the soft silk of his hair.

He seemed to ignore her. "Each time I hold you ... each time I touch you, I wonder whether this will be the last time. I cannot bear it. How do people bear it?"

"You just do," Tallin said. "If you have to. But why must we stop? I know you've talked about your duty, but surely there's a way?"

He shook his head again and let out a long breath, ruffling the fine hairs which had come loose from her plait and lay against her cheek.

"No. It cannot be. I wish it could be different," he said, tears still thick in his throat. "But know this, whatever comes, whatever happens, I love you and I always will. You are my first and only."

"I will always love you, too," she whispered, feeling her own eyes fill with tears. She couldn't imagine life without Kirian now, and the idea of returning alone to her tethered life at the monastery after what they had shared seemed intolerable.

"Do not be so certain of that," he murmured darkly.

"What?" she frowned, surprised by his sudden change of tone. "I know you're upset but don't be foolish. I know how I feel."

"Now, perhaps," he said. "But you may change your mind."

"Why in the gods name would I?"

He didn't answer, and within minutes she heard his breath even out as if he were sleeping. She lay awake for what felt like eternity after, staring into the darkness as her arm went slowly numb where Kirian rested his weight against her. Numb could be good, she thought idly. Numb meant not having to feel. She had been numb for most of her life.

No, she decided, feeling the warmth of the man lying beside her and the way the thought of his face made her stomach flutter. She didn't want to be numb, not ever again.

TWENTY-SIX

Her back throbbed when she awoke, the stone of the cave particularly unforgiving. She felt small bruised spots on her skin where she had pressed against the little crystals in her sleep. She had no idea how much time had passed or how long she had slept for. Time all seemed the same in this place, beneath the earth.

They crawled onwards through the narrow tunnels, her hands gritty and sore and her leggings wearing thin at the knees against the rough stone. Faolain was in front of her, and from time to time she would get too close and his tail would swipe across her face, sending fur up her nostrils and into her mouth. Several times this made her sneeze, Tallin desperately muffling the sound in her hand. Her whole body was tense with the need to be quiet, and her muscles were twisting and aching until she was nearly in tears with the pain.

She hoped that they would soon find a tunnel leading upwards towards above-ground and daylight. The thought became a mantra in her head which she repeated over and over as she willed herself to keep crawling. *Please let us find a way out. Please, a way out of here.*

Perhaps she was tired, perhaps she was thinking so hard about not making a sound that she did not stop when the others ahead of her came to a halt. She kept crawling, almost automatically, and her hand came down hard on Faolain's foot. The culai yelped loudly, and Tallin froze.

"Shh," Fianna hissed from the front of the line. Tallin held her breath, her ears straining for any sounds which might indicate that they had been heard.

She felt sick when she heard scraping sounds far ahead. It sounded like metal on rock, heavy and laboured. Not a noise that any one of them would have made. And it was all her fault for not paying attention.

Her ears pulsed with the effort of not exhaling, of listening for the danger. She wondered when the dwarves would strike at them. It had gone quiet again, and she began to hope that perhaps they had gone back to their work.

"Light," Kirian whispered from behind her.

Tallin touched her thumb and forefinger together. It didn't take much to conjure the spark of light which grew there, such was her fear. When she looked ahead and saw what lay in front of them, the light became almost phosphorescent before she waved her hand and it winked out, plunging them back into darkness.

The dwarves were lined up in formation, about ten body lengths ahead of Fianna. They stood expressionless, staring blankly towards them. They were like no creatures Tallin had ever seen before. They could have been carved from the stone itself, their glossy silver skin studded with gems in the same way the walls of the cavern they had slept in had been, except the gems in their skin had been turned to fine points. They were hairless, and their eyes were as black as soot.

Tallin didn't know how many of them stood there, waiting, but she had in the brief moment of light seen at least a dozen, and she knew there were more behind. She knew they had no chance of fighting, not here in these cramped tunnels where they could barely kneel let alone wield weapons.

The scraping noise began again, and then Fianna screamed and cursed. Before Tallin could spark her magic, she sensed the creatures surrounding her and felt small, cold fingers digging into her arms on both sides. She tried to kick out, but more of them grabbed her legs, pulling them apart and holding them tightly. She felt herself being dragged along the ground by her limbs, her breasts and belly bouncing painfully along the stone.

Around her, she could hear the unmistakable sounds of her companions being equally manhandled. Ystril was swearing loudly and thrashing; Ruari was crying. Faolain was growling and snapping, although Tallin thought that his teeth would probably have little effect on the wirry-dwarves. Fychan and Kirian were silent.

She was, too. She concentrated on tensing her body to keep it from hitting the floor and resigned herself to being the dwarves' prisoner. She hoped that, wherever they were taking them, there would be the chance for escape.

It felt from the air around them as if they were in a cavern even larger than the one they had slept in, though it was too dark to tell. The dwarves did not seem to need any light to find their way around. Tallin lay on the floor,

349

her wrists bound together with rope and one ankle shackled to something set into the wall. She didn't know where everyone else was, but she could hear them breathing, and Ruari's high pitched sobs.

She recoiled as she felt a dwarf touch her face. Its thick, stubby hand slid over her hair and forehead, and she squeezed her eyes shut as its fingers pressed against her eyelids and traced the shape of her nose. One finger pushed between her lips, and she tasted its skin, cold and metallic and earthy. It tapped her teeth and withdrew, continuing to feel its way along her jaw and chin.

The dwarf explored her body dispassionately, clearly trying to work out what she was and how she worked. It lifted her arm, curled her fingers, tapped at her ribs. It pushed painfully into the ligaments behind her knees so that she squealed and yanked frantically at the rope around her ankle.

It said something in a language that sounded like rusty daggers being scraped across stone and paused as if waiting for a reply.

"I don't know what you want," Tallin said, near to tears.

The dwarf spoke again, and she heard it shuffle away, presumably to poke and prod at someone else. When she heard Ystril swear shortly after, it seemed she had been right.

Not long after that, she heard Kirian shout out, and her magic burst into life without warning. She cursed and fought to tamp it down, but to her surprise, the dwarves didn't react. She could see Kirian lying face down on the floor, the dwarf sitting on his back not even flinching at being bathed in light.

"They're blind," she whispered to herself as she let the magic flow freely from her body, lighting the entire cavern.

Her eyes slid over the walls of the huge, hollowed-out room, the granite walls now familiarly studded with sparkling gemstones of all conceivable colours. In the light, they shone and sent bright rays dancing over the walls as if they were in some subterranean magical palace. The walls were also set with low iron rings to which they were all tethered. Ruari was lying flat on the floor with both his wrists shackled to the wall above his head. He drummed his feet frantically against the floor and sobbed.

Fianna was tied by her ankle, as Tallin was. She was curled into a tight ball, her head buried in her knees. She didn't look around in the light and didn't move.

Ystril stood, his ankles bound together and attached to the wall with two separate ropes. Several dwarves were trying to force him down on to the ground but, so far, he was resisting them. As Tallin watched, one of them began to bash a stone against his shin. Ystril yelled and swore, trying to get away.

Tallin watched as the dwarf on Kirian's back twisted his ankle at an angle which it was not meant to go. Kirian groaned gutturally, face pale in the silvery light of Tallin's magic, his head shaking from side to side as he gritted his teeth through the pain. Tallin's fingernails dug painfully into the palms of her hands, and she strained at the ropes which bound her until they chafed against her skin.

She sobbed as she watched the wirry-dwarves hurt her friends. Ystril had been sick, dark blood running down his scaly skin from where one of the dwarves had sliced his arm open. He was wobbling on his feet and looked faint.

Tallin remembered a spell she had read about in one of the older tomes in the abbey's library. She remembered Brother Yip had frowned and told her to put the book back, as it had been discredited years ago and was only kept for posterity. Yet the book had drawn her, she remembered, as it was one of the few writings which mentioned elemental light magic. The spells had been far from the usual creation and protection spells the monks had taught her. She had read the old book cover to cover in the early hours of the morning and late at night when her tutors were tucked up in bed.

Now, she tried hard to remember what she had read and sent up a prayer to Ceremor that the old magic still worked.

The light wobbled as she began to chant under her breath, shadows drawing back towards her. She closed her eyes and focused, tried to picture the pages of the book in her head. Her hands grew warm.

When she opened her eyes, there were shapes suspended in the air in front of her. She shook her head, inwardly cursing. They were meant to look like arrows, not carrots. She flicked her fingers and the carrot-shaped lights disintegrated into darkness.

"Try again," she muttered to herself, and ran through the words one more time.

This time, when she opened her eyes the magic

looked like arrows. Their tips were sharp, and she whispered another prayer as she sent them flying towards four dwarves who clambered over Kirian's prone body.

They hit their targets as if guided.

The first arrow to land struck the largest dwarf in the eye. He slumped over Kirian's back, bleeding silver blood like tears without making a sound.

The arrows landed silently, and the dwarves died the same way.

Kirian looked up at her through the shadows, his eyes red-rimmed. He smiled at her, blood on his lips but relief written clearly on his face.

"Thank you," he mouthed. She nodded and focused on creating more arrows.

Tallin lost count of how many arrows she had needed, but before long, there was a pile of corpses littering the floor, and she sagged against her bindings, weak with exhaustion. She had never used so much magic, never drained herself of so much emotion. There was nothing left now, no trace of the hatred or rage that had fuelled her attacks. She just needed to sleep.

"Get us out of here," Ystril hissed at her.

She shook her head. "Too tired."

That was all she remembered.

TWENTY-SEVEN

When she opened her eyes again, the room was in darkness. She called forth a wisp of light, ignoring the pain in her head which throbbed angrily at the request for more magic. The corpses were still piled around the room, the wounds on their bodies glimmering in the half-light as the magic winked off the glossy blood. Everyone was still in the same position they had been when she had passed out. She had no idea how long she had been unconscious for.

"Is everyone …" she began.

"Shh," Kirian hushed her. "No more sound. We do not want more to come."

What are we going to do? she wanted to say. *How are we going to get out of here?*

Nobody else seemed to have the answer anyway.

Tallin's wrists were raw and weeping, and her ankle was twisted from all her efforts to free herself from her bindings. It felt as if she had been trying for hours. Her throat was dry and sore, and it felt as if her tongue had expanded to three times its size. She needed a drink badly.

She had tried everything she could think of. She'd tried to make her magic so bright that it would sear through the rope, but no matter how hard she concentrated the light was always pale and cool. She tried to make a dagger, using the same enchantment that had created the arrows, but the resulting object was too unwieldy to cut through the ropes.

Sighing, she sank down on to the floor, waiting for her slow death.

She had passed out again, though she had no idea for how long, when she was woken by a sharp pain across the back of her hand. She pulled it to her lips and pressed her mouth against her hand, tasting blood which welled from a thin cut across her skin. Her thoughts ran from *how did this happen* to *wait, I'm not tied any more* before she focused on the small shadow in the darkness which was moving among them.

Fychan. She had never been so glad to see the aulin. Fychan had used the dagger from Tallin's ankle sheath to cut through the ropes. Tallin had no idea how she had managed to get away from the wirry-dwarves or stay hidden for so long, but her presence now was something of a miracle.

She was freeing them all, quickly and soundlessly.

Once the ropes were all cut, Tallin forced another wisp of light to illuminate the cavern. There were four tunnels leading off in different directions. Tallin couldn't remember the way they had been brought in, and neither could anybody else. They had all been disoriented in the darkness. They would just have to choose a direction and hope for the best.

Kirian, using his sensitive's intuition, chose a damp, mossy tunnel which sloped downwards away from the cavern. Tallin wondered if they ought to be heading upwards rather than down into the earth, but she decided to trust Kirian's judgement. In a ragged line, they hobbled, crawled and limped back into the network of tunnels which connected this cavern with others, and – Tallin fervently hoped – with the surface world. Tallin's ankle throbbed, but crawling on her knees, she tried her best to ignore it. Kirian seemed to have had the worst of the dwarves' ministrations, and his left knee was swollen like a ball. He pressed on regardless, but Tallin had seen in his eyes the amount of pain he was in. She wished she could take it away, but she had never been much use at healing magic.

The farther into the caverns they crawled, the colder and damper it got. Tallin felt the ache of the chill down to her bones, and her fingers felt as if they were no longer attached to her body. She could hear Ruari in front of her trying desperately not to whimper aloud.

None of them would be in any fit state to fight if they were set upon again.

There was one scare. Kirian, at the front of the line, suddenly came to a halt and everyone else froze behind him. Unmistakeably, Tallin could hear the steady scraping, marching sound of dwarven feet. The noise was muffled but getting louder.

Nobody moved. It felt as if nobody breathed.

The sounds grew fainter, and Tallin let out a long, relieved breath as she realised that the dwarves had headed down a different tunnel. They crawled on, slowly and painfully.

"Fychan sees light," the aulin suddenly exclaimed. Her voice was loud in the enforced silence of the tunnels, and Tallin's first reaction was to panic. Then the meaning of her words sank in.

"Where?" Kirian hissed.

"Follow," the aulin said.

Hope flared in Tallin's chest as the little creature disappeared into a narrow tunnel on the right that none of them had seen in the darkness. Ystril could barely squeeze through, having to wriggle at odd angles to fit his shoulders through the gap.

Sure enough, after a short time Tallin could see a silvery ray of light shining from above, making a little pool on the rocky floor before them. She had no idea how Fychan had known it was there.

Her eyes followed the dust motes which glittered and spun in the column of light, and her heart leapt as she saw – distantly yet quite unmistakeably – the sky. Grey, overcast and heavy with rainclouds, but undoubtedly the great Glendoran outdoors. She could taste the freshness of the air on her tongue.

They gathered around the fissure in the roof of the tunnel and stared upwards.

"How are we meant to get up there?" Ystril asked.

"Rope," Fychan said. "Fychan can climb up like before."

"What would we do without you?" Fianna said.

"Die, I think," Fychan said blithely.

"Yeah, you might be right," Fianna said, "but possibly better not to say it."

With a length of rope tied around her thin waist, Fychan began to scale the walls, using the inlaid gemstones as footholds. Tallin wouldn't have been able to fit a toe on them, but Fychan was small enough to use them as climbing aids. It wasn't long before she reached the curve of the ceiling.

"Careful," Fianna said softly.

"Fychan is fine."

The aulin leaned back away from the vertical wall and dug her long, claw-like nails into the stone of the ceiling. She began to swing from the stone, hand over hand, her fingers bleeding. She looked like a monkey, Tallin thought, a tiny, agile creature clinging and swinging her way towards the daylight.

Faolain whined, his ears flat against his head. He was clearly more worried than his mistress, who had nearly reached the edge of the hole.

Fychan knew what she was doing, though. Tallin watched as she swung herself up through the opening, disappearing from view for several minutes. Just as Tallin was beginning to feel a slow growing panic, Fychan's face peered down through the hole and she dropped the end of the rope, which slithered rapidly to the floor.

"Fychan tied it to a rock," she called down.

"Thank you, Fychan," Kirian said. "Right. Ruari, you go first."

The rope bore the boy's weight easily enough. He wasn't naturally athletic and struggled to pull himself up without anything to grip on to or push against, but eventually he made it to the top. Faolain went next, the rope tied tightly around his belly as Ruari lifted him up into the light.

It wasn't only the sky that was grey and dull, Tallin thought as she hauled herself out of the tunnel and lay on her side, blinking. They had emerged on to a rocky plain, desolate and bare. The wind whipped them, cutting through their tattered clothing and making Tallin shiver. She thought it had been cold in the tunnels, but this was worse.

"Where are we?" Fianna asked, as she clambered out of the hole.

"Somewhere in Tir Diffaith," Kirian said blandly.

"I know that," Fianna said. "But where?"

"I have no idea."

"That's helpful," Ystril said.

"If we need to get to Caer Gwynfor, how do we know which way to go?" Tallin asked.

Kirian shook his head. "There is no way of being sure until we find some sort of landmark, though my intuition is pulling me northward."

Ystril shrugged. "Well, better than being underground at least."

"No wirry-dwarves," Fychan said.

"Come on, then," Fianna said. "Pretty sure standing around here in the open isn't a great idea."

Tallin glanced up. The sun was barely visible, watery and pale behind the clouds, but from its position it seemed like it was already well past middle-light. They had maybe a few hours to travel before darkness fell. Fianna was right. They didn't want to be so exposed when the time came to rest.

It was tough on foot. With every step, Tallin wished she still had her old mare. Her feet were blistered, and there were scabs on her heels to match those on her knees from the tunnels. By the time the sky started to darken, she was hobbling like a newborn deer.

Kirian and Ruari weren't faring much better. When the boy began to fall behind, Fianna suggested that they stop for the night. The terrain hadn't changed, and they were all cold, hungry and dehydrated. Tallin didn't think they would get much sleep.

Perhaps it would have been easier if she hadn't. Her dreams that night were more violent and vivid than they had been since she left the monastery. It was as if Gwion knew how close they were getting.

TWENTY-EIGHT

She could feel the cold marble of the castle floor through the soles of her boots, could feel the uneven surface worn by thousands of feet which had walked this path since long before she was born. Her eyes swept over the grey, bare walls, running dark with water from the cracked and leaking roof. Her nostrils prickled in the fetid air, rich and damp with mould and moss, and the unmistakeable underlying stench of decay. The scent was sharp on her tongue, and she grimaced even as she kept walking forward towards the shimmering crystal orb which lay cushioned on its ornate stand, incongruous in the ruins of its surroundings.

She knew, now, what this was and what it held. It was a treasure beyond all other, and she had to destroy it.

She half limped, half ran towards it. When she lay a hand upon it, the colours in it began to race as if in panic, and she felt voices in her mind. Oh, the voices – it felt as if there were hundreds of them, all speaking the same words. *Help me. Please.*

The orb was hot under her palm, and her skin began to blister. Ignoring the pain, she grasped it in both hands and raised it above her head, preparing to dash it hard against the stone.

"That will not work in a dream."

The voice was rich, deep and mellifluous. The sort of voice which would hold you spellbound, should its owner burst into song, she thought.

It didn't seem likely that he would. Instead, he was walking slowly along the centre of the hallway towards where she stood. He was tall and stocky, draped head to toe in a rich, forest green cloak with a large hood which covered his face. She had no idea what he looked like, but she could smell him. A sharp tang of ozone and a bitter scent of wood smoke hit her senses, and her nostrils flared. *Magic*, she knew; he had been casting recently. Something powerful and beyond her own understanding.

She put the orb back down on its stand, trying to ignore the desperate wails which trailed through her mind.

"If this is a dream, how do you know it?" she asked, trying to control the wobble in her voice. She seemed so weak and reedy compared to him. She wondered what Kirian had been thinking, imagining that she could ever be a match for the power this man radiated, even in her sleep.

The man laughed. She felt the vibrations in her own chest.

"Oh, my dear, I know everything."

"You knew we were coming."

Gwion chuckled again. "Of course. I knew all along."

"Then why haven't you tried to stop us?"

"That would suggest that I thought you were a threat."

"We've made it this far. Perhaps we are stronger than you think," Tallin said defiantly, trying to stand as straight as she could. She hoped her hands weren't shaking too obviously.

"You are not. You are all weak compared to me. Even that mysterious companion of yours," Gwion said, more than a hint of amusement in his tone. "You will find out, if you carry on with your foolish mission. I can squash you like an insect without even lifting a finger."

"Why are you doing this?" Tallin asked.

"Why not?" Gwion stepped towards her, but she was still unable to make out his face beneath the hood. "Wouldn't you want to live forever, if you could?"

"Not like this," Tallin said. "I've seen those who come back. They're shells. They aren't people."

"I'm not talking about them," Gwion said, waving a gloved hand. "Collateral damage. You haven't seen what I am capable of. What if our bodies could be as strong as our minds? Imagine that. That's what I'm trying to do."

"You're sick."

"Hardly," Gwion said. "Nobody will ever be sick again, if I succeed."

"You won't," Tallin said.

"You have no idea what you are doing," Gwion said. "A world where nobody dies, and you're trying to stop it. How very selfish of you."

"It's unnatural," Tallin said. "What you're doing is wrong."

"So if I could bring back your friends, you'd say no?"

"I'd say no. And we're going to stop you."

"Well, then. I look forward to meeting you."

Tallin saw a flash of white teeth beneath the hood and then the man bowed low, his cloak sweeping the floor, before turning on his heel and sauntering away.

TWENTY-NINE

Tallin sat up sharply, rubbing her eyes. Her back ached from lying on the ground, but she ignored it. The dream had been beyond disturbing, far more than a usual nightmare.

"Is there a problem?" Kirian asked, leaning on one elbow.

"Gwion just spoke to me," Tallin said.

"The necromancer?"

"Yes. I went to the castle in my dream. He told me that he knows we're coming. He doesn't even care."

"I am not surprised," Kirian said. "I suspect, though, that he is more worried than you might think."

Tallin shook her head. "Why would he be? He's far more powerful than I am. I don't know why you think I could even try to be a match for him."

"You are stronger than you give yourself credit for," Kirian said. "You have just not had the chance to hone your skills."

"The monks tutored me for years," Tallin said.

"They have failed you, then," Kirian said. "You have been taught silly little spells which are beneath you, and have been protected from those which can make best use of your power."

"Well, thanks. Nobody ever called me silly before."

"You are not silly. I meant it as a compliment. You are capable of more."

"It's a bit late to be learning now," Tallin said.

"You are scared." Kirian shuffled over to her and wrapped an arm around her shoulders.

Tallin snorted. "You don't say."

"I will help you as best I can," Kirian said, "and I promise you I will be by your side no matter what happens."

Tallin felt the remnants of the dream begin to dissipate, her heart slowing to a normal rate.

"Thank you."

"Come on. We should move on."

Kirian got to his feet and offered Tallin his hand. They trudged on across the grit and stone of the plain. It began to rain.

"Cold," Ruari said miserably.

"Walk faster then," Fianna said.

The sky was beginning to darken again, and they were all wet to the skin and shivering by the time the terrain began to change. The ground beneath their feet became more solid, with less loose shale cutting into the soles of their boots. Rocky outcrops sprung up around them, and Tallin found her calves aching as the gradient became steeper.

They sheltered from the worst of the rain underneath the large, imposing rocks which at least offered some cover from the elements.

"I feel we are on the right trail," Kirian said. "The castle was built in the mountains."

"Makes sense," Tallin said, "especially given Gwion's intrusion into my dreams last night."

"He was in your dream?" Ystril frowned. "How is that possible?"

"His tie to magic is strong," Kirian said. "He will be able to communicate with others who have powers."

Tallin grimaced. "Lucky me."

It wasn't long before they found the remains of an old stone road, cracked and broken but unmistakably a pathway, winding its way up into the hills.

"Nobody has passed this way in a while," Kirian said. "It is an old highway from the days of the ancients. It will lead us to the castle. We are close."

Tallin shivered. After all these miles, all these days, here they were. She still had no idea how she was going to defeat Gwion and seal the shroud. Yet the time had come, whether she was ready for it or not. A tingling chill ran down her spine. *Someone's praying to Afallach*, as her mother used to say. She hoped he was listening. They needed all the help they could get.

It was early evening of the following day by the time the castle finally came into view in the distance. The skies were grey and heavy with rainclouds, and the wind sent sharp, icy fingers through the tears in their clothing. Tallin wondered aloud how anyone could live here all the time without slowly freezing to death.

"Mountain elves are a hardy race," Kirian said. "They have plenty of the Jotunn blood still in them."

"Where are they all, then?" Ystril asked.

"There are not many left," Kirian said. "They are not the most fertile of people, and they are spread sparsely across the land. It is rare to have encountered as many as we have."

"I'm not complaining," Ystril said.

"We killed them," Ruari said, frowning.

"We had to." Fianna ruffled his hair. "They would have killed us, otherwise."

"But why?" The boy looked up at the warrior with a puzzled expression.

"I don't know," Fianna said. "Perhaps we'll get the answer in there."

Caer Gwynfor loomed over them at the top of a long, gentle slope. It was imposing even at a distance, the walls so dark they seemed almost black in the hazy twilight. Arrow loops dotted the walls, darker patches in the grey stone. Tallin wondered when the last archers had taken their place in defence of the old building. She wondered if anyone was there now, looking down on them.

"What do we do now?" Fianna asked, not taking her eyes off the castle.

"He knows we are coming, so he must know we're here," Tallin said.

"I wonder if there will be a welcoming committee?" Ystril mused.

Tallin rolled her eyes. "I don't think there's going to be canapés."

"Are we ready for this?" Fianna asked. "It's getting dark, we're all tired. We don't want to blow it now because we're half asleep."

"You have a point," Kirian said.

"I don't know," Tallin said. "Are any of us actually going to get any sleep, even if we do find somewhere to stop?"

"I'm not," Ystril said.

"After the dreams I had last night, I know I'm not either," Tallin said. "I vote we make our stand now. Tonight."

And so it was settled. It would happen in the next

hours, and by the time the sun came up they would know whether the shroud was repaired and whether the world was as it should be once more.

It was eerily quiet as they drew nearer to the castle. Even as they had crossed the rocky plains, there had been sounds. The shirring of crickets, the whining of polflies and the occasional burst of birdsong. Here there was nothing. Other than the sound of their footsteps, they could have been in a vacuum. The wind had dropped, and the night was still and heavy.

"How are we to get in?" Fianna whispered. Tallin could only see one entrance – a vast wooden door behind a portcullis, barred with rusted iron. There was no way they would be able to force it open.

"An old castle like this would have had an external grain store somewhere," Kirian said, "and there would normally be a chute connecting it to the main building."

"So we're going to have to crawl through a grain chute?" Tallin felt her heart sink. She had had enough of claustrophobic spaces.

"No," Kirian said. "We will not fit. If we can find it, Fychan will have to go."

The aulin nodded her agreement.

It was full dark by the time they crept through the bushes which grew around the castle walls, gnarled and thorny. They caught in Tallin's hair and clothes, and she made an exasperated sound as one of the branches scratched her cheek deep enough to draw blood.

They circled the building slowly, watching for any sign of movement. The bare, open windows remained unlit by candle or magic, and there were no sounds to indicate their presence had been detected. Kirian led them through an area which would have been an old courtyard, perhaps where the guards would have trained their skills. It was empty now, and strangleweed grew abundantly through the cracks underfoot.

The castle gardens were even more overgrown. Once, perhaps, they would have been lovely. Tallin imagined the unruly, thick bushes being trimmed into delicate shapes like those in the gardens of the abbey. She wondered if, once, wild roses had grown here, or whether there had been a little herb patch like the one Brother Lyam was so proud of back home. Now, the trees and shrubs were grey and twisted, and the soil was so dense with weeds that nothing else had a chance at life.

It was Ruari who eventually found the old iron-bound trapdoor set in the floor of a dilapidated stone outhouse.

"Hey," he called. "Door."

It took several minutes to get the trapdoor to open. Fianna untied the rope from around her waist and threaded it through the handle. Ystril took the other end, and they both pulled so hard that they ended up on the floor. At least the door had cracked open, a rush of stale, dusty air making them cough.

Tallin looked down into the opening. She couldn't see the bottom, the steel sides of the grain chute disappearing into nothingness. She shivered.

Fychan stood beside her, silently gazing into the darkness.

Tallin turned to Kirian. "We can't ask her to do this."

"We have no choice," Kirian said, his face solemn. He crouched down and looked Fychan in the eye.

"Fychan," he said, "we are relying on you to get us in to the castle. We need you to wait until it is safe and then find your way to the portcullis. There will be a lever. We need you to operate it and lower the door."

"Fychan not strong enough," she said.

"You have to try," Kirian said, and the aulin nodded shakily.

Fianna lowered Fychan slowly into the chute, the rope tied loosely around her waist. She descended for an age, the rope almost playing out. Finally, there was a sharp tug on the rope, and Fianna wound it back in.

"She's in," Fianna said.

"All we can do now is wait and pray," Kirian said.

They hunkered down in some bushes overlooking the castle door, and they waited, and they prayed. Time ticked slowly by. Tallin felt sick with nerves.

"What if this fails?" she whispered to Kirian, who looked even paler in the wan moonlight.

He looked at her, a desolate expression on his face. "I do not know."

THIRTY

Tallin could barely sit still. She twisted her fingers in her lap, picked at the dirt under her nails, and tugged at loose threads on her tunic. She wanted nothing more than for this night to be over, one way or the other.

So, she supposed, she should have been happier when the portcullis slowly rose with an ear-splitting clanking. The heavy wooden door swung open, exposing a courtyard strewn with rubble and yet more strangleweed. Silence fell.

"Fychan?" Ruari called. There was no reply. Faolain whined pitifully and, before they could try to stop him, dashed off through the open doorway, disappearing from sight.

"Come on," Fianna said. "We need to follow him."

"I have a bad feeling about this," Ystril said.

"Seriously?" Fianna asked. "I can't think why."

"Sarcasm is unbecoming," Ystril said.

"That's rich, coming from you."

"Please," Tallin said, "let's not argue. We need to

stick together."

The aulin wasn't in the courtyard where the lever mechanisms for the portcullis and door were found.

"So who opened the door?" Ystril asked.

Tallin raked her gaze across the ground, examining every boulder and every shrub. "More to the point, where's Fychan?"

"If that damn culai hadn't raced off, maybe we would be able to find her," Fianna said.

Kirian was already on the other side of the courtyard, standing at the top of a stone stairwell, looking down.

"I think perhaps he went this way," he said.

The door at the bottom of the stairwell hung ajar and led to a large, dusty room which had, many years ago, been the kitchens. At one time it would have been the heart of the castle, warm and bustling and busy. Yet it had been a very long time since any meals had been prepared there. The great fireplace was long cold, filthy with dirt rather than ash and soot. Cobwebs decorated the walls and surfaces, and Tallin shuddered as a large cockroach skittered across the toe of her boot.

"Who wants a sandwich?" Ystril asked cheerily.

"Shut up, Ystril," Fianna said.

They moved on, down long corridors dotted with small rooms cluttered with the rusty remains of iron bedsteads.

"Servants quarters," Kirian said.

Tallin gazed around. She remembered this part of the castle from her dreams. It was unsettling to see how accurate they had been, as if she had really walked through these halls.

There was no sign of Fychan or Faolain.

"The dungeons," Tallin said, tugging at Kirian's sleeve. "In my dreams, the constructs he was building were in the dungeons. If he's got Fychan, he's probably taken her there."

Fianna cracked her knuckles. "I guess it's time, then."

"It is." Tallin sighed and leaned against the wall. It was damp and cold. "I still don't know if I feel ready, but I doubt I ever will."

"You mentioned constructs?" Ystril asked.

Tallin nodded. "He's been putting the souls into an army he has built from scrap.

"Our people would call them golems," Ystril said.

"It means the same thing," Kirian said. "Animated matter. We are not sure what he plans to do with them."

"Whatever it is can't be good," Tallin said.

"He's putting people into golems." Ystril pulled a face and turned to spit on the floor, as if trying to expel a bad taste from his mouth.

"And they can live forever in that body," Tallin said, "as long as they are not destroyed."

"It's sick," Fianna said. "We need to stop him."

"He wants his immortality," Kirian said. "That is how he intends to achieve it."

"I'd rather die," Fianna said. Tallin nodded in agreement.

"We all would, I think."

"Let's go then," Ystril said.

Tallin led the way, trying to cast her mind back to her dreams to show her the right path. It wasn't long before she found a door which looked familiar, and, pushing it open, she saw that it led down into the basement of the castle.

"This way," she hissed, and began her slow descent.

"How many golems are there?" Ystril asked from behind her.

"I don't know," she said. "Not too many, not the last time I dreamed about them anyway. He was having some difficulty with the souls. Of course, I don't know if my dreams are accurate."

She rounded the corner at the bottom of the stairs, and came to an abrupt halt. It was exactly as she remembered it in her dreams. The cells of the dungeon had been dismantled, and instead there was one room as wide as the castle, supported by pillars of stone.

Constructs lined up in rows along the back wall of the room, ten deep, twenty wide. In front of them was what appeared to be a workshop, large stone slabs holding limbs and heads in different stages of completion.

"Not all of these are active," Tallin whispered. She could sense the fear rolling off the people standing behind her. Even though she had known what to expect, she was terrified too.

The constructs were easily ten feet tall, the tops of their heads brushing the stone ceiling. They all looked different, created from a jumble of scrap materials, but each of them had a small sliver of glass embedded in its throat.

"That is what holds their power," Kirian said. "That is where they are imbued with a soul. Destroy that, and you destroy the construct."

His words were loud in the cavernous room. Several constructs shifted and opened what Tallin supposed were their eyes. They glowed green with magic, the light shining brightly from their eye sockets and washing over the remainder of their body.

The nearest one turned its head towards them and began to move.

"Now look what you've done," Ystril grumbled.

"We were going to have to face them sooner or later," Fianna said, and readied her sword.

Tallin frowned. "Why are only four of them moving?"

"The others do not have souls yet," Kirian said. "But only four? That doesn't make sense."

"We can talk about what makes sense later," Fianna said. "For now, we need to deal with these."

The construct who had moved first, the tallest of the four, began to wail as it neared them. Its voice appeared to emit from the glass in its throat, and as Tallin watched in horror, she saw the soul trapped within the glass beating against it desperately, trying to get out.

"This is torture," she said. "We will be doing them a favour by destroying them."

Ystril pushed past her, slashing at the construct with his sword, aiming at the soul. It raised a heavy, granite arm to defend itself, still wailing. Ystril's sword clanged off the stone and he recoiled, shaking his arm in pain.

"Swords are not much use unless you can get through to the throat," he muttered. "It's like fighting a wall."

"Tallin," Kirian said, "try using magic to restrain them."

The other three constructs were shuffling towards them in a bizarre kind of formation. Their gait was lopsided, and they raised their hands in a way that was clearly intended to be threatening. Tallin just felt sorry for them.

As the first construct aimed a blow at Fianna, which she sidestepped easily, Tallin began to focus her mind.

She called a ball of light into the palm of her hand,

where it crackled and burned with an intensity which turned it so white that even she could barely look at it.

Muttering a prayer to Ysgwyn, the god of battle, she let the light fly at the construct. It washed over it in a blinding flare, mixing with the green of its own magic. The construct didn't even hesitate. It took a few wobbly steps, but kept coming.

Tallin felt a pressure against her leg and looked down to see Ruari beside her, pulling her dagger out of its sheath.

"What are you doing?" she asked, alarm in her voice.

"I kill them," Ruari said. "Watch."

Light on his feet, the boy ran round behind the nearest construct and leaped on to its back. The creature roared and tried to shake him off, but he gripped with his knees as if he were riding a horse. Slowly, he inched up the construct's back until he was hanging around its neck.

Tallin watched as he stabbed the dagger into the glass once, twice, three times, grunting with the effort of his blows. On the fourth contact, the glass shattered and the soul hissed out, dissolving into the air in tiny flecks of colour. The construct ground to a halt, a dead shell.

It didn't take long, after that. The lumbering creatures were slow and laboured and appeared to be suffering great pain before anyone even touched them. Shattering their throats felt like a mercy.

"No sign of Gwion," Tallin said. "That seems odd."

"He must know we're here," Fianna said. "Someone opened that door."

"Agreed," Tallin said. "The orb where he keeps the souls is in the main hall. He's probably protecting that."

"Then that's where we have to go," Ystril said.

Nobody argued. Tallin led the way once more, rising through the bowels of the castle. The air became fresher as they climbed, although Tallin thought that was probably due to the cracks in the ceiling. Ivy was growing through the walls, as if the plants, not content with having overrun the garden, wanted to come inside too.

"The main hall is just through these doors," she whispered, pausing outside a set of double doors which would probably have been impressive before the rain rot and woodworm set in. Once, she thought, they would have been carved and gilded. Now, only the suggestion of the figures sculpted into the wood remained. One appeared to be a dragon.

They waited, listening. No sound came from beyond the door.

"Go on," Ystril hissed.

"After you," Tallin said. Now they were here, she did not want to go through the doors into the hall. She knew the orb would be there, and she did not feel ready to face it.

THIRTY-ONE

When she finally stepped through the door, it was the first thing her eyes fell upon.

The second was the figure standing in front of it, wearing the same hooded cloak as he had in her dream the night before.

The third was the small army of constructs that stood alongside him, headed by one which was even taller and shinier than any in the dungeon. There must have been fifteen of them there, standing in four lines, each with a soul glowing brightly behind the glass in its throat.

"What took you so long?" Gwion asked. His voice was exactly the same as in her dream. It held the same tone of arrogant contempt.

"Gwion, I presume," Ystril said.

"Who else?" Gwion said. "And you must be Ystril. I have been waiting for you."

"What do you mean?" Ystril asked.

"I know why you're here," Gwion said.

"We're here to free the souls of the dead," Tallin said. "What you're doing is cruelty. Those poor people in the dungeon, trapped like that... it's torture."

Gwion laughed. "My dear, those were merely my early attempts. Do you think I would have left my valuable work down there for you to ruin?"

"You're enslaving them," Ystril said.

"Not at all," Gwion said. "I am giving them eternal life. Just as you were seeking."

"Can you bring him back?" Ystril took a step towards the man, his face hopeful.

"I can bring anyone back," Gwion said. "Nobody ever needs to die again."

"Ystril," Tallin lay a hand on his arm. "You can see that these aren't people."

Ystril whirled around, pulling his arm away from Tallin. "Don't touch me," he hissed. "They might not have the bodies we recognise, but that doesn't mean they're not people."

"Are you serious?" Tallin frowned. "You can't condone this. You've seen what's happening out there, with the corpses."

"But if they can be given new bodies, maybe I can be with Fedlia again."

"You can," Gwion said. "He will live again, and you can live for ever beside him. You need never be parted."

"Yes," Ystril said. "I will do anything if you can promise me that."

"Your friends here are trying to destroy all my plans. If they succeed, Fedlia will be gone."

"I will stop them," Ystril said, a determined set to his jaw.

"No," Tallin said. She couldn't believe what was happening. "No, Ystril, you can't do this."

"Fedlia is all that matters," Ystril said. "We could bring back Ithal." He looked at Fianna. "We could bring back Cearul."

"This is wrong," Kirian said. "Souls have to pass through the shroud. It is the way of things."

Gwion pushed back his hood and stared at Kirian. The man looked surprisingly ordinary, Tallin thought. Dry, weather-worn tan skin, a bushy red beard pulled into plaits at the ends, small bright eyes. He looked harmless.

"Well, well," Gwion said, "if it isn't Afallach himself. Is this world so feeble that even its gods need help to defeat a mere mortal such as I?"

Kirian's face became very still. "I am simply doing my duty."

"What?" Tallin stared at him. "What does he mean?"

"I think it's quite clear what I mean," Gwion said. "Ah, hasn't he told you? He hasn't, has he?"

"It is not something that tends to come up in conversation," Kirian said coldly.

Tallin looked from Gwion to Kirian, bewildered. "What are you saying?"

"It matters little who I am. What matters is returning these souls to where they belong and sealing the shroud," Kirian said.

"Well, it matters to me," Tallin said.

Fianna lay a hand on Tallin's shoulder. "He's right. This isn't the time."

"Quite so," Gwion said. "Now, then, won't you hear me out? Ystril has already decided. Perhaps I can convince all of you."

"You know you will not," Kirian said.

Gwion waved a hand. "Not you, obviously. But as we've already discussed, you're not important here."

"Nothing you can say will convince me that what you're doing is right," Tallin said shakily. She felt as if the ground was shifting beneath her feet and needed to regain some control. "I've seen things I never imagined in my worst nightmares. It can't continue."

"I agree," Fianna said.

"Oh, do you?" Gwion said. "Do you really?"

He closed his eyes and muttered some words, and the largest of the constructs lit up with a green glow.

"Fi?" it said, the voice scraping and with a metallic edge, but unmistakeable.

"Cearul?" Fianna fell to her knees, her eyes widening.

"You see?" Ystril said. "Eternal life. We never have to grieve again."

"He gets it," Gwion said. "I don't know what you've seen out there in the world, but my research is just beginning. I might have made some mistakes, but when I am done, we will all be able to live forever like this. I'm not doing this to take over the world. I just want my daughter back."

"Your daughter?" Ystril asked.

"She was only eight. She drowned. All this is for her," Gwion said. "She was the only person who ever mattered to me."

"Fi, please," Cearul said. His great metallic legs shuffled a few steps forward.

"We burned you," Tallin said, her head feeling as if it were full of tangled wool. "You died."

"Yes, thank you for that," Gwion said. "One of the problems I'm having at the moment is those who are newly passed are returning to their own bodies. I can't work out why. It's only if the bodies aren't available that they come through the orb."

"I thought," Fianna began, her voice breaking, "I thought you'd gone."

"I am here," Cearul said, taking a few more slow steps.

"Will you join us?" Gwion said, a wide smile breaking across his face. "Will you help us?"

"I want to," Fianna said, walking over to the construct inhabited by Cearul and looking into its shimmering green eyes.

"Then do," Gwion said. "You can be together again, just like Ystril will have Fedlia, just like I will bring back my Yannis."

"Cearul," Fianna said, lifting one hand to the construct's face. She winced as her palm touched him. "Tell me you're well."

"Fi," Cearul said again. "Fi."

"Tell me you're well."

"It hurts, Fi," Cearul said.

"No," Gwion said, his voice rising. "He lies."

"If it is truly him," Fianna said, "he would never lie to me."

"It hurts," Cearul said again. "It hurts. Please, no more."

"This is what you are doing," Kirian said. "You are not saving these people. You are torturing them."

"You heard him," Ystril said. "He doesn't want to harm them. He is still researching."

Tallin's fists clenched. "That doesn't make this acceptable, Ystril. These people are in agony. This is Cearul. We all loved him."

"I'm sorry about Cearul," Ystril said, "but I still believe that he can bring back Fedlia. I'd do anything for that chance."

"Even condemn others to suffer?" Kirian asked.

"People suffer all the time," Ystril said coldly. "You should know that, Afallach."

"That does not mean I condone it," Kirian said, equally sharply.

There it was again. *Afallach.* He wasn't denying it. The thought whirled in Tallin's mind so that she was struggling to process anything else that was going on. Kirian was the Soulkeeper. How could she not have known? Why hadn't he told her?

So much for her non-believing. She almost laughed aloud at her train of thought, reining it back in quickly when she saw that Gwion had fixed his attention upon her.

"So, my little plaything of a god, if giving life is so unacceptable, what do you intend to do about it?"

She opened her mouth to speak, but Fianna got there first.

"We're going to stop you," Fianna said, "any way we can."

Gwion sighed and shook his head. "I didn't want it to happen this way," he said, "and I take no pleasure from this, but I seem to have no choice in the matter."

He muttered an incantation under his breath, his skin lighting up with the same green light that emitted from the constructs. Every one of them sprang to glimmering life, the souls twisting and battering against the glass.

"I am truly sorry," Gwion said, speaking directly to Fianna, "but you are going to die by your lover's hand."

"He wouldn't," Fianna said, standing firm as Cearul lifted an arm.

"Oh, I forgot to mention one thing," Gwion said. "As I am effectively their Creator now, they obey me. It's you or him. I wonder who will win."

Cearul swung his great, iron-clad hand and hit Fianna solidly in the ribs. She fell to the floor, crying out in pain. Cearul stood over her, emitting a long and agonised wail before stamping on her ankle. Tallin heard bones crack.

She hurriedly cast a shielding spell, surrounding Fianna with a bubble of light which would protect her from the worst of the damage, at least while the spell held. She didn't know how long that would be. The other constructs were beginning to shuffle closer now, and some of them had blades welded to their hands. Tallin felt a wave of despair wash over her. In that moment, she thought there was no way they could win this fight. Not with Ystril having betrayed her and Fianna lying crippled on the ground. Even with her body suffused with emotion, she wondered how long it would be before her own energy stretched thin and her body gave up. *Kirian was wrong*, she thought. *I don't have the power that's needed here. We needed an army, not magic.*

"Come on," she shouted at Kirian. "If you're a god, then prove yourself. Help us."

"I am not Ysgwyn," Kirian said. "I am no fighter."

"You must be able to do something," Tallin said. "Other than lie to us all, of course."

Kirian looked pained. "I did not mean to."

"Right, right, just never had the chance to tell me, I get it," Tallin said. "I'll deal with that later. Now, we need help. Come on."

Cearul was battering at the shield of light surrounding Fianna, wailing the entire time. It was the most agonised sound Tallin had ever heard. Fianna lay on the ground, curled into a foetal position, audibly sobbing. Tallin had never seen the woman look so broken, not even after Cearul had died.

She would not be able to help them now.

It wouldn't be long before the other constructs reached them. They moved slowly but with purpose, and there was no doubting their intentions. Tallin backed away, trying to focus on her magic, trying to think of a spell, an enchantment that she might be able to use to stop them in their tracks. She wished, once again, that the monks had taught her more useful ways to harness her power.

Tallin looked over at Ystril. The koroni was standing

shoulder to shoulder with the necromancer. He watched impassively as the mechanical army advanced upon the people he had called his friends.

"Ystril, please," she called. He ignored her.

Gwion's eyes were closed and his lips were moving as he pushed the army of souls onwards. Trails of magic seeped from his skin, from his arms, from his chest. The glittering emerald rays sank into the constructs and kept them coming forward, one shuddering, laborious step at a time.

"Golems don't want to do this," Ruari said from behind Tallin.

"They cannot resist," Kirian said.

Tallin pulled light from the air, glittering motes of dust trapped in her hands as she threw a silver ball of magic at Gwion. The man summoned a barrier around himself, and Tallin's spell washed over it harmlessly.

The constructs continued to shuffle painfully through the hall. Tallin looked around in panic. Kirian and Ruari stood beside her, and Fianna was attempting to get to her feet. Her right ankle was badly swollen and looked broken, but she gritted her teeth and rested her weight on it anyway. She lifted her sword and stared at what remained of her lover.

Tallin shifted her hands and drew a sigil in the air. It was a symbol of a cloak, and it glimmered briefly with the effects of her magic before dissipating. With a wave of one hand, Tallin sent a surge of energy rushing across the room, coating Gwion with white light. He stuttered, and his magic briefly died.

In that moment, Tallin saw Cearul hesitate, one thick arm raised above Fianna's head as she held her shield firm.

"No," he said, slowly drawing back his arm. "No."

"What are you doing?" Gwion shouted. "Kill them."

Cearul lowered his arm and turned to face his captor, shuddering with the effort of denying him.

"No," he said again.

Tallin felt a wave of hope rise in her chest. She stared at Gwion, channelling all her rage and fear into a spell she cast on instinct. All her training, her years of dutifully reading the right books and holding her power in check, fell away. She drew in a deep breath, exhaled, and closed her eyes.

"Like starlight," she heard Ruari say from behind her.

She knew, even from behind her eyelids, that she had pulled all the light from the room and crystallised it into a single point, held in the palms of her hands. She felt it skittering over her fingers and pulsing in her veins. It was a strange sensation, almost like an itch deep beneath the skin which could never be scratched.

"You think you can match me?" Gwion laughed. Tallin flicked open her eyes and met his gaze.

"We'll see," she said, and sent a stream of white light in a sparkling ribbon across the room. It wrapped itself around Gwion's chest, trying to tighten.

Gwion simply inhaled, his chest filling with air, and the magical bands around him burst into blue flame and burned away.

"Not a bad try," he said, "but you're going to have to do better."

He retaliated with a stream of flame, which Tallin had to duck. It sizzled as it caught the edges of her hair, and a bitter burning smell permeated the room.

Cearul was shaking, the metal rivets holding his limbs together grinding and squealing. He was making noises of exertion as he fought against the compulsion to attack. As Tallin flung herself down to avoid another fireball, she noticed that the other constructs had stopped advancing, too. One of them had begun stumbling towards Gwion, who was backing away and hurling spells at it. The fireballs bounced off the construct without effect.

"You can't do it, can you," Tallin said, her breath coming in loud pants. "For all your power, you can't manage to destroy your own creations."

Gwion ignored her, continuing to fling streams of fire. He managed to land one direct hit on the throat of the construct, which screeched and shuddered as the glass melted, but by this point the others had also begun to stagger towards their former master. Gwion's face contorted as he struggled to fight them off.

Meanwhile, Ystril had raised his sword and was pointing it at Cearul's throat.

"Do as you have been instructed," Ystril said.

"I will not," Cearul said.

"Don't you want to live?"

"This is not living," Cearul said, his voice strained.

"Then let me help you," Ystril said, pressing the tip of his blade against Cearul's throat. His soul, a bright pink smudge behind the glass, whirled frantically.

Tallin saw the blur of movement seconds before Ystril fell to the ground, Fianna's sword buried deep in his stomach. She had no idea how the injured woman could move so fast when even now she was having trouble staying upright. Cearul put out a hand to steady her.

"I had to," Fianna said, looking down at Ystril, who lay on the ground clutching his stomach. Dark blood seeped out between his fingers and began to puddle on the floor. "I'm sorry."

"Fi," Ystril said, his voice wheezing through pain. "I just wanted to live again."

"I know," Fianna said, leaning down to grip the pommel of her sword. "I wish things could be different too. But not like this. Not like this."

Tallin got to her feet and began to focus once more on her magic. She felt drained, her legs wobbly and her fingers shaking with the effort of summoning more light to her aid. Yet she knew that now was her chance. Gwion had been surrounded. Four of his own army had backed him into a corner and were stabbing at him. He held them off with a brightly-glowing crimson shield, but he seemed to be weakening.

The spear of light Tallin sent flying from her fingertips burst through the magical shield, dissolving it into scarlet sparks which rained to the ground and disappeared. Before Gwion could cast again, one of the constructs swung a thick stone hand and hit his shoulder with a crushing blow, sending him sprawling to the concrete.

As Tallin watched, panting and shivering, a small grey-brown bundle ran out from underneath the dais on which the orb stood and fastened itself around Gwion's neck.

"Faolain," Ruari called.

The little culai sank his teeth into the necromancer's throat and growled low as he shook his head from side to side. Gwion roared and rose to his feet, grabbing the struggling animal and flinging him across the room with the force of powerful resistance magic. Faolain bounced off the wall and collapsed to the floor, where he slid along for a few yards and lay unmoving.

Ruari raced over to him, bending over his body. Tallin could hear the boy's cries. She pulled together the very last of her strength, gasping and shivering, sending light-crafted arrows sailing in wonky trails through the air. One hit its target, sinking into Gwion's left shoulder, sending him spinning back to the ground.

Gwion tried to stand. He flopped along the ground like a stranded fish.

"What have you..." he sputtered, then coughed.

Tallin walked slowly over to the man and looked down at him. His tongue was swelling, his neck thick with clotting blood. She could see Faolain's poison already darkening his skin.

She knelt beside him and drew her dagger.

"You do not deserve this," she told him, as she pressed the tip of her dagger against his chest. His eyes rolled white, terrified.

"Please," he whispered, his voice muffled and pained. "Save me."

"You deserve to die slowly, but I cannot watch suffering, even yours," Tallin said, and pressed down. The dagger broke through his flesh and sank into his heart, ending his life just the way it had for the old horse, all those weeks ago. Gwion died with less grace, Tallin thought. He squealed and thrashed around and urinated in his trousers. She grimaced and stepped back.

"It's over," she said, staring at the man's body.

"Not quite," Kirian said, walking up behind her. "We still have the orb."

Tallin closed her eyes. "What do I need to do?"

"The orb must be destroyed," Kirian said, "and I will guide the souls back to Everlasting. Magic created the rift. I will need your magic to seal it again, to stop the souls being trapped in between."

"I don't know if I have any left in me," Tallin whispered, feeling her legs give way as she sank to the floor.

"You must," Kirian said. "If you cannot seal the shroud, the souls will keep coming back."

"Does this mean Cearul will die again?" Fianna asked.

"Cearul is already dead," Kirian said. "He will return to Everlasting and be at peace."

"Please," Cearul said.

"And what about you?" Tallin raised her eyes to Kirian. "Afallach."

"I cannot change who I am," Kirian said. "I am sorry I could not tell you."

"Why?" Tallin asked. Her voice was reedy and plaintive, and she winced inwardly.

"Would you have believed me?" Kirian asked. "It took weeks for people to listen to me, thinking I was insane. If I had told the truth then, I would have been locked away and forgotten about."

"But afterwards," Tallin said. "You let me fall in love with you, knowing you were lying."

"I told you we could not be together," Kirian said.

"You should have told me why," Tallin said.

Kirian sighed and sank to the floor beside her. He had tears in his eyes.

"I know," he said, "and I am sorry. I just wanted to

be happy, for a while. I wanted it for myself, just once. It was selfish of me."

"It was real for me," Tallin said.

Kirian squeezed her hand. "As it was for me. Never doubt that. I love you, Tallin."

Tallin stared at him, the familiar face of her lover that she had come to know so well. She had learned every inch of his skin, every mark and freckle on his body. She had loved him as a man, and discovered him to be a god. Her mind was still struggling to process the knowledge that everything she had believed was false and that the gods her people worshipped were real – so real as to be almost like her. So much so that she would never have recognised him as less than human.

More than human.

The exhaustion which had dogged Tallin for days finally washed over her body, bringing her to tears. She put her head in her hands and sobbed. She cried for Ithal, who would never again smuggle her extra orange buns after dinner. She cried for Fianna and Cearul and the love they had shared and lost. She cried for Faolain, whose broken body lay matted in the dirt. She even cried for Ystril, who had been desperate enough to betray his friends for the sake of his love and had paid the ultimate price.

Kirian sat silently beside her, his hand resting on her back. She found comfort in his touch, even now. Yet she knew she would have to say goodbye.

Fianna was already saying hers.

She stood with her arms wrapped awkwardly around the construct that was Cearul. He could not hold her in return, but stood like a statue, making a low humming sound.

"When you died," Fianna said, her voice hesitant and thick with emotion, "when you died, I was so angry with the world. For a while, I didn't want to carry on. I was angry that you died so easily. I was angry that I never had the chance to say goodbye."

She wiped at her eyes furiously. "I was going to give up and go home, back to the abbey, and wait for the world to turn itself inside out. I didn't have the energy to care. Then something changed."

Fianna took a deep breath and swallowed hard.

"I began to suspect that I was carrying our child," she said. "Now I am sure of it. You're going to be a father, my love. And if he's a boy, he will have your name."

Cearul made a rasping, choking noise. It sounded as if he were trying to cry.

"Tell our child," he said, his voice low and broken. "Tell them how much I loved their mother."

"I will," Fianna said, tears running freely down her cheeks. "And I will tell them how brave and kind and handsome their father was, and how very much I loved him too. I will miss you always."

She pressed her lips to the cold stone of Cearul's cheek, stroking her hand along the metal plates which joined his arms to his shoulders.

"Now we're going to let you go, my love. Rest well," Fianna whispered.

"It is time," Kirian said, his voice soft and low in Tallin's ear.

Tallin nodded. "Tell me what to do."

"We need to create an enchantment which means that when we break the orb, the souls will be absorbed into my earthbound body," Kirian said. "I will then return to the other plane. When I have gone, there will be a hole in the fabric of this time. I will teach you how to seal it. When this is done, it will all be over. The dead will be safe."

"Kirian," Tallin said. "Will I ever see you again?"

Kirian smiled sadly. "Everyone does," he said. "But if we are lucky, you will live for many years, first."

"Will you remember me?"

He took her hands in his, and she gazed into the infinite blue of his eyes, not wanting to let him go.

"Always," he said. "I could never forget you."

"Then wait for me," she said. "I will not be long."

"I want you to live," he said, his face a mask of desperate sadness. "Live in a way that I never can. And when the time comes, I will be there for you. I promise."

She blinked away the tears that sprang to her eyes, feeling as if her heart was trying to force its way out of her throat.

"I love you," she said, instead.

"Like I never imagined," Kirian whispered, and kissed her.

THIRTY-TWO

They stood ready, Kirian with the orb in his hands. It was almost too large for him to hold, and was so full of colour that no clear space remained.

"So many," he said reverently, and dropped it.

The glass shattered as it hit the ground, spraying across the hall in a shower of glittering crystal. The souls rose from it in confused clumps of colour: indigo, fuchsia, jade. Tallin thought it was beautiful. It was as if the early morning mist was made of rainbows.

In the middle of it all, Kirian stood, his arms outstretched and his head tilted back. The souls began to cling to him, orbiting his body as if magnetically drawn. Some of them went into his mouth, his nose, through his eyes. Tallin gasped and shuddered. She felt Ruari's hand on her arm.

"He needs to do it," the boy said.

Tallin nodded, unable to speak. She watched as Kirian's chest swelled, watched him rise on to his toes and close his eyes. The air smelled of ozone, sharp and fresh, and she could hear a low rumbling sound. There was a blinding, white-hot flash which made them all cry out and shield their eyes, and when she finally looked up, blinking, Kirian had gone. All that remained was a sizzling, twisting ball of light, the gateway to the Everlasting. She knew what she had to do.

Swallowing down her grief, she poured it all into one last final effort of magic. A high pitched whine rent the air as she began to pull at the sphere, strands of silvery light peeling away and winding around her fingers.

"Like yarn," Ruari said.

Tallin supposed it was, if only yarn were made of sunlight. The strands felt hot and alive against her skin. She gritted her teeth and focused.

The light diminished as more and more of it floated towards Tallin, as if she were knitting in reverse. Her fingers were burning, blisters rising where the light touched her. She swallowed hard and ignored the pain, whimpering softly as the tear in the shroud grew smaller. Finally, the last fragile thread wound itself around Tallin's wrists. Her fingers glowed with a spectral sheen, then the light winked out.

She stood in the middle of the room, her shoulders hunched, her entire body shaking. She felt too dazed to cry. It was over.

"You did it," Ruari said.

"We did it," Tallin said, mechanically. She wanted to close her eyes and never open them again. Perhaps then, she wouldn't have to see Ystril's body lying in a pool of blood, she wouldn't have to see the constructs collapsing to the ground in a chorus of squeals and clatters, she wouldn't have to watch Fianna crouching over the construct that had been Cearul, choking and sobbing. She wouldn't see the vast, empty space in the middle of the hall where Kirian had been.

There was a piercing squeal and Fychan appeared through the broken-down double doors at the top of the hall. She raced at top speed across the floor, dodging the bodies of the constructs, flinging herself at Faolain's body.

"No, no, no," the aulin sobbed, curling herself around the culai's fur. "Fychan couldn't find you. Fychan is too late."

Even muffled in Faolain's soft body, her wails were gut-wrenching. They had all lost so much, Tallin thought. None of them would ever be the same people they were at the beginning of this journey. But they had succeeded.

She wondered why it didn't feel that way.

EPILOGUE

It had taken them nearly half a year to get back to the abbey. When she looked back at it now, Tallin still felt amazed that they had managed to return home. The only trouble was, it had never felt quite like home again. She always felt as if she was marking time.

Not that she hadn't filled her days. Watching Fianna and Cearul's daughter grow had been a constant joy. Jira had the courage of her mother and the compassion of her father. She had become a scholar, rather than a fighter, and she had written texts on magic and religion that were renowned throughout the land. Few half-elven people commanded the respect that she had achieved. Tallin was constantly proud of her.

It helped, of course, that Tallin and Fianna had been able to tell her tales that nobody else ever could. It had taken many years, but finally they were able to reminisce with a smile instead of sadness.

It was odd, still, to think about the gods being so real. Even stranger to imagine that one of them had been her lover, over half a century ago. She could see his face in her mind as if it were yesterday. Nobody in all the years since had been able to live up to what she had felt for him. Tallin thought that wasn't surprising. He was a god, after all.

And he would be coming for her, soon.

She lay on her bed, looking out of the window at the stars in the sky. It was a peaceful night, and a gentle breeze ruffled the curtains and filled the room with the scent of jasmine from the gardens below.

Ruari had come from the plains to visit her that morning. It had been nearly twenty years since she had last seen him, and he had grown even more rotund than she remembered. He had brought his elven bondmate, Ishke, and two of their four children. None of them had known quite what to say.

Goodbye seemed like the easiest word, and the hardest. There had been tears in his eyes when he had left, and she knew that it would be the last time.

She thought about goodbyes. There had been so many.

Isbel, just before last Brumalia. The first person to have welcomed them home to the abbey, racing across the old stone bridge with squeals of pure joy, so delighted that Tallin could barely resist a smile herself. She had been a loyal friend for all these years. The end was quick for her, a cough and a fever and four days later she was gone. Tallin missed her terribly.

Fychan, only three years after the defeat of Gwion. She had known that aulin lived short lives, but it was still a shock. Tallin and Fianna had wrapped her body in dilis leaves and buried her under the roots of the largest tree in the woodland behind the abbey. Fychan hadn't feared death, Tallin remembered. She'd just wanted to see Faolain again.

Tallin understood that all too well.

The pain in her chest which had been her constant companion for days seemed to have gone, and her body felt almost weightless. Tallin tried to lift her arms, but they would not move. She sighed, turned her head to rest her cheek against the soft satin of the pillow, and closed her eyes.

She opened them in the small walled garden outside the abbey that she loved so much, wild roses creeping up the stone. The air was cool and still, and she could hear the crickets singing.

"I knew you would be waiting for me."

"I made you a promise," Kirian said, gazing down at her as she walked up to him and took his hands in her own. They were warm and soft, just as she remembered them. She looked up at him with a jolt as she realised that her hands were no longer gnarled and arthritic, but smooth and unmarked by age.

She saw herself reflected in the pale depths of his eyes just as she had been that day, standing in the castle hall and watching the only man she had ever loved disappear into another world. She looked young and vibrant and happy.

"I missed you," she said, her throat tightening and tears pricking at her eyes.

"Fifty years for me is the blink of an eye," Kirian said, "yet this past fifty has felt longer than a thousand."

"Tell me you won't leave me again," she said.

He smiled at her. "Never."

"I love you."

"And I will love you for all eternity, if you will have me," Kirian said, brushing her long, dark hair away from her cheeks.

Tallin felt a lightness in her heart which threatened to bubble up and overwhelm them both.

"I will."

She kissed him then, as solid and real as he had ever been to her. It felt as if, at long last, she had come home.

"Are you ready?" he asked her softly, squeezing her hand.

She nodded and smiled. "Let's go."

They walked away, hand in hand, into the deepening twilight.

ACKNOWLEDGEMENTS

Like many people, I've grown up wanting to be a writer. More than anything, I wanted to write a book and to see my name on the cover. I spent many years thinking that writing an Entire Book was something that other people did, people who were more clever and talented than me. Throughout those years, I dabbled. I wrote terrible teenage poetry before being "emo" was a thing. I wrote short stories, I jotted down ideas. I went to University to study something totally unrelated to writing, getting bogged down in essays which sucked all of the fun out of the craft.

So first, I would like to thank David Gaider and Patrick Weekes, and their team of writers who produced the Bioware games Mass Effect and Dragon Age. Because, when I grew sick of academic writing, I picked up these games and they inspired me. I began to write fan fiction based in their worlds - because, I figured, the characters and universe were already there so it would be easier, right? Actually, I have to say, it's a good challenge to write someone else's character and get it right. And, damn, I enjoyed every word of it. Writing was fun again. Without those games, this story would not exist.

It also wouldn't exist if I hadn't signed up for a local college's evening class in creative writing. The fanfiction got my creative juices running again; the evening course steered me in the right direction and helped to provide me with the structure, skills and motivation to shape my ideas into an actual living thing. So a very large thank you goes to the tutor of that course, Angharad Hill. Thanks, Angharad, for the challenges you set for me and for the encouragement you have given to me throughout this process. I'd also like to thank my fellow students, whose feedback and support have been invaluable. You know who you are!

To the fellow writers I've met online, thanks for giving me a place where I can bounce around my ideas and share snippets of my writing and where I can share in your writing too. Particular mention goes to fellow fanfiction writers and to the Writers Retreat Facebook group for all their encouragement and support.

Thanks also to my good friend and cover designer Carl Freeman, and to my editor Remy Thomas, for helping this collection of words find shape as an Entire Book, something that I can hold in my hands and be proud of.

To my friends and colleagues, thank you for putting up with me and for being vaguely interested in my scrawlings. And to my family, who have no choice but to put up with me.

To my husband Andrew, whose ongoing love and support has allowed me the headspace to actually make the words go.

Finally, thank you for buying this book. I am privileged that you have chosen to read it, and I hope that you have enjoyed it.

You can contact me via my blog

www.elainemilton.com or at Elaine@elainemilton.com, follow me on Twitter @emiltonwriter or on Facebook @elainemiltonauthor.

75797803R00249

Made in the USA
Columbia, SC
29 August 2017